Praise for Tracy Brogan

My Kind of You

"In this relaxed contemporary, Brogan (*Love Me Sweet*) creates a charming small town where even the scandals and secrets are relatively wholesome. Events sweep readers along, making them long for the idealized community Brogan portrays."

—*Publishers Weekly*

"Recommend this romantic story to fans of women's fiction."

—*Booklist*

"This story is filled with lively characters who jump off the page. The author knows how to capture her readers' attention. The scene where the hero tells the heroine that she's 'the kind of woman a man wants to make promises to' was romantic and sweet."

—*RT Book Reviews*, 4 Stars

Crazy Little Thing

WALL STREET JOURNAL BESTSELLER

RWA RITA® FINALIST, 2013, BEST FIRST BOOK

"Heart, humor, and characters you'll love—Tracy Brogan is the next great voice in contemporary romance."

—Kristan Higgins, *New York Times* Bestselling Author

"Witty one-liners and hilarious characters elevate this familiar story . . . Readers will love the heat between the leads, and by the end they'll be clamoring for more."

—*RT Book Reviews*, 4 Stars (HOT)

"Brogan shows a real knack for creating believable yet quirky characters . . . The surprising emotional twists along the way make it a satisfying romp."

—Aleksandra Walker, *Booklist*

"*Crazy Little Thing* by Tracy Brogan is so funny and sexy, I caught myself laughing out loud."

—Robin Covington, *USA Today*, *Happy Ever After*

"Tracy Brogan is my go-to, laugh-out-loud remedy for a stressful day."

—Kieran Kramer, *USA Today* Bestselling Author

The Best Medicine

RWA RITA® FINALIST, 2015,
BEST CONTEMPORARY ROMANCE

"With trademark humor, lovely, poignant touches, and a sexy-as-sin hero, *The Best Medicine* is Tracy Brogan at her finest. Charming, witty, and fun."

—Kimberly Kincaid, *USA Today* Bestselling Author

Love Me Sweet

RWA RITA® FINALIST, 2016, BEST CONTEMPORARY ROMANCE

"An upbeat, generous message about finding yourself, standing up for yourself, and living an authentic life . . . A sexy, slightly kooky romance that should please Bell Harbor fans."

—*Kirkus Reviews*

Jingle Bell Harbor: A Novella

"Brogan's hilarious voice and word play will immediately ensnare readers in this quick but satisfying small-town romance."

—Adrian Liang, *Amazon Book Review*

"*Jingle Bell Harbor* is a fun, funny, laugh-out-loud Christmas read that will surely put you right in the mood for the season."

—*The Romance Reviews*, 5 Stars

"This was an incredible read! I was definitely surprised by this book and in a great way."

—*My Slanted Bookish Ramblings*, 4.5 Stars

"*Jingle Bell Harbor* by Tracy Brogan is about discovering what you want, deciding what you need to finally be happy, and rediscovering a love of the holidays. It's a quick, easy read filled with laughter and enjoyable quirky characters. If you're in the mood for something light and funny, I would recommend *Jingle Bell Harbor* by Tracy Brogan."

—*Harlequin Junkie*, 4 Stars

"This is a really cute, uplifting Christmas novella. It's quick, light, and gives you warm fuzzies just in time for the upcoming holidays. There is plenty of humor to keep you entertained, and the quirky residents of Bell Harbor will keep you reading to see what else is in store."

—*Rainy Day Reading Blog*, 4 Stars

Hold on My Heart

"Successfully blends a sassy heroine and humor with deep emotional issues and a traditional romance . . . The well-developed characters and the sweet story with just a touch of heat will please readers looking for a creative take on romance."

—*Publishers Weekly*

"Launched in hilarious style by an embarrassingly cute meet, this delightful romantic comedy will keep the smiles coming."

—*Library Journal*

Highland Surrender

"*Highland Surrender* features plenty of action, romance, and sex with well-drawn individuals—a strong, yet young heroine and a delectable hero—who don't act out of character. The story imparts a nice feeling of 'you are there,' with a well-presented look at the turbulent life in sixteenth-century Scotland."

—*RT Book Reviews*, 4 Stars

"Treachery and political intrigue provide a well-textured backdrop for a poignant romance in which a young girl, well out of her depths, struggles to reconcile what she thinks she knows with what her heart tells her. *Highland Surrender* is a classic sweep-me-away tale of romance and derring-do!"

—Connie Brockway, *New York Times* Bestselling Author

My Kind
of Forever

Books by Tracy Brogan

Trillium Bay Series

My Kind of You
My Kind of Forever

Bell Harbor Series

Crazy Little Thing
The Best Medicine
Love Me Sweet
Jingle Bell Harbor: A Novella

Stand-alone

Highland Surrender
Hold on My Heart

My Kind of Forever

A Trillium Bay Novel

TRACY BROGAN

Montlake
Romance

Text copyright © 2019 by Tracy Brogan

All rights reserved.

Published by Montlake Romance, Seattle

www.apub.com

Amazon, the Amazon logo, and Montlake Romance are trademarks of Amazon.com, Inc., or its affiliates.

ISBN-13: 9781503902893
ISBN-10: 1503902897

Cover design by Laura Klynstra

Printed in the United States of America

For Tiffany. Thanks for getting me over the hump.

Chapter 1

"Good luck, kid. You're going to need it." Harry Blackwell dropped a well-worn set of brass keys into my unsuspecting palm and stepped toward the open door of the mayor's office—an office which, until last week's election, had been his. For twenty-eight years, he'd served Trillium Bay's community. Before that, his older brother had been the mayor, and before that, their father, and his father before him, and even *his* father before *him*. You get the picture. A Blackwell patriarch has been running the show around here on Wenniway Island pretty much ever since a fiery comet crashed into the earth and killed off all the dinosaurs. That is, until now. Now it was my turn.

That's right. Me. Modest, pragmatic Brooke Therese Callaghan, science teacher turned public servant. Not only had I toppled the Blackwell dynasty, but I was also the first female, and the youngest, mayor ever elected in Trillium Bay. Unprecedented stuff, and trust me, no one was more surprised by my landslide victory than I was. Except for maybe poor old Harry Blackwell.

He took a shuffling sidestep, his scuffed brown loafers scraping softly against the hardwood floor as his long-suffering assistant, Gertie, stood in the background with both hands pressed to her heart, as if the sight of him departing was more than she could bear. She listed to the left, her bony hip bumping up against a gigantic mahogany desk strewn with stacks of manila files, tattered papers, and a plethora of office-y type things. A dented black stapler. A wire in-basket. A dusty bust of Ronald Reagan.

"Where are you going?" I asked as he continued to amble toward the door. "I thought we were meeting to go over . . . things." I wasn't entirely sure what kind of things because, truth be told, I was wholly unprepared to be the mayor. Like a bride who thinks a lot about the wedding but very little about the marriage, I'd focused most of my energy on the campaign without a great deal of strategizing over how to run things in the event that I actually won. But won I had, and having earned the trust of my *constituents*, I was now determined to be the best damn mayor the town had ever seen. Luckily for me, while Harry may have had size-fourteen feet, his shoes should not be all that hard to fill.

"I'm out of here. Goin' fishin'. Gertie can bring you up to speed."

I glanced at his assistant just as Gertie dashed a fat tear from her splotchy cheek.

"Um, I'm sure Gertie will do a fabulous job filling me in, but don't you and I have lots to talk about? I'd like to learn as much from you as I can before you officially step down. You've got so much knowledge and expertise." Out of necessity, I chose to appeal to his battleship-size ego, because even though Harry Blackwell wasn't the most dynamic character, or the most inventive, or ambitious, or insightful for that matter, at the moment, he was my best source of information. Plus, admittedly, the people-pleaser in me wanted him to be happy about this turn of events, which he clearly was not. I'd tarnished his reputation and usurped his power. That was evident in the harsh set of his fleshy jaw.

He plucked a raggedy khaki fishing hat from a spindly coatrack and dropped it on his nearly bald head. "It's already official. I resigned this morning. The tribe has spoken and voted me off the island, so no sense in me sticking around where I'm not wanted. Next week I'm heading down to Florida to visit my grandchildren. You can keep the Reagan statue, but I'll be back for my autographed photos with George and George W."

My breath cut short and I looked to Gertie once more, hoping in vain for some reinforcement, but his assistant just let another tear dribble down her face, her pale brown eyes magnified to triple their size behind her thick reading glasses. She looked like a praying mantis.

"You already resigned? But . . ." My tongue felt suddenly clumsy and thick. "But I'm not supposed to take office until January. It's November. If you've already resigned, then who is in charge right now?"

He crooked a bushy, bristly white eyebrow and looked down at my still-open palm. "See those keys?"

I nodded.

"Looks like you're in charge."

He took advantage of my surprise to slide around and lurch out into the hallway. He was pretty agile for a grumpy old man.

"Best to you, Gertie," he called out, and the bell rang over the lobby entrance as the door rattled open and slammed shut. The sound reverberated against the walls, and inside my chest. The keys grew twice as heavy, and twice as cold, matching the new sensation of foreboding in my lungs. I'd been nervous about our scheduled meeting today. Anxious to get started because I strongly suspected my learning curve wouldn't be steep so much as it would be a straight trajectory upward. Being born and raised on Wenniway, I'd participated in my fair share of committees over the years, and you couldn't live on an island this size without being aware of what things had an impact on the community, but negotiating those decisions and presiding over the city council were far above any of my previous experiences. My gaze lifted from those keys back to Gertie's stricken expression.

"I suppose you'll want to fire me and hire someone younger." She squared her shoulders in a blatantly false display of courage. Her peony-pink lipstick seldom stayed within the actual boundaries of her lips, making their current trembling even more obvious, but her worry was misguided.

"Fire you? Are you crazy? I'm going to need all the help I can get. Please don't leave me." No false flattery there. I was completely sincere.

"Really?" The trembling stopped, and a wobbly sort of smile slanted all her pinched features. Gertie wasn't beautiful by anyone's standards, with jet-black bangs cut too short and straight across her pale forehead, and a reed-thin body that made stick figures look voluptuous, but she had a sweet and efficient quality to her. Never married, she'd devoted her life to the running of this island's government. She was as instrumental in the inner workings as Harry had ever been, and some even went so far as to speculate that she was the real brains behind anything that actually got accomplished. I hoped that was true because it looked like Harry Blackwell had prematurely evacuated.

"Of course I want you to stay, Gertie. You were Harry's right-hand gal, and I've heard that nobody knows the rules and regulations and bylaws like you do. I need you." Relief flooded Gertie's expression, followed by a slight blush, and I got the sense that Harry hadn't spent too much time telling his assistant she did a good job. As a teacher, that was something I could certainly relate to. With a winter population of just over six hundred people, the island had only one school, and that school had only three teachers. I'd been one of them for the past thirteen years, and in all that time, I'd been thanked by parents exactly never times. Teachers are often taken for granted. Like Gertie.

"Oh, thank you, Mayor Callaghan." She all but saluted.

"You've known me since I was a little kid, Gertie. I think it's okay to call me Brooke."

Her smile widened, exposing seriously crooked teeth as she nodded. "Of course. Can I get you some coffee, Mayor . . . um, Brooke?"

Coffee? No one ever got me coffee at school. I could get used to this. "That would be lovely, Gertie. Thanks so much. I take it black."

An all-too-brief flutter of power rushed to my head but was gone as soon as it arrived because, as Gertie walked out, I took my first good, long look around. The mayor's office, *my office*, was a study in chaotic disarray. Dingy walls with marks where pictures had once hung and been moved, gray metal filing cabinets, most with drawers that were too full to close, and cracked pleather furniture with permanent butt dents. And every surface stacked a mile high with papers. This place was one spark away from a raging inferno, and setting it on fire might be the best place to start. I sensed the implementation of a new filing system on the horizon. And some fresh paint on the walls. Surely there would be money in the budget for one gallon of paint?

Gertie returned and handed me a stained, chipped mug with a Wenniway Island logo on it that dated back to the mideighties. Maybe there would be cash in the budget for some new cups, too?

"Thanks, Gertie. I appreciate it. Now, maybe you can take me on a tour of this obstacle course? The first thing you might want to know about me is that I'm obsessively tidy, so all this"—I gestured to the room at large—"this is going to need to be organized."

Gertie's hands clapped together. "Really? Oh, that's the best news I've heard in ages. Harry never let me throw anything away. And he didn't know how to use a computer, so everything had to be printed for him. Even his emails."

"He didn't know how to use a computer?" We good people of Trillium Bay pride ourselves on not just clinging to bits of the past, but embracing and celebrating it, like all the old Victorian architecture and the fact that we don't allow cars, but that was no reason for the *mayor's office* to be without a computer! I mentally moved that item to the top of my political agenda. *Bring modern technology into the city government.* I'd successfully managed to get some decent computers for the school, so this shouldn't be that different. Although reliable internet service was another thing entirely. The whole island suffered from spotty service and sluggish loading times. If I could fix that problem, I'd be a local hero.

Gertie's shellacked, bobbed haircut remained solidly in place as she shook her head. "Harry didn't trust computers. He said the interwebz were created by godless individuals to bring pornography and Amazon drones into our lives. I finally convinced him to let me have one, but there isn't one in his office. Not that there'd be room for one. I haven't seen the surface of that desk since Michael Jackson was at the top of the music charts."

"That's a very long time."

"Tell me about it."

"Well, I guess we should get started then."

Seven hours and twenty-six garbage bags full of shredded documents later, we'd barely made a dent. I still considered the time well spent, however, because Gertie, as everyone suspected, had her finger on the pulse of just about everything happening on the island, and listening to her talk was like an immersion class in small-town government. I, of course, already knew who all the players were, since I'd known most of them my entire life, but Gertie had the inside scoop on the inside scoop. She knew all about how Sudsy Robertson had voted against the new bike-helmet ordinance because his wife loved to ride but thought helmets made her cheeks look fat. She knew that April, May, and June Mahoney were pushing for new zoning laws so they could turn their parents' old house into a bed-and-breakfast and were bribing other members to vote in their favor by plying them with cookies and muffins and rum balls. And she knew that Vera VonMeisterburger, the village librarian, somehow managed to steer every conversation toward the island's current fruit bat shortage, even when it wasn't on the meeting agenda. Actually, everyone knew that, because Vera couldn't *not* talk about the island's fruit bat shortage. That little tidbit was not news. Still, the rest of it was helpful. My father, Chief of Police Harlan Callaghan, sat on the city council and must surely know all this, but being a man of few (or no) words, he hadn't shared any of it with me.

"I think people are excited to see what you can do with this job, Brooke," Gertie said, pulling another trash bag from the box. "But I should probably warn you: they're not going to go easy on you. I wouldn't be surprised if they thought they could push you around because you're so young."

That brought an unexpected smile to my face. I was thirty-six, not sixteen, and I knew how to get things done. Being the oldest of three sisters had its benefits—not to mention the fact that I'd become the de facto woman of the house after my mother died. I was just fourteen when that happened, but old enough to step up and take care of my family. My father was around, of course, but children, and girls in particular, seemed to be a mystery to him. I understood that, and it was easier for me to just handle things on my own, so I was quite accustomed to being in charge.

"I hope people are excited about me being the mayor, and I also hope to prove to everyone that they made the right choice." My heart gave a little thump as nerves gripped me. While my victory may have been decisive, I wasn't naive. I knew why I'd been elected. The good folks of Wenniway Island hadn't chosen me because of my vast intellect or political brilliance. It wasn't my witty, insightful rhetoric or fresh ideas, either. They'd chosen me because Harry Blackwell was a bajillion and a half years old, scientifically speaking, and had no more relatives to follow in his footsteps. They'd chosen me because over the past few years, the business owners of Trillium Bay had grown increasingly frustrated with his stodgy lack of foresight and his refusal to adapt—as evidenced by his inability to use a computer and his less-than-inspirational campaign slogan: *If it ain't broke, don't fix it.* And they'd chosen me because, as a homegrown girl and a teacher, they'd figured I could handle not only the work but the personalities. I knew the score. Like an expert poker player, I understood that playing the cards in my hand was only half the game. The other half was all about learning how to play the *players*.

Chapter 2

I'd walked down Main Street of Trillium Bay hundreds, if not thousands, of times. Today, it looked just as it always had. A thoroughfare of Victorian hotels and storefronts, fudge and taffy shoppes with ornately carved signs, and T-shirt shops designed to look like old fur-trading posts. During the summer months, the wooden sidewalks and the street would be jam-packed with tourists, but as autumn arrived, the crowds dwindled to just a few weather-resistant visitors, construction workers there for winter projects, and a handful of locals. Even so, the ever-present clip-clop of horses' hooves and the jangling of harnesses added to the nostalgia factor. Outsiders thought this town was quaint, but to me it was just home. And although today it looked the same as yesterday, something was *different*. I guess I was different, because now I was the *mayor*.

Just two days ago Harry Blackwell had dropped those keys into my hand, and yesterday I'd stood before Judge Brian Murphy at the Trillium Bay Courthouse to be officially sworn in to my new job. My old job as teacher was being divided between my two previous coworkers until a replacement could be found. The search had begun the day after the election, and a long-term substitute was scheduled to arrive by the end of the week. Everything seemed to be happening in double time, but the pieces were falling into place, and now here I was on my way to my first official meeting.

"Good afternoon, Brooke. Where are you off to all dressed up today?" Mr. O'Doul waved a knobby-knuckled hand from the front steps of his grocery store, clutching a well-worn broom in his other fist. At eighty-nine, he looked every bit his age, and his mind was about as sharp as a crayon, but he was much loved around here, and a bit of a celebrity because his grocery store was (allegedly) the oldest of its kind in the entire United States, although I'm not sure who bothers keeping track of such things. Actually, the source of this information was old Mr. O'Doul himself, so the truth of it was anybody's guess. "Never trust anything you hear from an old Irishman," my grandmother Gigi always said, and she should know because she'd married and buried three of them.

I stopped in front of him. "Good afternoon, Mr. O'Doul. I'm on my way to the city council meeting."

"Oh, are you now?" His wave turned into a not-very-threatening finger point nearly touching me on the left breast. I'd give him the benefit of the doubt for that and blame his poor eyesight.

"Hey," he said, "when you see that Harry Blackwell, you tell him that the missus and me don't like those striped awnings that the Tasty Pastries Bakery just put up. A real eyesore, those awnings."

I had to wonder if old Mr. O'Doul could even see that far, as the pastry shop was a dozen storefronts away from his, but maybe he and his wife passed by them on their way to Sunday morning church, or Wednesday evening square dancing. "Harry Blackwell isn't in charge of that anymore. He has resigned and now I'm the new mayor."

His sudden squint of confusion added to the multitude of lines on his already craggy face. "You're the new mayor? Aren't you still in school?"

"I was a teacher. Now I'm the mayor."

"Did I vote for you?"

"I don't know. I hope so."

He pondered this for a moment before his bony shoulders offered up a dismissive shrug. "Well, I probably voted for you, so please get rid of those ugly awnings. My wife doesn't like them, and when the missus is unhappy, she stops feeling romantic, if you know what I mean." His rheumy eyes gave off a feeble sparkle even as his finger hovered ever closer to my boob. While there was a bit of a gray area regarding just where my obligation to serve the people of Trillium Bay began and ended, I was not about to claim responsibility for the success or failure of Mr. and Mrs. O'Doul's geriatric sex life. Or anyone else's sex life for that matter. I didn't have one of my own to worry about, so theirs was nowhere on my radar.

I patted (swatted) his hand away. "I'll do my best, Mr. O'Doul. Have a nice day now." I continued on my way before he could further engage me in some other pointless commentary. I was already running late and needed to stop by the post office before the meeting. I'd left my house in plenty of time but had foolishly allowed my sister to talk me into wearing not only her navy-blue business suit, which was too tight in the ass, but also her stupidly high-heeled shoes.

"I don't need to wear a business suit, Emily. No one dresses up for these meetings," I'd said to her that morning when she'd stopped over at my place for coffee.

"This is technically your first day as the mayor, Brooke. You have to set the tone. You want them to take you seriously, right? You can't go in there in old jeans and a ratty old sweatshirt."

"I wasn't going to wear old jeans and an old sweatshirt." Probably.

"What were you going to wear?" She'd crossed her arms and looked at me in the same cross-examining way she looked at her daughter when her daughter wasn't being completely honest, and the flush on my face had given me away.

"I was going to wear *new* jeans and a *new* sweatshirt." I vaguely recalled resisting the urge to stick my tongue out at her. Or maybe I did stick my tongue out. Either way, I'd lost that battle, and now I was teetering along the sidewalk like a drunk on stilts. How Emily managed to get around on these wobbly chopsticks was a mystery, but she'd insisted that the red-soled pumps *made* the outfit, and maybe they did, but this pair was a size too big and pitched me forward at such an awkward tilt that I was shuffling more than walking. Three times in the past ten minutes, I'd taken a step forward only to have a shoe stay behind. Let that be the first lesson learned from my new job: don't pretend to be someone I'm not.

I continued on, past the Espresso Yo'self Coffee Bar and the Sugar Pie, Honey Bunch Bakery with the flowered sign in the window that said WE'VE GOT BIG BUNS, AND WE CANNOT LIE. Then, as if to spite me, the spindly heel of one borrowed shoe plunged into a crevice of the sidewalk and stuck. My foot popped out and I launched forward, nearly face-planting onto the sidewalk. I caught an arm on the railing just in time and righted myself before looking around to see if anyone had witnessed my gazellelike gracefulness. A few tourists glanced my way, but seeing that I was okay, they continued on with their day. *Nothing to see here, folks. Move along.* I turned my eyes back to the shoe, glared at it, and at the sidewalk in general. Did we have money in the town budget to repair sidewalk crevices? I certainly hoped so, but first I had to get to the damn meeting. I hopped gingerly back a step and nudged the stuck shoe with my toe. It was wedged in there tighter than me in the Spanx Emily had also insisted I wear. (I hate her, by the way.) I kicked at the shoe with a little more oomph. And then again, with too much oomph that time, because the cursed thing dislodged from the sidewalk, soared through the air like an Olympic javelin, and landed with a wet, squishy squelch, stiletto heel piercing right into the center of a generous pile of horse manure. Naturally. Horse manure. No cars, remember? Bikes and horses. Pooping horses.

Well, crap.

Literally.

Old Vic and his team of street sweepers were very efficient at keeping the roads in town clean, but sticky equine refuse was a common thing, especially on a damp day like today, and it's not that unusual to get some on your shoes if you don't watch where you're going. This was a new twist, though. And quite the dilemma. I pondered my next move while posing flamingo-like on the sidewalk and gazing at the errant shoe perched precariously atop the pounds of poo. It looked like the tackiest decoration on the world's least appetizing wedding cake.

"Nice going there, Cinderella. Need some help?" A masculine voice floated over my shoulder just as a stranger moved into my peripheral vision. He stepped into the street and plucked the red-soled bane of my existence from the mound of horsey excrement. A brown leather jacket strained across his back as he bent over, and when he turned around to face me, I gripped the railing more tightly and momentarily considered swooning. He was tall. Quite tall, and undeniably handsome, all dark-haired and angular-jawed and chivalrous-like, rescuing me in my moment of need. He smiled a Prince Charming smile as if to show me that even his teeth were handsome. Yes, swooning was definitely an option, but sadly, I'm not the type. Though currently in a spot of distress, I'm no damsel. Not even a little bit. I'm Brooke Callaghan, a reasonable, sensible, practical woman, not some fluffy-headed girl prone to whimsical bouts of dramatic emotion. No swooning for me, even if he was hot-damn handsome. I offered back what I hoped was a dignified smile. As dignified as it could be, considering the fact he'd just pulled my shoe from a pile of horseshit.

"Thanks," I said. "That was very nice of you."

"You're welcome. Looks like no harm was done." He tapped my shoe against the edge of the sidewalk, effectively removing any organic matter, then set it next to my foot before straightening up. He was tall enough that I had to tilt my head back to look at his face. Broad, too, with muscular . . . everything. I reconsidered the whole swooning thing, but instead said the first thing that popped into my head.

"Would you like some hand sanitizer?" *Really, Brooke?* I reached into my bag without waiting for his answer, mostly so I could look down and hide abruptly burning cheeks. *Hand sanitizer?*

I heard his soft chuckle as he said, "Um, sure."

Thirteen years as a teacher had taught me that hand sanitizer is always a good thing to carry around, and this just proved it. I was a problem-solver. I shouldn't be embarrassed. I was prepared for anything. I was going to be a phenomenal mayor. My accidental prince held out a hand, and I squirted enough goop into his palm to sterilize a six-person hazmat team infected with Ebola while cleaning up a nuclear power plant explosion. I was a little enthusiastic with my squeeze.

"Thanks. That ought to do it." He rubbed some in and shook off the excess. He might have chuckled again, but I wasn't entirely sure because the cannon at historic Fort Beaumont boomed just then, making me jump like a timid little bunny rabbit, which was ridiculous because I'd heard that damn cannon go off three times a day, every single day of my life. I was normally immune to it, but not today apparently. The cursed shoes had thrown me off-kilter both physically *and* emotionally.

"Don't worry," he said. "I think that's just the cannon at the old fort. It seems to go off pretty regularly."

The irony of a tourist telling me about the island made me smile, and this guy was most certainly a tourist because I'd never seen him before. I would have remembered! And, if I were the type to make split-second assumptions (which I am), I'd bet a year's salary he was on the island to get married. Trillium Bay hosted dozens of weddings each year, and this guy had that utterly well-groomed . . . groomy look to him. His jeans fit just right and weren't the big, baggy dad pants with all the pockets, and his shirt underneath his jacket was snug against his torso, but not too snug. It was black, with a tiny, indistinguishable logo, instead of something broadcasting his love for some college sports team or a cape-wearing superhero. Yep, a groom. Most certainly.

"Yes, they fire the cannon at noon, two, and four. Have you been on the island long?" I slipped my foot into the shoe and tried to regain my composure while at the same time preparing to make a hasty-as-possible exit. Normally I would have chatted up a visitor. I would have mentioned a few touristy things he should be sure to do during his visit, and maybe mentioned that I lived here, but telling someone you lived on the island always prompted a myriad of questions. How did we manage in the winter? What was it like growing up in such a small community? How on earth did we function without cars? And as much as I might enjoy five extra minutes with this sentient Ken doll, I had somewhere important to be, and important governmenty things to do, like . . . well, I wasn't entirely sure yet because my tenure as mayor was literally days old. Nonetheless, there were things. I needed to go attend to the things.

"I've been here a few days," he said. "How about you?"

My smile widened, and I swallowed down a chuckle. "I've been here awhile. Thanks again for your help. Someone will be along any minute to clean that up." I pointed a thumb at the horse poo, not wanting him to think our streets weren't well tended to. "Have a wonderful stay on the island."

He nodded, hesitation flickering across his face until his smile tilted upward again. "I will, thanks, but I have to ask you . . . by complete coincidence, I've been following you for about ten minutes, and this is the third time you've lost a shoe. I find that peculiar."

My cheeks sizzled again, and it had nothing to do with the weak autumn sun, or even his nearby hotness. My face was heating up because, really, what he meant was *what kind of a klutz can't walk and keep her shoes on at the same time?* Which was a very legitimate question. Unfortunately, my answer was *the kind of klutz who lets her sister talk her into things.* In my defense, Emily is ten times more stylish than I am. She's taller, and slender, with gorgeous strawberry-blonde hair. The kind of hair that always makes men look twice, if not three times.

Especially men like the one standing before me, eyeing me with curiosity but not a hint of attraction because my hair is curly and brown and solidly average. Basically, on a scale of one to ten, Emily's an eight. Our younger sister, Lilly, is a twelve, and I hover somewhere around a six, unless it's really humid and then I plummet to a scary, witchy-haired four. Growing up I was often referred to as *the smart one*, and I was never sure if that was a compliment or a concession. Either way, I'd long ago come to terms with that, and hopefully, with my new role in the community, I could prove to everyone that yes, I *am* the smart one. However, this was not an auspicious beginning.

I looked down at my feet. "Um, they're not actually my shoes. They're my sister's and they don't fit. Obviously." Nervous laughter rose from my throat unexpectedly—because it had just hit me. In this prince-rescues-the-damsel scenario, I wasn't Cinderella. I was the aesthetically challenged stepsister. I was Drizella. Awesome. "Anyway, I'm on my way to a meeting, so thanks again."

I turned with a little wave and peered down the street to estimate how many steps were between me and the post office. *Too many.* I'd never make it without another foot-popping mishap, especially with that soon-to-be-somebody's-husband watching me. Choosing the lesser of two embarrassing evils, I kicked off both shoes, hooked them with two fingers, and headed off down the sidewalk to the echo of him chuckling. Again.

Chapter 3

Fifty-five steps. It was fifty-five steps to the Trillium Bay Post Office. I'm not sure why I counted, but I had, and now I knew. Fifty-five. I twisted the old-fashioned crystal doorknob and pushed open the door, hearing the antique brass bell above the frame jingle upon my entrance. Constructed in 1884, the post office harbored that wonderful timeworn-building smell, dampness tinged with dust and several coats of paint. The scent was both familiar and soothing, especially when it also smelled of cookies. Shari Bartholomew had been the postmaster here since before I was born, and not only did she always have the most up-to-date gossip, but she also loved baking. It wasn't unusual to find a plate of cupcakes or cookies waiting to be shared, and I needed a quick dose of simple carbs after the whole shoe-in-the-poo, sexy-stranger ordeal.

Shari looked up from a project in her lap and smiled brightly as I walked into the tiny lobby. Wenniway Island didn't have delivery service, so the post office was a popular visiting spot as neighbors stopped by daily to get their mail. Since most days it only took her a few hours to sort through everyone's letters and magazines, Shari entertained herself between customers with a variety of crafty projects. She'd gone through a lengthy knitting phase one winter until virtually everyone on the island had a hat. And a scarf. And mittens. And an afghan. She'd also tried her hand at watercolor painting, calligraphy, origami, cup stacking, and for a short while, internet poker, until she realized the money part was real. Now she seemed to be doing something with glittery beads and a glue gun.

"Hi, Shari. What do you have there?" I scanned the room for a plate of treats as she held up a coaster-size, cone-shaped piece of thick fabric gloriously adorned with pink and gold rhinestones.

"Pasties," she said, beaming. "Isn't this one pretty?"

I halted in my tracks. "Um, yes. Why are you making pasties? Please tell me they're not for Mr. and Mrs. O'Doul."

She giggled. "Of course not. They're for exotic dancers. I've started selling them online. You'd be amazed what some of these girls will pay for customized pasties."

"I'm already amazed. That is certainly a niche market."

Shari's smile was infectious. "This one gal, Vixen—although I suspect that might not be her real name—has asked me for an entire line inspired by all the major holidays of the year. I'm not entirely certain what to do for Yom Kippur, but I'm always up for a creative challenge. Would you like a brownie?" She set aside her tray of beads and got up from the chair.

"Yes, I would love a brownie. Is there any mail for me?"

"I think there are some catalogues. Why are you carrying your shoes? Isn't it a little cold for going barefoot?" She moved behind the tall counter, where a long row of wooden mailbox slots lined the wall. She'd worked here for so long that most of them weren't even labeled. She just knew where everybody's mail went.

"Emily made me wear them, and they're too big." I sounded like a sullen teen, as if my sister had done this to me on purpose. She hadn't, of course, but I needed to blame someone. Most days I would have told Shari all about the cute guy and my pseudo-Cinderella moment, but I was sort of embarrassed, and not in the mood to get into the details. Pretty soon I'd consider the whole encounter funny, but at the moment, not so much. Knowing this town, she'd hear all about the incident by the end of the day anyway. I hadn't noticed any of the locals paying attention to me or my disobedient footwear, but few things happened on Main Street that were not discussed at length in living rooms all around the island by nightfall.

The bell jingled again, and a short, stocky man in a rust-colored suit entered. He had a smattering of pale hair across his head and dark, beady eyes that darted around the room before landing on me like a pinch to the arm. I'd never seen eyes like that before. I'd also never before encountered a suit with such wide lapels, unless it was while watching old cop shows from the 1970s with my dad. Did they even make polyester anymore? His smile was lopsided as he grinned at us with his yellowish teeth and closed the door firmly behind him.

"Good afternoon, lovely ladies. How are you on this fine day?"

"Just fine, and yourself?" Shari said, leaning her elbows on the counter. I set the shoes down and slipped them on. It wouldn't do for yet another tourist to see the new mayor barefoot. Even this guy with his questionable sense of style.

"I'm fantastic, thank you. I'm hoping you can help me out. I'm looking for some information." His voice was loud and fast and strident, like a used car salesman trying to convince a reluctant buyer that a beat-up old Buick was really the ride they wanted. "Just a little information is all."

"Okay," Shari answered politely. "What kind of information?"

He pulled a couple of business cards from his pocket and handed one to each of us. They were flimsy and looked homemade. I could even see the perforation marks around the edges, and the logo was rudimentary and ill-conceived . . . B.S. INVESTIGATIONS.

"I'm Bill Smith, private investigator from Miami, Florida."

"Private investigator?" Shari glanced over at me.

"Yes, from Miami, Florida," he said again, as if that were significant. "I'm looking for a man."

"Oh, honey, aren't we all?" She smirked at me knowingly. Her errant husband had taken off a few years before, much to the stunned surprise of everyone, especially her. "I should have been suspicious," she'd confided in me once. "We never took vacations, then all of a sudden he went out and bought himself a set of luggage."

The investigator smiled at her, but it wasn't so much a friendly smile as it was an insincere, patronizing one. Like the kind of smile you get from a dog when that dog knows he's in trouble. Something about this guy set my teeth on edge. Something more than his icky, petroleum-based clothing.

"I'm looking for a specific man. I'm hoping you might be able to tell me if this one looks familiar." He pulled a couple of old photographs from another pocket. They were faded and tattered around the edges. He slapped them down on the counter in front of Shari, and I leaned closer to get a better look. The images were hard to make out, but one picture appeared to be a man with short dark hair and a scruffy mustache. He was smoking a cigarette and holding up a beer, and in the other picture, he was sitting on a beach next to a woman with blonde braids. It wasn't much to go on, and clearly these were not current. They were old Polaroids.

"Do you have any idea what year these were taken?" I asked.

"Around 1980. Why? Does he look familiar?" His creepy eyes got even more intense. I found his pupils unnaturally large, which I might not have noticed if he hadn't been staring at me like we were having a no-blinking contest.

"Not really, but whoever this is probably doesn't look like this anymore."

Shari put on her reading glasses to get a better look. "What's his name?" she asked.

"James Novak, as far as I know, but he might be going by something else these days."

She stared for another moment, then pushed the photos back toward Bill Smith from Miami, Florida, and shook her head. "Can't say that I've seen him before. What's he done, anyway? I mean, why are you looking for him?"

The investigator leaned in, his voice lowering. "Can you keep a secret?"

We both nodded even though, in truth, neither one of us had ever kept a secret. *No one* on this island could keep a secret. Or if they could, I guess I didn't know about it.

"He's a master jewel thief. One of the best."

"A jewel thief?" Shari's hand flew to her throat as if to ensure her necklace was still there. "On Wenniway Island?"

He nodded vigorously. "I believe so. I tracked down one of his associates, who said he'd been here as recently as last year."

"An associate? What kind of associate?" She clutched the pendant more tightly.

"A fence. He and Novak have worked together for decades, and based on what he told me, it's possible Novak lives here."

"Lives here?" I said, my surprise canceled out by the complete impossibility of it all. "That's ridiculous. We get a lot of tourist traffic in the summer, Mr. Smith, so it's possible he's visited, but he certainly hasn't spent significant time here. This is a very tight-knit community, and we all know each other. And we've never had an issue with expensive jewelry being stolen. Not even from our elite guests at the Imperial Hotel."

A jewel thief? Living on Wenniway Island? That was crazy talk. And dangerous talk, too, because news of a criminal even *visiting* Trillium Bay could hurt our tourism industry. If this guy went around asking stupid questions like *can you keep a secret*, then this story would spread faster than warm syrup over a stack of hotcakes. I needed to end this fast. "I suggest you take the pictures to my father. He might be able to help you."

"Your father?" The man's sandy-colored eyebrows rose right along with his voice.

I nodded. "Yes, my father is the chief of police on Wenniway Island. Harlan Callaghan. He'd be glad to help you."

The investigator hastily scooped up the photos and stuffed them back into his pocket, his smile tightening. "Well, that's an excellent suggestion. I'll do that. Thank you for your assistance, ladies."

"Would you like me to walk you to the police station? It's on my way," I said as he scuttled back toward the door with the speed of a cockroach.

"No, that won't be necessary. I'm sure I can find it. Good day to you, ladies."

The brass bell jingled, and he was gone.

Shari and I stared at the door for a few seconds until she turned to me, excitement shining in her eyes. "A jewel thief? Right in our very midst, and we never even knew it. Who'da thunk it? Who do you think it is?"

"It's no one, Shari. That guy is nuts. You know everyone who lives here, and even if some random jewel thief did pass through here once, it must not have been for very long."

"Well, of course it's no one who lives here, but maybe he's visiting here now? Maybe he's here for a big heist. Do we have any famous visitors scheduled to stay at the Imperial?" She seemed awfully excited at the prospect of a felon wandering around our town.

"Not that I know of, and think about it, Shari. What kind of criminal comes to a tiny island to hide? We all know each other, so he'd totally stand out. Plus, the occupancy rates at the hotels plummet this time of year. If a thief was going to come here, he'd come in the summer when there are lots of people and lots of distractions. Right?"

"I suppose." She did not sound convinced.

"Listen, we need to keep this one quiet. I can't have that guy scaring people. He gave me the heebie-jeebies with those ferret eyes of his." I rubbed the skin on my arm, trying to remove the feel of his stare.

She waved a hand, dismissing my concerns. "Oh, that guy wasn't so scary, and no one is going to be afraid of a jewel thief."

"Well, maybe they should be. All the regulars who come here for the summer in their expensive boats will go someplace else if there's a sudden crime spree or we get a reputation for harboring criminals."

She rested her cheek on her palm and gazed off into fantasyland. "I think it's glamorous, and don't you think all those other ports where rich people like to park their yachts have the same issues? You think the French riviera doesn't have a burgling problem?"

"I think exotic ports probably do have crime problems, but that doesn't mean we want them here. And seriously, didn't that investigator seem a little off to you? He sure wasn't too interested in talking to my father."

Now Shari pursed her lips and frowned as if I was being beyond silly. "Of course he doesn't want to talk to your father. Private investigators and cops never get along. For goodness' sakes, haven't you ever seen a movie? A television show? The police always want to do things by the book. You know, follow the letter of the law and all that, but the private investigators just want to get the job done, even if it takes a little criminal creativity. Honestly, Brooke, you need to broaden your horizons and learn more about life. Subscribe to HBO, why don't you?"

She did not seem to have the same grave take on this situation that I did. "Thanks for that tip, Shari. I'll just grab a brownie and go. I'm late for the city council meeting."

So far, my first day as mayor was not going quite as planned.

Chapter 4

I shuffled into the Palomino Pub after leaving the post office, not because I needed a drink (although now I sort of did) but because that's where the weekly city council meetings were held. Originally the building had been a trading post used by French and Indian fur trappers, then for a while it was a barbershop where grizzled, bearded men could get a shave and a hot bath for two cents a bucket. Soap, naturally, was extra, and I suspect most men didn't bother with the extravagance. Early in the 1900s, the building became the township offices, and Mayor Blackwell, whichever one was around then, decided meetings should be held there every Wednesday at 3:30 p.m. Then, after World War II, once families started to vacation again, tourism took hold on Wenniway, and this building became a saloon. Council meetings continued to meet there, though, because apparently no one ever thought to change the venue.

Personally, I considered a bar to be a questionable location for the local government to tend to its duties, so my first order of business (well, after organizing and painting my office, installing computers, fixing the damn sidewalks, and rooting out any criminal element on the island) was going to be to relocate our meetings to someplace more professional, less publike. Maybe the library or community center. At least to someplace that didn't smell like old beer and fried pickles. Partly for the message it sent, but also because, as reliable rumor had it, the board members did a fair amount of drinking during meetings. Booze and politicians may go together like mice and cheese, but that didn't mean I had to encourage it. Even if the fried pickles were delicious.

I stepped inside the pub and paused to let my eyes adjust from sunlight to the dim interior. Dark-paneled walls surrounded a collection of unadorned tables and cozy booths.

"Hey there, Cinderella."

I spun around at the sound of that voice, and there, behind the glossy yet dinged-up wooden bar of the Palomino Pub, wiping a highball glass with a red checkered towel, stood Prince Charming. His jacket was gone, and now he wore a dark green T-shirt with the white outline of a horse on it. The logo of the Palomino Pub. Wut? Why?

"What are *you* doing here? Why are you behind the bar?" My voice had a definitive *blurt* quality to it, tinged with annoyed surprise. Not because I was annoyed he was there. It's just that I don't like surprises, and today seemed to be full of them.

Fortunately, he didn't seem to take offense. His responding smile was all mischief and charm. "I work here. My shift started ten minutes ago."

"What do you mean you work here? Since when?" Still blurting. My people skills were sadly lacking today.

"Since yesterday. I'm Leo, by the way. And if you don't mind me asking, why are you wearing your sister's shoes if they don't fit?"

"Because they go with the suit, which is also my sister's." I was feeling oddly defensive for no discernable reason. His questions were completely logical. It's just that my answers were so . . . stupid. I don't like feeling stupid.

"Why are you wearing your sister's suit?"

"Because I'm the mayor," I practically shouted, and even as it came out, I realized that made no sense. I needed to get hold of myself. It wasn't his presence that had me so edgy, it was that weird private investigator and his crazy idea of a jewel thief running around Wenniway

Island. And my first city council meeting. And my shoe in the poo. And, okay fine, his presence, too. Clancy was supposed to be behind the bar. He owned this place, and he was the bartender. No one had told me about a new guy, and news of a cute newcomer was typically a front-page story. How had he gotten hired here without the local gals causing a kerfuffle? And a stampede.

I took a deep breath, a trick I'd had to utilize quite often as a teacher, and tried to gather my thoughts. "Let me start again." I stepped toward the bar, careful to keep my shoes on, and extended my hand. "I'm Brooke Callaghan. I grew up here, and I'm the new mayor of Trillium Bay."

He set down the towel and glass, and our palms met in a very ordinary handshake. He was still stupidly handsome, but I could handle it. Because I was a grown-ass woman and not a hormone-saturated teenager.

"The mayor, huh? Interesting."

"Interesting? In what way?"

His smile stayed relaxed. "Um, just interesting. I don't think I've ever met a mayor before. Especially a barefoot one." His gaze flicked down to my feet and then traveled back to my face. I felt a flush following the trail of his eyes because it seemed as if he might be flirting with me, but no one ever flirted with me, so it probably wasn't that. In all honesty, I wouldn't recognize flirting if it bonked me in the head with a rubber mallet. That ship had long since sailed: the downside of growing up in a small, isolated community. No one bothered to flirt with me anymore.

"Brooke, honey! There you are. Congratulations! I heard Harry turned tail and ran as soon as you stepped into his office." Dmitri Krushnic stepped out from the small room off to the side of the main bar area where we held our meetings. His generous smile exposed a significant gap between his two front teeth, and he was wearing his beekeeping hat because he always wore his beekeeping hat, but he swept it from his head and bowed before me with a dramatic flourish. It was like being welcomed by a musketeer.

Never one to follow the polite rules of society, Dmitri let his salt-and-pepper hair flow freely past his shoulders, and on all of Wenniway Island, he was one of my most favorite people. Despite his eccentricities and our significant age difference, he'd always treated me as an adult, as an equal. He'd also been the one to sit with me after my mother's funeral, and his kindness that day was something I'd never forget. I'd adored him ever since.

"I don't think I scared him away, Dmitri. I think he just didn't want to help me. Thank goodness for Gertie. Say, have you met the new bartender? Apparently, he works here now." The *why didn't anyone tell me?* was obvious in my inflection.

Dmitri was upright once more and nodded, tossing his hat onto one of the tables. "We have met. The kid makes a good gin and tonic. I'll have another, by the way." He held up an empty glass, and I saw a chance to implement my first policy change.

"How about we hold off on the cocktails until after the meeting."

Dmitri walked to the bar and set the glass down before turning back to me.

"You expect me to sit in that tiny room and listen to Vera VonMeisterburger drone on endlessly about our fruit bat shortage without having a bit of anesthetic in my system?" he asked.

"Vera's bat shortage crusade is not on today's agenda."

"It was never on Harry's agenda, either." He lifted his glass again, shaking the ice and winking at the new bartender. What had he said his name was? Oh yes. Leo. Leo, the tall, dark, handsome good Samaritan/bartender.

"I intend to stick to the agenda," I said firmly to Dmitri, then looked at Leo with my stern teacher face. "Hold off on the cocktails, please. Nothing but soft drinks for at least an hour."

"You got it, Mayor," he said, picking up another glass to dry.

Dmitri shook his head, his forehead furrowing in a mild scowl. "Kid, you don't work for her. You work for Clancy McArthur, the owner of this fine establishment, and never in his life would Clancy deny a patron a refreshing libation. Especially if that patron had to listen to . . . Why, hello there, Vera!"

I heard the door open, and the scent of mothballs and camphor assailed my nose as the Trillium Bay librarian bustled inside, a well-stuffed, purple canvas bag over her shoulder. Her nearly white hair was woven into two uneven braids that hung to her ample waist. If Dmitri was my most favorite person, Vera was my least favorite. In fact, with just a few exceptions, I suspect she was everyone's least favorite. Few on the island had escaped her wrath at one time or another, and an overdue book was enough to trigger her laser-beam glare. It burned through your skin like a flamethrower. We'd all been scared to death of her as kids, and somehow it was the kind of fear one never outgrew.

"Good afternoon, Dmitri. Madam Mayor." Everything about her demeanor said severity, until she turned and spotted the new guy. Her face transformed into a sublime gaze of appreciation. "Why, hello there," she purred. "You're new. What's your name?"

I watched his Adam's apple bob as he swallowed. Vera had that kind of instantaneous impact on people. "Leo. Leo Walker. You must be Mrs. VonMeisterburger." His smile stayed steady, if a little forced, and kudos to him for remembering that mouthful of a name.

"That's *Miss* VonMeisterburger, Mr. Walker," she said coquettishly, running an age-spotted hand down one skinny braid. "So nice to meet you. Are you the new bartender?"

He nodded. "Yes, ma'am. Can I offer you something to drink? Iced tea? Lemonade?"

She didn't bat a lash. "Dewar's. Neat. Care to join me?"

He didn't bat a lash, either. It was impressive. I'd seen grown men tremble under her stare, but he was cool as a professional gambler bluffing with a pair of threes. "Perhaps another time, ma'am. I never drink on the job."

The door opened again as other city council members ambled in, effectively saving Leo from any further disturbing advances from our frisky librarian. There was June Mahoney in floral pants that stretched across her vast backside like an entire field of poppies. She was a long-time archnemesis of my grandmother, Gigi. They'd recently called a truce to the generations-old feud, but it was fragile, sure to topple at the slightest insult. Behind her was Olivia Bostwick, all ninety-five pounds of her, most of it in the form of a helmet of curls circa 1975. She'd been the longtime nemesis of my sister because Emily had broken the heart of Olivia's son about a thousand years ago. Grudges were a bit of a hobby around here.

My father came in next, tall and gruff with mirrored sunglasses hooked in the neckline of his uniform. Sometimes he skipped the city council meetings because he couldn't stand the bickering and wheel-spinning, but I guess he didn't want to miss my debut as the ringmaster of this particular circus. I felt a little flutter of appreciation, since he wasn't one to make a fuss about such things. Sentimentality was not his strong suit. In fact, I'd never even dared to ask if he'd voted for me.

Semiretired and leathery-skinned Sudsy Robertson of no-bike-helmet fame came in next, wearing plaid pants and a pink cashmere sweater. He owned a dozen businesses on the island and only left his golf game to attend these meetings to ensure that no new laws, regula-tions, ordinances, guidelines, edicts, rulings, statutes, directives, or even suggestions interfered with any of his moneymaking ventures. He loved the island, but he was a capitalist first and foremost. The rest of the council, excluding my father, were more like a homeowners association hulked-out on mega-steroids and fueled by Red Bull. They considered it their sacred duty to micromanage every aspect of island life. We had bylaws about everything from the size of window boxes allowed on people's houses to what color the storefronts on Main Street can be.

There are rules about flowerbeds and flagpoles and chicken coops and sheds. Rules about pub hours, speed limits for bikes, and even laws about where it's okay to feed the ducks and where it isn't. Managing such minutiae was about to become my job.

I walked into our private meeting room as everyone called out drink orders to Leo.

"Let's keep those drinks nonalcoholic, please," I said loudly. There was dead silence for a moment, then everyone burst into a loud, unanimous guffaw. So much for my power play. Apparently, I'd have to make it an official bylaw if I wanted everyone's drinking habits curtailed in the future.

As we settled down around the rectangular table, we were joined by Monty Price, our town lawyer; Ben Hawthorne, who ran the cemetery board; and Maggie Webster, president of the chamber of commerce.

"Welcome, everyone. I'm sure Gertie will be along any moment," I said, standing up at the end of the table. "I'd like to call this meeting to order."

"But we need the pickles," Sudsy said. "We can't start the meeting without the fried pickles."

"I think we can," I said. They all exchanged horrified glances, as if I'd said *let's start the meeting by first removing our clothes.* "Gertie has the printed agenda, but since I emailed it to each of you in advance, you should all have it on your phones." Another round-robin exchange of blank expressions, and my heart sank just a little bit. "Does anyone have the agenda on their phone?"

"How on earth am I supposed to bring my phone, Brooke?" June Mahoney asked. "It's attached to the wall of my kitchen, and the cord isn't that long."

My heart dropped again and rattled in my chest, like an elevator with the cables snapping one by one. I'd thought my experience as a teacher would be an advantage in this new role, but I hadn't considered that my demographic had shifted significantly. These were not a bunch of kids, well versed in and wholly dependent on their electronic devices. These people were old. Old people who'd grown up on an island where movies were still watched on VHS tapes. Time to recalibrate my messaging.

I heard the pub door slam just then, and seconds later Gertie came flying around the corner, a bundle of papers in her hands.

"Sorry I'm late, everyone. I had a little trouble with the printer." She rushed around the room, her track shoes squeaking on the wood floor as she passed out the agendas; then she plopped down into a chair and demanded breathlessly, "Where the hell are the pickles?"

❀

"I didn't mean to eavesdrop," Leo said after everyone else had left and I remained seated in the small meeting room holding my aching head in my hands. "But it sounds like you have your work cut out for you."

Wow. Did I ever. I'd just spent the past two hours listening to so-called adults bickering about a litany of arbitrary topics. Should Polly's Popcorn Shop be allowed to sell day-old products? Could the street sweepers add five minutes to their afternoon break? Who was going to play Santa during the Christmas Parade if Harry didn't come back in time? And the biggest topic of the day? Did everyone see the awnings Tasty Pastries had put up, and who on earth had approved that?

"It's like they couldn't even hear me talking," I said, looking up at him for a response, just to reassure myself that I was, in fact, speaking out loud.

He picked up an empty glass with one hand while wiping a ring of condensation off the table with a damp rag. "I'm not sure they could hear each other talking. Seemed like a lot of monologuing without any listening."

"But I had an agenda." I shook my paper, now covered in notes that I'd scribbled in the margins about all the *other* things I wanted to discuss, at him. Things I *would* have discussed if I could have gotten a word in edgewise. The only one who didn't interrupt me was my own father, but that's because he didn't say anything the entire time. Not unusual for him, but I had hoped to demonstrate a little more power over that cluster of clucking hens. Even Dmitri wasn't any help. "They were worse than teenagers. I have so many great ideas, but all they care about is the awnings."

Leo wiped another spot off the table. "What ideas?" He gazed down at me, and I noted how dark blue his eyes were. Depths-of-the-ocean kind of blue. The kind of eyes that made every glance feel significant, even if it meant nothing at all. A flutter of something long-forgotten tickled inside my veins. Attraction. Followed by an immediate need to ignore it.

"Oh, all kinds of ideas." I smiled tiredly and pushed myself up, because it was nearly five thirty and the Palomino Pub would start filling up with the evening crew pretty soon. "I'll get out of the way now so you can have the room for dinner guests."

"Speaking of dinner," he said, "I'm new around here, so I was wondering, what restaurants do you like?"

"Oh, we have lots of great places to eat. All price ranges. The Windemere Grill is right down on the corner. There's the Imperial Hotel dining room if you want something elegant. The Feast Well Bistro, Carmen's Café, and Tate's Tavern on the Bluff are good, too. At the tavern, you can watch the sun set behind Petoskey Bridge. It's a great view. And for breakfast, I recommend Link & Patty's Breakfast Buffet. The pink piggy décor is a little much, but the pancakes are the best."

"Are you suggesting we have dinner *and* breakfast?" His dark eyebrow arched just as the corner of his mouth quirked in a ridiculously endearing fashion.

I pushed in my chair with an abrupt scrape. "Excuse me?"

"I was inviting you to dinner. You were inviting me to breakfast."

That flutter of attraction multiplied even as my mouth fell open for a second. I'm sure it was a great look on me. "I wasn't. And you weren't. Were you?"

He laughed, and even though it might have been at my expense, the sound of it sent a flush over my skin and a tingle to places that hadn't tingled for a very long time.

"I was inviting you to dinner, but not very well, apparently. I've been on the island a few days, but I don't know anyone here, so would you like to have dinner with me?"

I was starving. And he was handsome. And new in town. And looked to be roughly my age. There was no history, no baggage, no reason to say no. But it had been so long since anyone had asked me out, it nearly felt improper. Everyone knew me around here. Everyone would know that we'd had dinner, and certainly everyone would have an opinion about it. And it's not as if we could go someplace *private* because there was no place private on the entire island. And there was that issue of the flutter. I didn't want to be fluttering. Fluttering led to heartbreak.

He leaned against the table. "Unless you think your boyfriend wouldn't like it."

I recognized that ploy well enough. That was man-speak for *do you have a boyfriend?* I didn't, though. I didn't even have a dog. I lived alone on Ojibwa Boulevard in a sweet little house with a white picket fence, surrounded by lilac bushes. I'd lived there since I'd turned twenty-three and returned from college to begin teaching at Trillium Bay School. And I was long overdue for dinner out with a man. Desperately overdue. But I was the mayor now, and everything I did, especially in these first few months, was going to be scrutinized with microscopic intensity. Plus, I didn't know anything about this guy, other than the fact that he was movie-star delicious and made a mean gin and tonic. He could have all sorts of secrets behind that slow, easy smile. I'd known a man with secrets before, and it hadn't turned out well for me. I'd need more information before I could make an educated decision. If he was the new bartender, he'd be around for a while. Dinner could wait.

"No boyfriend," I finally said. "But I'm pretty new at this job and I actually have a ton of work I have to do." That was an excuse, but it wasn't untrue. I did have work, and what I didn't have at the moment were any emotional reserves to spend on an evening attempting to be witty and engaging while trying to pretend that the flutter wasn't there. "Could we do it another time?"

His smile stayed in place, and I felt an illogical twinge of disappointment that he seemed to show little disappointment of his own. I guess he really was just looking for someone, *anyone*, to have dinner with. So much for feeling special. The flutter evaporated, replaced by a pragmatic sense of self-protection.

"Sure. You let me know when. Other than working, my schedule is wide open."

He picked up the few glasses remaining on the table and walked from the room.

Well . . . so much for that.

Chapter 5

Sunday evening dinners at my grandmother's house had become a family habit ever since Emily moved back to the island last summer. She, along with her thirteen-year-old daughter, Chloe, now lived with Gigi, and Emily's boyfriend, Ryan, was a frequent fixture there as well. He lived in one of the few condo villas on the south side of the island, an area where the buildings had been constructed sometime within the past fifty years. You know—new stuff.

On this particular Sunday, we were gathered on the front porch. It was a surprisingly warm evening by November standards, and we were taking advantage of the last bit of sunshine, knowing that winter was on its way. I'd been filling them in on the city council's antics, and deliberately avoiding any mention of the alleged jewel thief, when my father arrived. He walked up the wide steps, shoes thumping softly on the old wooden stairs.

"Evening, ladies. Ryan." He nodded at each of us as we said our hellos.

Ryan stood up to shake his hand. "Chief. Nice to see you."

Gigi and I were on the porch swing surrounded by well-worn chintz cushions and a couple of fuzzy throw blankets. She was polishing off her second martini while I nursed a weak vodka and cranberry. Emily and Chloe lounged nearby on a wicker outdoor sofa with one of Gigi's cats reclining between them. I didn't know which cat it was because I'd stopped paying attention to that a long time ago. Gigi was forever taking in strays. They'd hang around for a while and then eventually move on. Half the time she didn't even bother to name them. She just called them all kitty.

"I'm afraid I have a bit of sad news," my father said as Ryan settled back down on the other side of Emily.

"Sad news, Grandpa?" Chloe looked up from her phone.

"Yep, sad news for certain," Harlan said, leaning against the white-washed post and sliding his hands into the pockets of jeans that were at least as old as his granddaughter. Like most people born here, Harlan Callaghan was nothing if not frugal, and one did not discard a perfectly good pair of pants, even if they did date back a decade or two. "Bridget O'Malley has finally called it quits," he said. "Poor old girl kicked the bucket, as it were."

"She died?" Emily said. "When?"

"This morning. She was quilting with some of the other old gals over at Delores Crenshaw's house, and they all thought she'd just dozed off. Not sure how long she sat there until they figured it out."

"That's terrible," Chloe said, pulling the cat into her lap for comfort. "No one even noticed?"

"Well, keep in mind, Niblet, those quilting ladies are none too young themselves, and Bridget just turned a hundred and three years old. She napped all the time, only this time she didn't wake up."

This news was not really a surprise, but still a shock. Bridget O'Malley had been as much a fixture of the island as most of the historic buildings. In fact, her own house was now a special landmark, what with its pink exterior and the dubious honor of being the most fire-prone house in Trillium Bay. She tended to use her smoke alarm as an oven timer. Smoke poured from her windows so often you'd have thought she lived in an active volcano. Or had a pet dragon in there.

We sat in silence for a moment until Gigi said, "Well, I suggest we make a toast, and in that case, I'll need to refill this glass. Harlan, get me a martini, won't you?"

He glanced at me and I held up two fingers, indicating she was on her second. We tried to keep track—not that it did any good.

"I'll get it for you," Emily said, standing up. "Dad, you sit down. Can I get you a beer?"

"Well," he said, "since we're toasting . . ." as if he'd ever turned down a beer after a long day of work. He settled into a vacant chair near his granddaughter and gave Chloe's hair a ruffle, then looked back to me. "That was some council meeting the other day. Vera needs to get a grip. If I have to hear one more thing about bats, I'm going to lock her up in jail."

"Is that an option?"

"Probably not. Not unless she stages some sort of protest and things get out of hand."

"I've only spoken to that crackpot woman once in my life," Ryan added with a visible shudder, "and still, the nightmares."

Ryan Taggert had come to the island last summer for a hotel renovation project, but one look at my sister, and he'd taken root and stayed. Currently they were working together on remodeling a bed-and-breakfast over on Blueberry Lane. I liked Ryan, and I liked him with my sister, but deep down I had to admit that their romance triggered some unwanted envy in me. I didn't begrudge them their happiness, but it reminded me of everything my life currently didn't have. No significant other, no marriage on the horizon. No kids. That was stuff I'd wanted. Something I'd always assumed I'd have, but the dating pool on the island had pretty much dried up for me. Sure, there were guys like Leo Walker. The type who came to Trillium Bay for a few months or so and got all the single ladies revved up and hopeful, but those guys never stayed. That wasn't what I wanted. I didn't want temporary. I wanted a forever kind of guy.

The screen door banged shut as Emily returned with a tray of drinks. She handed the three-olive martini to Gigi before doling out the beers, keeping one for herself. She sat back down on the sofa so close to Ryan that she was nearly in his lap. They were like Velcro, those two. Another pang of guilt-tinged envy rippled through me, but I pushed it away.

"No martini for me, huh, Mom?" Chloe asked.

"You know the rule. No drinking until you're fourteen," Ryan teased.

Chloe's sigh was purely for dramatic effect. "Guess I'll just have to toast old Mrs. O'Malley with this lemonade."

Gigi held up her drink. "To Bridget O'Malley. She never returned anything she borrowed, and she died owing me thirteen dollars and twenty-seven cents, but she made the flakiest pie crusts this island has ever seen. May she rest in peace."

"One hundred and three," Chloe murmured after sipping her lemonade. "That's like my life times"—she calculated in her head—"times eight. Wow. Did she have any family? Did she ever get married?"

Harlan shook his head. "Nope. Never."

"That's so sad. She must have been so lonely." Chloe stroked the kitty as it stretched across her legs.

Gigi popped an olive into her mouth and talked around it. "She wasn't lonely. Oh, sure, she never had a husband of her own, per se, but back in the day she had plenty of husbands who belonged to other women. So I guess she did return some of the things she borrowed."

Emily gasped. "Gigi, little ears are present!"

Chloe's expression turned from sympathetic to indignant. "Seriously? Little ears? What am I, seven? It's not like I don't know anything about sex, Mom."

Emily covered her ears with a *la, la, la*, even though I knew for a fact that she and my niece had discussed virtually all age-appropriate aspects of sex, love, and romance, which, as we all know, are not always synonymous.

Chloe's humor returned. "Would it make you feel better if I called it the 'special hug'? Isn't that what you used to tell me? Married people have a special hug?" She fell back in her seat, shaking with laughter, and I found myself giggling along with her.

"Speaking of special hugs," Gigi said. "I have a little announcement of my own."

All the laughter abruptly halted as we turned as one toward Gigi. I didn't dare guess where she was headed with this, but my instincts told me it would be something I could not un-hear. Everyone else seemed to be staring at her with the same concern. Gigi was not one to use caution when speaking.

She took a loud slurp from her martini before continuing. "As you know, my dear third husband, Bert, left us a while back, may he rest in peace, along with Conroy, and of course Harlan's wonderful father." Gigi made a hasty sign of the cross to send off a blessing to each of her three dead spouses. "But woman cannot live on bread and gin alone, and so I've taken a lover."

Awkward silence was followed by the sound of my father slapping a hand to his forehead. "Good Lord, Mother," he groaned. Ryan made a tight sort of gurgling sound before taking a hefty drink of his beer, and I exchanged a long stare with my sister.

"What? It's a healthy thing to do. I'm vibrant. This baby got back." She patted the tight curls of her gray hair and took another sip from her glass.

"You go, Gigi!" Chloe cheered.

"I'm not so sure it's healthy for any of us to have to hear about it, though," I said, wishing I could rewind time about sixty seconds so I could have gotten myself a stronger drink. It was bad enough to feel jealous of my sister's romance. Now I had to be jealous of my own grandmother?

"Why not discuss it? Aren't we all modern women?" Gigi was seemingly undeterred by our collective unrest.

"I'm not." My father held up his hand. "I'm not a woman, and I'm not modern, and I don't need to know about any of this. What you do in your . . ." He cleared his throat. "In your private time is your own business, and it is not necessary to keep us informed. Ever again."

Ryan nodded vigorously. "I'm with the chief on this. I learned to mind my own business when my dad started doing the 'special hug' with someone half his age. Oh . . . sorry, Chief."

My father closed his eyes and pinched the bridge of his nose, because the "hug-ee" in question was my youngest sister, Lilly. She and Ryan's widowed father had fallen head over heels in love last summer and were now traveling the world together. And *hugging*—a detail my father tried very hard to forget.

"Well, I had no idea you two were such prudes," Gigi scoffed. "Why is it, do you suppose, that men simply cannot handle a woman being in charge of her own sexuality?"

"Gigi," Emily said, "although I don't disagree with your point, maybe we could have this conversation another time. It's sort of a complicated subject, and I'm starving."

"Oh, all right, fine. I'll feed you puritans your dinner, but first I need to tell you the rest. My lover and I have decided to move in together. I'm not ready to get married again, but we want to give things a trial run, so Emily, you and Chloe may continue to live here in my house, and I'll be moving in with Gus."

"Gus?" Harlan's voice exploded like a grenade. "Gus Mahoney?"

Gigi took a prim little sip of her martini before answering. "Yes, Gus Mahoney. You all wanted the Callaghan-Mahoney feud to end, and so it has. Gus and I have been secretly dating for a few weeks now, and he's really quite charming. So unexpected, considering he's got those awful sisters, but it turns out he doesn't like them any more than I do. I never knew."

April, May, and especially June Mahoney had made it their mission to annoy Gigi all throughout her life, and Gigi gave them back as good as she got. The fragile truce that had been engineered last summer was sure to collapse under the weight of this new development.

"Do the Mahoney sisters know anything about this?" Emily asked, her voice falling to a strangled whisper.

"Gus is telling them this weekend, and it's not as if they'll have anything to say about it. It's not their business."

"It's going to become everybody's business, Gigi," I said, "and June Mahoney is going to drag you to the top of Bent Rock and pitch you into the lake. There's no way she'll let this happen."

"It's already happened. I mean, we haven't moved in together yet, obviously, but there has been all sorts of fornication. Trust me, that ship has sailed."

"Jeeeezus," Harlan muttered.

"I think it's cute," Chloe stated. "And Susie Mahoney is my best friend, so now it's like we're all practically related."

It wasn't cute. It was all kinds of gross and disastrous. The first real scandal of my new administration. August Mahoney was a good ten years younger than my grandmother and covered in such quasi-pornographic tattoos from his days in the marines that his sisters forbade him to ever go anywhere shirtless. "Have you seen the tattoos?" I had to ask.

Gigi's coy smirk spoke volumes, leaving no doubt that some of that fornicating was being performed in full light. "His tattoos aren't so bad. He had a few of them altered, you know—had little bras and panties added to all the naked ones."

Emily's stare in my direction was equal parts horror and humor. She was looking at me as if I should be *doing* something about this, but what?

"Mother, you cannot move in with Gus Mahoney," Harlan said. "You just . . . can't."

"Why?"

His face flushed, and I could see perspiration beading on his forehead. My father was not easily flustered. In fact, I'm not sure I'd ever seen him lose his cool. He was more of the silent, brooding type, but not today. He looked ready to pop a cork.

"You just can't," he ground out. "People will talk."

"Good. Let them. We haven't had a good old-fashioned scandal around here in ages."

"But I'm the mayor now, Gigi," I reminded her. "What you do affects the whole family."

"I wouldn't worry about that, Brooke. Every single person on that city council has a skeleton or two in their closet, and so do most of the people who live here. And you know what they say about throwing glasses at stone houses, or however that saying goes. Gus and I are two consenting adults, and what we do is our own business, and if I want to live with him, I'm going to live with him. Now, who wants some pot roast?" She stood up and walked into the house, slamming the screen door in her wake.

I looked around at the collection of expressions on my family's faces, and no one said a word until finally Ryan stood up.

"I'm starving. Maybe during dinner, we could talk about something more pleasant. Less traumatic? Like world hunger, or Vera VonMeisterburger, or how poor old Bridget O'Malley sat dead for hours in a roomful of quilters?"

Chapter 6

Saint Bartholomew's Catholic Church was filled to the sills of the stained-glass windows with mourners who'd come to pay their final respects to Bridget O'Malley. Surveying the funeral crowd, I couldn't think of anyone from the island who wasn't in attendance. Gigi, my father, and I were sitting in the fifth row, on the right, just as we did every Sunday. Catholics are all about routine, you know. Woe to the unsuspecting visiting Protestant who might sit in the wrong pew. It threw off the entire hierarchy. Emily, Chloe, and Ryan were sitting in front of us, and over to the left, I spotted Gloria Persimmons. At thirty-one years old, she was typically a study in tie-dye, neon, and sparkly accessories, but today she wore a very subdued black dress, although it was adorned with pink dots that, upon closer inspection, turned out to be little iguanas. Her mammoth boyfriend, Tiny Kloosterman, sat patiently beside her as she dabbed at her nose with a tissue. Tiny was the foreman of my sister's construction crew, and the quintessential version of a menacing-looking guy who was actually an overstuffed teddy bear.

At the organ, Delores Crenshaw's nine-year-old great-granddaughter was hammering out a medley of Bridget's favorite tunes with far more gusto than talent. Because nothing says *welcome to the afterlife* like hearing "I'm Looking Over a Four Leaf Clover" banged out by a nearsighted third grader. The sounds reverberated around the lousy acoustics of the historic church until even the statue of the Virgin Mary started looking impatient and uncomfortable.

At last Father O'Reilly took his place near the altar and offered up some prayers and a wonderfully brief but heartfelt speech about a life well lived. He gamely glossed over some of Bridget's less-than-stellar qualities. Like that thing about the adultery. The eulogies were brief as well. Percy O'Keefe talked about how Bridget liked to make him meatloaf because he took care of her yard. Maggie Webster told a story about Bridget teaching her to crochet when she was a little girl, and Dmitri told a very engaging, if somewhat off-color, story of how Bridget once caught him hanging laundry out to dry when he was wearing nothing but a pair of boxers. The stories were sweet but lacked substance, and I began to realize that, since most of her peers had long since preceded her to that great big Fudge Shoppe in the sky, those of us who were left didn't remember that much about her. It made me sad to think she'd left so shallow a mark, but with no family there was no one to claim her legacy.

Gloria sniffled loudly, and it was oddly comforting. Some reassurance that there was *someone* who seemed to be taking this hard. In fact, judging from the noise, Gloria appeared to be quite distraught. I'd known they were friends, and that it was often Gloria who'd brought Bridget to Sunday services, so her grief made sense. Even so, she was pretty damned emotional. Then again, Gloria never did anything halfway. She was all in, all the time.

Delores Crenshaw seemed to be taking it hard, too, clutching a lace handkerchief to her red nose. "I tried to offer her a macaroon," she told Gigi and me as the service ended and we all filed out into the churchyard. "I thought she was just being passive-aggressive. You know, ignoring me because everyone knows my macaroons are tastier than hers, so I gave her a tough little nudge on the shoulder. Damned if the poor woman didn't tip right over and fall to the floor. Now I feel terrible. I'd just had that rug cleaned."

Technically it wasn't Delores's fault, but maybe she *should* have felt terrible. I mean, it's bad enough to have someone keel over in your house without anyone noticing, but to be the person who knocked the body to the floor? Yeah, that's awkward.

"There, there, Delores," Gigi responded with a consoling pat on the back. "We all know it's Midge Clairmont who makes the tastiest macaroons. Yours are very gummy." This, of course, only sent Delores into another fit of tears.

"Nice going, Gigi," I whispered as we stepped away to make room for the pallbearers. They looked somber in their dark suits. Dmitri, with his hair pulled back into a ponytail; Harvey Murdock, who owned several fudge shops; Brian Murphy, our local judge and frequent drinking pal of my father's; and enormous Tiny Kloosterman, who, in all honesty, could have hoisted the pine box onto his shoulder all by himself and jogged with it all the way to the burial site. Instead, they walked slowly and deliberately from the front of the church, gently loading the casket onto the funeral carriage.

The weather was appropriately gloomy and overcast, but the carriage still gleamed. I stared at it, noting that in some ways it was beautiful, all glossy black with gold accents, but of course, I could never see that thing without remembering the day I'd walked behind it, holding hands with ten-year-old Emily and five-year-old Lilly as it carried our mother away. She'd died very unexpectedly from a heart defect that no knew she had until it was too late. Our father had walked ahead of us that day, head down, never once looking back to see if we were okay. That kind of set the stage for the next twenty years: me taking care of my sisters, and my father assuming we'd handle things without his intervention. It wasn't that he meant to be neglectful. Even at fourteen, I understood that he was lost without my mother, and clueless about raising daughters. Gigi was around, of course, but I decided pretty early on that I'd rather just take care of things myself.

With Bridget O'Malley loaded into the back, the carriage driver clucked at the horses, and the processional slowly wended its way along Lake Shore Avenue, down Big Pine Lane, past the newly remodeled Clairmont Hotel, and on to Croton Hill, where the Wenniway Island Cemetery was located. Gravestones from as far back as 1764 dotted the landscape, some so old and weathered that the names and dates had long since worn away. As the casket was lowered into the ground, Stan MacPherson and his two sons played "Amazing Grace" on their bagpipes, and I felt unexpected tears prickle behind my eyelids.

"Bridget would have loved this," Gigi said with a sigh, gazing up at the pale sky. "She always did love a good funeral. She said black made her look taller, and damned if it didn't."

"She loved sparkly pinks, too," Gloria whispered loudly from behind us. Her voice trembled, and Tiny pulled her closer to his beefy side. They'd been dating since last summer, ever since my sister had encouraged Tiny to invite Gloria to a square dance. Ever the attentive boyfriend, he dutifully took Gloria's wadded-up tissue and handed her a new one. "I really loved that old bitch," she gurgled, and burst into a full-blown sob. The bagpipe music moaned to a pitchy halt, and Clancy McArthur called out, "First drink at the Palomino Pub is on the house! Time for a right proper wake."

Like thirsty lemmings, we followed. We were the world's least organized parade, or perhaps the world's least threatening gang. Somewhere near the corner of Perkins and Main, someone started singing "O Danny Boy," and so it went as we strode purposefully to the pub. Bridget O'Malley was most certainly sitting on a cloud right above us, singing along.

"Why, hello, Madam Mayor," Leo said, smiling broadly as I walked into the pub a few minutes later and wound my way up to the bar. His presence caught me off guard. With all the funeral and mayor-ing stuff over the past few days, I'd kind of forgotten about him, but one look at that face and it all came back to me. Handsome, helpful Leo Walker who now worked at Clancy's pub, and who looked right at home with his shirtsleeves pushed up to his elbows and a beer in each hand. Trigger the fluttering.

"What can I do for you?" he asked.

Realistically there were a couple of different answers I wanted to give him. *Seduce me. Marry me. Help me forget that everyone on this island seems to be having sex except for me, including my grandmother and the ancient O'Douls.* But I opted for a straightforward and non-flirtatious response instead. "I'll have a vodka tonic, please."

"Coming right up." He quickly filled a glass with ice and pulled a bottle from the shelf behind him. "Take a seat. Talk to me for a bit."

I suppose it's the least I can do, what with him not having any friends on the island. I am the mayor, after all. "Okay." I settled onto a stool and watched as he expertly filled the glass. Not that filling a glass is all that complicated, but he held the bottle up high and then gave it a little flip when he was done. This is not a skill that is remotely useful unless you are a bartender, but still, I was impressed.

Someone jostled me and Dmitri appeared, nudging a few people aside to settle himself on the barstool next to mine. He'd attended the funeral service without his beekeeping hat, but now it was back in place, with the netting pulled up around the brim. He'd taken off his dark suit coat and replaced his dress shoes with hiking boots. An odd pairing with his dress slacks, but I'd seen him in stranger outfits.

"So, tell me about this FBI agent you and Shari talked to," he said. His voice was loud over the din of the crowd, and Leo turned to stare.

"FBI agent?" Leo said.

I shook my head at them both. "He wasn't an FBI agent at all. He was some skeevy private investigator from Florida with some ridiculous story about a jewel thief hiding out on this island."

"A jewel thief?" Leo's brows rose with interest as he set my drink down in front of me on a little cardboard coaster.

"Gin and tonic, kid," Dmitri said, then turned to me. "What makes you think it's so ridiculous?"

"It's ridiculous because we know every single person who lives on this island, and we know the regulars who just come for the summer, and not a one of them is a jewel thief."

"How do you know?" Leo asked, scooping ice into a glass.

I resisted rolling my eyes. "I just do."

Dmitri leaned forward, toward Leo. "Well, I've heard some things. Some mighty interesting things."

I took a gulp of my drink. "Of course you have, Dmitri, but that doesn't make any of them true."

Actually, the only thing I knew to be true at this moment was that Dmitri was always hearing *mighty interesting* things, and he wasn't above embellishing a story just to make it even *more* interesting. He was a professional rumor mill on an island full of people eager to encourage him.

"What kind of things?" Leo asked. He seemed intrigued, but I guess that was to be expected. I mean, the *concept* of a criminal on the island was exciting, but I'd need to warn him to take everything Dmitri said with a block of salt. And follow it with tequila and a lime.

Dmitri adjusted his hat. "Well, I don't like to kiss and tell, but I've been known to have a dalliance here and there with gals who work up at the Imperial Hotel."

"You mean like hookers?" Leo's eyes widened.

"We do not have hookers on Wenniway Island!" This time it was my voice that carried, but fortunately no one seemed to be paying any attention to me. As usual.

"No, no. Not hookers," Dmitri said. "Housekeepers, waitresses, cashiers. Working girls but not, you know . . . *working girls*. Anyway, I had a lovely little interlude with a maid two summers ago, and she told me about some very interesting items she'd once seen in a guest's room."

"Such as?" I demanded.

"A bag full of identification badges. Driver's licenses and passports with the same photo but different names. And some tools that she didn't recognize, but when she described them to me, I told her they sounded like lock-picking tools."

"Seriously?" I looked at him intently, trying to discern if this was honest-to-goodness fact or his unique brand of fiction. "Dmitri, if that's true, she should go talk to my dad."

"Alas, she's gone. She left the island at the end of that summer, and I haven't spoken to her since. This may sound cavalier, but I can't recall the dear thing's last name. It was a brief yet passionate affair." He took a big gulp from his drink.

"And you never told my dad? Or hotel security? How is that even possible?"

"She was afraid she'd lose her job if anyone found out that she'd gone through a guest's belongings. Apparently, the items weren't left out in the open. They were zipped up inside of a suitcase. I didn't tell anyone, because I was protecting a dear friend." He gave me a sideways glance as if to remind me that he was indeed capable of keeping a secret. He'd been keeping one for me for quite some time now.

"That's wild," Leo said, seeming to be fully engaged. "Did she say what name he was checked in under? Or the names on the other ID cards? Maybe it's some jewel thief we would have heard of. Like somebody famous."

As much as I hated to be any part of this discussion, I found myself drawn in. "The private investigator said one of his names was James Novak."

Dmitri set his glass down. "He said James Novak?"

I nodded. "Yes, and the pictures he had were from the eighties. Sound familiar?"

He stared at his drink as if deep in thought. "No. I've never heard of a James Novak, and I don't remember my friend mentioning any names, either. Wait. Maybe she said he was checked in as a Michael Jones?"

Leo leaned closer still. "Michael Jones. There's got to be a million of those around. Did she tell you what the guy looked like?"

Dmitri took a slow sip from his glass, eyeing Leo over the brim. "I don't recall, exactly. Maybe she said he was short and stocky? And swarthy. You saw pictures, Brooke? What do you think he looked like?"

"Grainy and pale. The pictures were pretty much useless. But seriously, Dmitri, you need to share this with my dad. If you are, indeed, telling the truth."

He had the nerve to look affronted, as if we didn't all know his propensity for exaggeration. It would be just like him to insert himself into the drama just for the fun of it, and my dad would not want to be bothered with some tall tale from bored, overly imaginative Dmitri. But if what he said was true, then my father definitely needed to know.

"Of course I'm telling the truth. What possible reason could I have for making that up?"

"No reason at all," I said, as both an agreement and a warning.

"Exactly." He stood up. "And now you have insulted me and besmirched my good name. I shall leave in a huff." He wasn't actually insulted. I knew him better than that. He was leaving because he'd already told me his little anecdote about the maid, and now he wanted to hurry off and tell someone else. Hopefully one of those people would be the chief of police.

"Huff away," I said as Dmitri flung himself into the crowd.

"So, what do you think about that?" Leo said, eyebrows raised. Like Shari from the post office, he seemed more excited than distressed. Was I the only one who thought having a criminal on the island was a bad thing?

"I think that Dmitri likes to make things up, and any story he tells needs to be corroborated by at least two more reliable sources."

"You don't think that stuff the maid found was from the jewel thief?"

I wanted to say *no, of course not,* but if Dmitri was being honest, then that certainly opened up a whole host of possibilities. "I don't know what to think. Except that I think I'd like to have another drink."

Leo smiled, and I wondered if he knew just how good-looking he was. It seemed unlikely that he hadn't noticed. He had some facial scruff today, and I wondered if it would be prickly or soft. I wanted to reach over and touch it, but that just wasn't something the mayor could do. Such a shame.

"You know what you need, besides another drink?" he asked.

For you to take off your shirt? "No, what?"

"Dinner. With me. And don't tell me that you have to work, because I haven't even said which night yet and you can't possibly have to work every single night."

I'd spent the last few days regretting having turned him down the last time. I didn't think I had the resolve to say no again. I couldn't ignore the attraction I felt. Especially considering the scruff. And so what if people wanted to talk? Gigi moving in with Gus was far more exciting than boring old me having a casual dinner date with the cute new bartender. And everyone would be far more focused on the jewel thief. And so what if I hadn't had time to do any background checking to see if there were unsavory tidbits from his past that I should know about. It's not like we were going to jump into bed. It was just dinner. I could handle it. Because the truth was, Leo Walker was a hot commodity. Emphasis on the *hot,* and if I didn't go out with him soon, someone else would most certainly scoop him up. Local shop owner Eva Culpepper had been eyeing him since the moment she'd arrived at the bar. This invitation might be my last chance.

"Okay," I said. "How about tonight?"

His eyes lit up. "Perfect. I'm done here at six."

I was about to respond, but before I could say more, a commotion in the corner captured our attention. It was Gloria.

"Everyone? Everyone? Could I have your attention for just a quick second?" She'd stepped onto the small carpeted stage in the corner where live music was performed on Saturday nights. She gripped the microphone tightly in her pudgy fingers, although it wasn't on. She didn't need it for volume, and I really, sincerely hoped she was not about to sing something in honor of Bridget. If she did, dogs all over town would start howling.

"Everyone? Hello!" she bellowed again. "If I could have your attention for just a teensy, weensy sec, I have something I'd like to share."

The room quieted, ice clinking in glasses the only sound as the crowd turned toward the stage.

She pushed a strand of bleached-blonde hair from her pink cheeks and smiled. "Hi, everybody. As most of you know, Bridget was a special friend to me. When I was little, she taught me how to swear in German." Laughter circled the room. "She taught me how to make pie crust, although I could never get mine to be as flaky as hers, and I seriously suspect she left out an ingredient every time just so mine wouldn't be as good. I often sat by her at Sunday church services, and let me tell you, that woman could speed through a rosary like nobody's business." Gloria's voice broke, and Tiny reached up and handed her a fresh tissue. She clung to his hand for a moment, and he nodded at her, smiling.

She took a big, deep breath, blowing it out in a nervous huff. "Okay, well anyway, we are here today to celebrate her life and her wonderful spirit. I don't want to take anything away from that, but I think Bridget would be okay with what I'm about to say." She took another big breath and shouted, "Tiny and I are having a baby!"

The room was silent for a speck of a second, then erupted with well-wishers shouting well wishes. Gloria giggled and bobbed, and waved her hands, shushing them. "Wait, there's more. There's more. This dear man of mine . . ." She gazed lovingly at Tiny, all three hundred muscle-bound pounds of him, and dabbed at her tears. "When I told Tiny that he'd knocked me up and was going to be my baby daddy, well, this handsome fella didn't hesitate for a second. He dropped right down on one knee and he said, 'Glo-glo, baby, what the hell. Let's get hitched.' So, we're getting hitched!"

The second round of cheering was even louder and more raucous than the first.

"So, if you're not busy Friday after next at four o'clock," she shouted over the din, "my *fiancé* and I will be over at the courthouse making it all legal-like, and then we'll be having a reception someplace. I don't know where yet, but you're all invited."

Laughter and cheering circulated around the bar once more, bouncing off the walls and ceiling. Shots were poured, toasts were made. The sadness of Bridget O'Malley's passing gave way to the celebration of a new family being formed. I felt that pesky pang of longing as I saw the way Gloria and Tiny gazed into each other's eyes. I wanted what they had. Well, not exactly what they had, because those two were unique in some rather unflattering ways, but I did want to experience the kind of love they obviously felt. Someday.

I smiled over at Leo as he passed a tray of drinks to Clancy. "That is a match made in some weird alternate universe heaven," I said. "But I think they're going to be very, very happy."

"I hope so," Leo said, shaking his head. "But that is going to be one huge baby."

Chapter 7

Leo and I had agreed to meet at Tate's Tavern on the Bluff at seven that evening, giving me plenty of time to get home and waste half an hour agonizing over what to wear. I wanted an outfit that would say fun and flirty, but not too flirty. Nothing that would say I was trying too hard, but not something that would say *bookish civil servant*, either. I thought about calling Emily for advice but scrapped that idea pretty quickly. She'd have me in something strappy and low-cut, and that just wasn't me. Last time I took her advice, I ended up barefoot, so I settled on jeans that made my butt look good and a flowy red shirt that I'd bought ages ago and never really had a reason to wear. I put deodorant on three times, brushed my teeth twice, then reminded myself that I was being utterly absurd. It was just dinner. Dinner was all I wanted. And besides, he'd only asked *me* because he didn't know anyone *else*.

The walk to the restaurant would've only taken about fifteen minutes, but the wardrobe decision had taken more time than I'd realized, and so, like most islanders would do, I hopped on my bike and arrived on the dot. During the summer tourist season, Tate's was always crowded, but as I entered the room, I discovered only a few dozen diners. I spotted Judge Murphy and his wife at one table, and Link and Patty Sommerville at another. I waved and kept going because I'd also spotted Leo over in a corner booth. Good choice. We'd have a sliver of privacy there.

Leo stood up as I approached, and there was an awkward second where I wondered if we were going to hug or something, but since I'm not much of a hugger, I just smiled and kind of fumbled with my purse as I slid into the seat.

"You look nice," he said.

"Thanks, so do you." I laughed a little too breathlessly and decided to blame that on the exertion of biking here, and not on the fact that he *did* look nice. Nothing special about his outfit. Just jeans and a striped collared shirt, but still. Mmmm, nice.

A previous student of mine brought menus to our table and offered up a broad smile.

"Good evening, Miss Callaghan. Sir. Can I get you something to drink?" She gazed at Leo for a long second, then all but winked at me. Cheeky girl.

We ordered wine and made small talk while we looked over the menu.

"That's quite a view of the Petoskey Bridge, as promised," Leo said a few minutes later, after we'd ordered our food. I followed his gaze and had to admit he wasn't wrong. Even having lived here all my life, watching the sky turn crimson and gold as the autumn rays glowed down from between clouds never got old. I regaled him with some bridge trivia, mostly to make conversation—not because I found it so fascinating, but visitors usually did.

"So, what made you take a job here on the island?" I finally asked. It was a question I'd been itching to get to because it was pretty unusual for someone to move here in November unless they were part of a construction crew scheduled to work on one of the hotels during the winter lull. Naturally the island was overrun with new employees during the summer—waitstaff, chefs, landscapers, and such—but Trillium Bay was excessively quiet during the off-season. Many of the hotels and restaurants even closed down for the winter so the owners could snowbird down in Florida.

Leo toyed with the edge of his cocktail napkin and paused before answering. "Well, I've been living in Chicago for the past couple of years, but the company I work for just went belly-up, and I suddenly found myself without a job. I've got leads on a few things, and I'm not too worried, but my family and I came here once when I was a kid, and I always thought about coming back." He gave a little shrug, making it impossible for me not to notice how broad his shoulders were. Did I mention he was handsome? He was. Leo continued talking. "I figured now was as good a time as any to check the place out again."

"You do realize there's not a ton going on here over the winter, right?" That probably wasn't a very mayor-like thing to say. The head of the tourist board would scold me for that, and in fact one of my missions was to increase our winter occupancy rates. Still, I felt as if I should warn him.

"That's actually perfect. I'm looking for peace and quiet and solitude."

Solitude? Well, that was a bad sign. He chuckled at my expression.

"Not complete solitude, obviously. Just a break from my regular work."

"Okay, what kind of work do you normally do?" I took a sip of wine, a crisp chardonnay. I normally preferred reds but decided purple teeth would not be in my best interest.

"I'm in private security, mostly," Leo answered. "A friend of mine started up a company after we did a couple of tours in Iraq. Great soldier, but not much of a businessperson, apparently."

Well, that explained part of it. Leo was a soldier. Mark that in the "automatically sexy" column. Something about a person willing to selflessly serve their country was undeniably attractive. That explained the muscles, too. No wonder I had the flutters.

"Iraq, huh? Scary stuff. Thanks for your service."

He shrugged it off. "Thanks for having dinner with me. I'll have to let you know about breakfast, though. I wouldn't want you to think I'm easy."

I laughed, wishing *I* was easy. I wasn't, but oh, if I was . . .

I lifted my glass in a salute. "Good to know you have such high moral standards. I promise not to pressure you into breakfast. Or anything else." *Oh, look at me, being all flirty and stuff. Must be the wine.*

"Well, now, don't be too hasty. You could at least try. Otherwise you'll hurt my feelings." His lips tilted into a grin, and good Lord. Did I mention he had dimples? Long dimples on either side of his mouth. As if I needed something else to draw attention to that mouth. If this guy bartended during the summer, he'd make a million dollars in tips. With his *I'll-take-care-of-you* kind of charm and his *let's-go-to-bed-in-the-middle-of-the-day* kind of gaze, visitors and local gals alike would be leaving him tens and twenties, not to mention their phone numbers. He was dangerous in all the best possible ways. The tremor that rippled through my torso was equal parts attraction and concern, because without much effort, I could see myself getting rather addicted to his . . . everything.

"So, you live in Chicago?" I said blandly, demonstrating my determination to steer the subject toward something less sexual. For my sake.

He laughed knowingly, clearly sensing my redirection. "Yep, for now, but my next job could take me anywhere. Or maybe not. I'm not sure. Maybe I'll stick around here for a while." He stared at me over the rim of his glass, but I wasn't going to read too much into that statement, even though the southern region of my body was wishing I'd offer him a long-term lease at my place.

"If you're used to Chicago city life, don't you think you'll get a little bored here?" There I went with my great endorsement of the island again. Seriously. What was wrong with me?

"Bored is kind of the idea." He turned away to look at the bridge for a second, seeming self-conscious for the first time, which only made him that much hotter. He chuckled nervously as he turned back. "Promise you won't laugh?"

"No." *See, I could be sassy if I wanted to.*

He seemed to take my sarcasm in stride. He leaned forward, and I felt myself doing the same.

"Okay. Well, I have this crazy notion about writing a book. There. I've said it." He sat back in his chair as if a burden had lifted. His guise was now guileless, with maybe even a hint of vulnerability.

"A book?"

Seriously? Authors were nearly as sexy as soldiers. Men not only able to identify nuanced emotions, but bold enough to put them on the page to share with the world? Not to mention the fact that most of my boyfriends had been fictional. Darcy. Heathcliff. Rhett. Jamie Fraser. The list of my literary boyfriends was long, and maybe it was just the teacher in me, but *oh, my.* Add another check mark in the sexy column.

Leo's nod was sheepish. "Yeah, and I know what you're thinking."

Wow. I seriously hope not.

"You're thinking how half the population says they're going to write a book someday, right?"

Sure.

"But I figured now was the time to give it a try. I've got some savings set aside, and lots of ideas. And I also figured that if I holed up someplace kind of isolated, there wouldn't be anything to distract me."

Ouch? He wanted solitude and no distractions? Awesome.

"At least I thought there'd be no distractions." He smiled again, and his gaze was direct. I flushed under his stare. Was he talking about me? I wasn't typically considered distracting. Academic, maybe. Tenacious, definitely. But I don't think I'd ever been much of a distraction to anyone.

Our food arrived just then, speaking of distractions, and the conversation wove in and out around other topics as we ate. My family, his family.

"My father was in the army, so we moved around a lot. I've lived in seventeen different cities, not including places overseas," Leo said as he pulled a roll from the bread basket.

"Seventeen cities? I haven't even visited seventeen cities." Shari was right. I really did need to get out more. "The only time I've lived away from here was during college. I went to Albion to get my teaching degree and promptly ended up right back here."

"Did you ever think about moving away for good?"

I had thought about moving away, once, but that wasn't a story I shared. Dmitri was the only one who knew how close I'd come to leaving, and that had been years ago. A far-off memory now of the life I might have had. "It's crossed my mind. Sometimes I wonder how my life would have been different if I'd moved, but my family is here, and all my friends. It might not sound very worldly to you, but I like it here. I liked being a teacher, and hopefully I'll like being the mayor, although if my first council meeting was any indication, I'm not so sure." I smiled and was only mostly kidding.

His smile back was supportive. "I'm sure you'll get the hang of it. I mean, I could only hear bits and pieces, but those people all seem to have pretty strong opinions."

"That they do." I didn't want to get into talking about the city council, so instead I turned the conversation back to him. "So, what kind of book?"

"What?"

"What kind of book do you intend to write? You said you had lots of ideas."

He took a drink of water before answering. "Um, honestly, I still feel a little foolish talking about it. Like I don't want to jinx myself, but one idea I have has to do with an old military fort. That's another part of the reason I decided to come here, because of Fort Beaumont. I figured I could do a little research, hopefully get inspired. Got any good stories about the island?"

I couldn't help but laugh at that. "I have hundreds of stories, and so does every person who lives here, but I'm not sure they're book-worthy. I could put you in touch with a couple of historians who live here, though. I'm sure they'd love to talk to you, and they might have more of what you're looking for."

His eyes lit up. "Really?"

"Sure. You remember Dmitri? The guy with the beekeeping hat?"

Leo nodded.

"He's in charge of the historical committee, and they're very active. History is sort of our thing around here, in case you hadn't figured that out already. There's a big section in the library dedicated to the fort, and I'm sure Vera would be happy to help you with any research."

He paused with his fork halfway to his mouth. "Vera, the librarian? I think I'd like to avoid her as much as possible, although that was some fascinating stuff she shared the other day about bats."

I tried to recall which stuff she'd said about bats. I'd heard it all so many times, it was simply background noise. "She has a long-standing and well-intentioned fixation on the island's bat shortage, but sometimes she's a little, um . . . tedious."

"Oh, I don't know about tedious," he said casually. "Personally, I found all that stuff about how fruit bats perform fellatio to be quite educational."

I gasped and nearly spilled my wine. I caught the glass just before it toppled over. "What was that, now?"

"She said fruit bats love the oral. I found that pretty intriguing." He popped a green bean into his mouth.

"I guess I wasn't paying attention," I said, both mortified . . . and yet slightly turned on. I hardly knew this man, so hearing him say the word *fellatio* felt overtly intimate, especially given that we were out in public. I glanced around, but no one seemed to be paying us any attention. Still, not the time.

"So, a book about the fort, huh?" I said, making him laugh.

"Something like that. Do they keep public records at the library, too?"

"Public records? I think they're mostly in storage at the courthouse. Why?"

He shrugged casually as he speared a roasted potato with his fork. "No reason, really. I was just thinking it might be fun to look at the different census records to get a feel for family names, maybe see which families have been here awhile and who is new to the island."

"New is a relative term in Trillium Bay. I'm sixth generation, and most of the established families have been here since the seventeen hundreds. Anyone who's lived here for less than, say, fifty years could be considered new."

"Sixth generation? Seriously?"

I nodded. "There seem to be two types of people around here: the ones who come and plant their roots and never leave, and those who last a year or two and realize this place isn't for them."

The sun set while we ate, and drank another glass of wine, and told more stories. Now the restaurant was dimly lit by wall sconces and candles on the table. The crowd had thinned even more until I eventually realized we were the only two left. It was time for us to go, but I wanted to linger. I had a little buzz from the drinks and from the novelty of conversing with a handsome man. For this evening, I was letting myself pretend that this was the kind of life I had. The kind with dinners out, with fun, flirty banter, and lots of potential. I wanted to indulge in all the ripples and trembles and breathlessness that he seemed to trigger in me, but a nagging voice in the back of my mind kept tapping at my mood. He wasn't permanent. All his stories involved travel, and even now Leo was having his own adventure—a temporary kind of adventure on my island—but he probably wouldn't stay. Not for long. Not for forever. I'd do well to remember that.

"Thanks for dinner," I said as we walked out of the dining room and into the tiny lobby. I could see the waitstaff putting chairs up on the tables and heard the hum of a vacuum starting up. When we stepped outside, the wind was brisk and I shivered. Leo put his arm around my shoulders and gave a squeeze, although I wasn't sure if it was a romantic gesture or just a guy trying to keep a girl warm. Either way, I leaned into it as we walked down the path to the bike rack.

"Thank *you* for dinner," he said in return. "It's not that late. How about a nightcap?"

Keeping the evening going a bit longer would be oh so nice, but the only places open at this hour would be one of the pubs, and that would dash my little bubble of the perfect evening. We'd most certainly run into people I knew, and I didn't want to tarnish this memory by cluttering it up with other locals. The lights from Main Street shone on us as I turned toward him and shook my head.

"Wish I could, but it's a school night."

"You're not a teacher anymore."

"I know, but I'm the mayor. I can't be seen cavorting with strange men at all hours of the evening."

He chuckled and said, "It's not even eleven o'clock."

"I know, but they fold the streets up at midnight. You're not in Chicago anymore, Mr. Walker. And I do have an early meeting tomorrow with some of the store owners. They have a list of demands they've been dying to present me with, and I have some prep work to do before that happens."

His sigh was big and sad, although not very convincing. He'd survive. "A mayor's work is never done, huh? Too bad. Another time, then."

We stood for an awkward second, and the undercurrent of attraction nearly pulled me closer. I let myself believe he was feeling it, too, but a foghorn sounded out in the distance, spoiling the moment.

"Another time," I said.

He smiled. "Okay, this is where we would normally get in a car, and I'd drive you home. Or you'd get in your own car and drive yourself home. What's the protocol here? Do I walk you?"

I laughed. "Not necessary. I rode my bike."

"You rode a bike? That's adorable."

"That's how we do things around here."

He shook his head. "Damn, I wish I had a horse tied up nearby so I could do one of those running and jumping and landing in the saddle moves."

I bit back a smile. "Is that something you know how to do? Because I'm picturing it right now, and I have to be honest. In my mind, you don't actually make it onto the horse."

His laughter rang out, followed by mine. A nice blending of sounds in an otherwise still night. "No, I can't say I've done that, but I'd be willing to give it a try. I'm not above making a fool of myself to impress a girl."

I fluttered inside. Again. "Well, consider me impressed. Good night, Leo."

"Good night, Mayor Callaghan. Pedal safely."

Chapter 8

"I have a problem, and I need the two of you to take care of it." Gigi plopped her big red leather purse down on the pink laminate table at Link & Patty's Breakfast Buffet, where my dad and I were having breakfast. I'd called him after my early meeting and invited him to join me so I could fill him in on everything Dmitri had said about the jewel thief staying at the Imperial Hotel. He was as dubious about the whole story as I'd been.

"Didn't you always teach me to take care of my own problems?" Harlan said to Gigi, stabbing at a piece of ham without even looking over at her as she slid in next to him.

"Don't talk back to your mother, dear. No one likes a wiseass. And all I need is one tiny favor. I need you two to push something through lickety-split with the city council."

I took her purse off the table and set it on the seat next to me. "If there's something you need, we can ask, Gigi, but we can't do something for you that we wouldn't do for other members of the community. That wouldn't be right."

She caught Patty's eye and pointed at my coffee cup, indicating she wanted some of the same. Patty nodded as Gigi looked back to me and said, "Oh, please. Every person on that city council has done favors for people, and what good is it for me if I have a son who is the chief of police and a granddaughter who is the mayor, if I can't get a special favor once in a while? I can't believe you two call yourselves politicians, and anyway, this is a very unique set of circumstances."

Harlan's expression remained dour. "I have never once called myself a politician."

"What is it you need, Gigi?" I asked, sensing this conversation could wander off in a multitude of useless directions.

"I need to get rid of three dead husbands."

"Excuse me?" Dad and I spoke in unison, causing several diners to turn and stare.

"Well, you know they're all in urns sitting on my mantel, and Gus says I can't bring them to his place, so I have to find somewhere else for them to live, er . . . I mean, someplace for them to be dead? Either way, Gus says they can't come to his house."

Patty arrived with coffee just then, splashing a little over the rim as she set it down. "So, it's true, then? You and Gus? June Mahoney was in here yesterday with Olivia Bostwick, and I could tell they were spitting mad about something."

Gigi dumped a container of creamer into the cup. "Please, Patty. We are trying to have a private family conversation here."

"In the middle of my diner during the breakfast rush? Good luck with that. And good luck dealing with those Mahoney sisters, too. Hope Gus is worth the trouble."

Patty turned and sashayed away as Gigi added two sugars to the cup and stirred vigorously. "As I was saying, Gus says no way to me bringing my dead husbands, but if they don't come with me, what am I supposed to do with them? Emily says she doesn't want to be responsible for them, and I can't just dump them out in any old place, on any old day. There needs to be some kind of ceremony, some kind of special send-off."

"Like a memorial service," I said. "That makes sense, but why is that something the council needs to be involved in?"

She paused a moment, as if choosing her words carefully, which is a thing I'd never seen her do before.

"Well, I'll tell you. I happened to be discussing this with Chloe, and she did a little research on that fold-up computer of hers. I tell you, you can find out just about anything about just about anything on the World Wide Web these days. And there's something called *apps*. I love the apps. Have you heard of Pinterest?"

"Stick to one subject at a time, please, Mom. I haven't had enough coffee yet today to deal with one of your rabbit holes." Harlan took another bite of ham, chewing it methodically.

"Oh, fine. So, Chloe researched how to dispose of ashes, and it turns out there are all sorts of fun things you can do."

"Fun?" Disposing of human remains did not seem fun to me, no matter how you did it. "I'm sure I'll regret asking this, but what kind of *fun* things?"

Gigi leaned forward, clearly encouraged by my interest. "Well, first of all, I could have their ashes compressed by a special machine that will turn them into gemstones. Isn't that fascinating? I think it's fascinating, but Gus says no way. He says if he doesn't want them on the mantel, he sure doesn't want them hanging around my neck, either."

Bodies turned into jewelry? I had to side with Gus on that one, although it was odd seeing her defer so easily to someone else's rules. "Gus sounds pretty bossy, Gigi. Are you sure you've thought this through? Can't you two just date instead of living together?"

"You're not turning my father into a gemstone, Mom," Harlan stated grimly.

She stared hard at him for a long moment. "I know. That's what I just said. I'm not doing that. And yes, Brooke, I've thought about it quite a bit. I've got Emily and Chloe living at my place, and that puts a bit of a damper on spontaneity for Gus and me, if you know what I mean. We'd like a little more privacy, and like I said, it's sort of a trial run. If things don't work out, I'll just move back to my place."

"Okay, so what happens if you get rid of everyone's ashes, and then move home? Won't you regret that they're gone?" Personally, I'd never been a fan of keeping those ashes around in the first place, but they'd been there for so long, moving them now seemed cold.

"I don't think I'd regret it. Not really. I mean, Conroy was always a slob, even when he was alive, and I have to admit, I'm tired of dusting him. And Harlan, your father would be just as happy if I simply dumped him out in our vegetable garden. Speaking of that, here's another option. You can send the ashes off to some company that will turn them into a pod that you bury in the ground, and then a tree grows from it. I could turn them each into a tree."

"You're not dumping my father out into the vegetable garden or turning him into a pod. Don't you think that would be a little . . . undignified?"

She turned and scowled at him. "Harlan Callaghan, you are being disagreeable just for the sake of being disagreeable. I'm trying to come up with a solution to a problem, so how about this? This is what I really want to do with them anyway, and this is what I'll need approval from the council for."

I felt myself bracing for impact.

"Fireworks."

"Fireworks?" I said as my dad pushed his plate away and crossed his arms, falling back in his seat with a thump.

"Yes, I love this idea," Gigi said with a grin. "We have their ashes loaded into fireworks and then launch them off into the sky, where they explode into a magnificent shimmer of beauty before floating gently back down to the earth. Or in this case, they'll land in the lake, which all three of them would approve of. Isn't that a fabulous idea?"

Harlan rubbed a hand across his face. "You want to turn my father's remains into a firecracker?"

"Not a firecracker. Listen to my words. A beautiful, wonderful . . . celestial shower of shimmering lights. I think it sounds magical."

Gigi was getting her Irish up, her frustration with Harlan visibly growing.

It didn't sound magical so much as it sounded weird, but then again, it was a little strange to have them all sitting on the mantel, too. Especially considering Gigi liked to decorate the urns for the holidays. My grandfather had been wrapped in tinsel, holly, and evergreen boughs. He'd had Easter eggs tucked behind him, and once in a while, if she remembered it was his birthday, she'd move his urn to the kitchen table, where we all had to eat cake while staring at it. All things considered, maybe Gus had been wise to say the dead husbands were not welcome in his home.

"I've contacted the company," Gigi continued, "and they can have the fireworks created and back to me in five or six weeks, which I'm hoping will be just in time for New Year's Eve. Wouldn't that be special? Ring in the New Year by sending them off in such a dramatic fashion? But of course, I can't launch fireworks without some help. I mean, I could, but I'm trying to be responsible. Aren't you impressed with me?"

"I don't like any of these suggestions," my father said. "Can't we just take them to the cemetery like normal people?"

"The cemetery is so boring. This is their last great adventure. I say we send them off in style. Now all I need is for you two to get the council to approve it, because I'll want to have some sort of dedication right before we launch them into space. You just remind those council members that I didn't even have to ask for their permission, you know. I could have just asked Percy O'Keefe to launch them off Bent Rock, and no one could have stopped me."

My father looked at me from across the table, resignation all over his face. Gigi was *tenacious* with a capital *ten*.

I shrugged. "I guess there's no harm in asking."

"It's the most ridiculous thing I've ever heard," my dad said, "but I know you, Mom. Now that you've sunk your teeth into this idea, you'll drive me crazy until I ask. So, yes, I'll run it past the council, but I'm also going to ask Father O'Reilly. There may be some sort of special permission we need to get from the church, you know."

"Rats!" She snapped her fingers. "I never thought of that. Okay, well, the next time you're playing poker with O'Reilly, make sure you let him win a few rounds before you ask him, and give him a few drinks, too."

"Plying a priest with alcohol and money will not change the teachings of the church."

She scowled. "Since when did you turn into such a Bible-thumper? I didn't raise you that way."

"Yes, you did."

"Did I? Well, good for me then, but in this case, I need the church to have a little flexibility. See what you can do."

"There you are!" The door of the restaurant banged against the frame as Emily came in looking flushed and annoyed. Wearing jeans and a flannel shirt, she still managed to look glamorous. It was so annoying. She strode over to our table, hands on her hips. "Dad, why is my work crew in jail?"

"Good morning to you, too, Emily," he said, sipping his coffee.

"Yeah, good morning. Why did you arrest my entire construction crew last night? I got to the work site this morning, and the only one there was Georgie, and she said that the rest of them were in jail."

Harlan chuckled. "Technically, yes, they are in jail, but no one was arrested, and they're free to go."

Emily visibly relaxed and slid into the booth next to me. "I don't understand. What happened?"

"The details are a little sketchy," Harlan said, "but from what my deputy could make of it last night, the boys were celebrating Tiny's impending fatherhood by plying him with shots of Fireball. Lots of shots of Fireball. He finally passed out at the Mustang Saloon, but since all the horse taxis were in for the night and he was too damn heavy to carry home, they dragged him by his feet across the street to the jail so he could sleep it off there. I guess the rest of them were either too lazy or too drunk to go home, too."

"So, no one is in trouble? They can all come to work today?"

Harlan laughed again. "Sure, they can all come to work, but I wouldn't expect much from them. They were a mess last night. And Tiny probably has a powerful headache from the Fireball. And the curb. And the steps into the station. No power tools or saws today, okay? I don't want somebody losing a limb."

Emily shook her head in dismay. "Great. That's just great. I need to start building days into the construction schedule to account for their shenanigans and hangovers. Geez. Give me those pancakes."

She reached for my plate, and I handed her my fork before someone got hurt.

Chapter 9

"She wants to launch her dead husbands into outer space? What is wrong with that woman?"

The pub's window glass behind June Mahoney may have just cracked a little at the shrill tone of her voice. It was city council meeting time again, and so far, this one wasn't going any better than the first one. My well-constructed agenda was once again being used as cocktail napkins by these bickering geriatrics, and since my father had been called away to help catch a runaway horse, I didn't have him to back me up.

"She doesn't want to launch them into space, June," I corrected for the fifteenth time. "She wants to send them up in a firework. Well, three, actually, one for each." I cringed internally, knowing that my version didn't sound that much better. "She'd like to do this at midnight on New Year's Eve."

June had been pacing the floor, the swish of her corduroy pants loud and irritating. She whirled back toward me. "Brooke, your grandmother has been a nutjob since the day she was born, but this just takes the cake."

Her aggressive stance sent my frustration level over the edge. "She is not a nutjob, June, and if your brother wasn't being so demanding, she wouldn't have to be doing this at all!"

June slammed her hand down on the table. "Don't you bring my brother into this. He is a sweet, guileless man, and your grandmother is just using him for . . . for her own sexual gratification."

Sudsy and Dmitri exchanged intrigued glances. "Gigi is in need of sexual gratification? If that's the case," Sudsy said, "I'm available Tuesday evenings, when Marilyn goes to bingo. Your grandmother is still a hottie."

I didn't for one second want to know if Sudsy was serious or not. "Could everyone please stop talking about my grandmother's sex life?" I glanced out the open door of the meeting room to see Leo chuckling behind the bar and might have felt embarrassed if I hadn't been so annoyed by the whole thing.

Gertie raised her hand. "Ladies, gentlemen, I feel we are veering off topic. May I suggest a nonbinding vote to see where everyone stands on the issue of launching dead bodies into the sky? It's possible we're closer to agreeing on this than we realize."

"Gertie, I think that's a great idea," Dmitri said. "Let's vote. All in favor of letting Gigi blow up her dead husbands, raise your hand." His hand popped up, and slowly, one by one, the other members voted in favor. The other members not including June Mahoney. Even Olivia Bostwick gave a tiny little wave of agreement.

"Olivia," June gasped. "Et tu, Brute?"

Oliva rolled her eyes. "It's just some fireworks, June, and nothing you do will stop Gigi from moving into your brother's house if he wants her there."

"Oh!" She flung herself down into a chair, which protested with a loud creak.

"Let's make it official then. The motion passes," Dmitri called out joyfully. "Let's have another round of drinks, shall we?"

"No more drinks," I said pointlessly.

"I have something I'd like to bring to the council's attention," Sudsy said as June pouted from her seat.

"Is it on the agenda?" I said. "If it's not on the agenda, then we're not talking about it today."

"How could I put it on the agenda? I only got the phone call this morning. Anyway, I have been contacted by a small Michigan production company, Grand River Films, and they'd like to use my Beech Tree Bed & Breakfast location for a movie! Isn't that something?"

Well, it wasn't on the agenda, but that was pretty good news. We'd had movie crews on the island a handful of times before, and they were always a fabulous source of revenue, not to mention being great for publicity.

"Think of the business this would bring, what with their crew needing places to sleep and eat. They hinted at some big-name stars, too. I think this could be a real boost to our entire economy, especially in light of our jewel thief situation."

"There's no jewel thief situa—" I said, or tried to say, before being cut off by Maggie Webster.

"Speaking of the jewel thief," she said, leaning over the table, "I heard he once snuck into the governor's mansion while the governor and his wife were sleeping and made off with her grandmother's pearls."

"That's not true," I said.

Gertie leaned forward, too. "Did you also hear that he's got loot buried all over the island? Just like a pirate. I wish I'd come across his secret map. We could all be rich!"

"There's no map," I said.

"Delores Crenshaw told me she heard that in the summer of 1992 he actually camped in that little cave by Bent Rock. He'd sneak out at night to get food from the restaurant dumpsters, and sometimes he'd bathe in the pool at the Imperial Hotel."

"No, he didn't," I said.

"I heard he's French and a descendant of the Marquette family. You know, as in Marquette Street, right here on the island."

"He's not," I said.

"I think he must be staying on the island right now. Why else would that FBI agent come around and start asking questions?"

"He wasn't an FBI agent," I said.

The room filled with voices and stories and hearsay and exaggeration, and absolutely no one was listening to me at all. I thought about stomping my feet or pounding my fist on the table. Maybe I needed a referee's whistle. Or a megaphone. That might do the trick.

"I heard he's stolen dozens of items from hotel guests but replaces them with cheap replicas so no one notices until it's too late."

"He comes from a vastly wealthy family and only steals for the pure joy of it."

"He donates money to children's charities and only keeps enough to live on."

"Mrs. O'Doul recognized the man in the pictures that the investigator showed her, only she couldn't recall where she'd seen him before."

"She probably saw him in her grocery store. He was probably stealing food and she didn't even realize."

I sighed and sat down, resting my elbows on the table. There was no point in trying to stop this flood of misinformation. I looked out into the bar again, and Leo smiled at me, replacing my frustration with the city council with a brand-new kind of frustration. Frustration of a sexual nature. A frustration that had been growing inside me since dinner the other night. I kept trying to ignore it because it was pointless. Even if Leo did pursue me, I wasn't interested in a meaningless fling because . . . because it would be meaningless. If I put my heart on the line, it was going to be for something substantial. Something real that could last. Still, I couldn't deny he'd gotten under my skin, and no man had done that in what seemed like an eternity. It wasn't just that Leo was handsome. It's that he was nice. We hadn't done anything together other than talk, and yet the conversation had seeped inside of me and had left a mark.

Leo disappeared from view but seconds later appeared in the doorway of the meeting room with a tray of drinks. He set a Jack and Coke in front of Sudsy Robertson, then knelt down near my chair. "Let me guess. The jewel thief?" he asked.

"Yep. They're on a roll." I took one of the drinks off the tray. I didn't care that it wasn't mine. It was clear and looked like a gin and tonic, so I slugged it down. Yep, gin and tonic.

Leo smiled an *I-think-you're-cute* kind of smile, and the corners of his eyes crinkled in a way that made me want to squeeze him. With my vagina.

"Have they said anything that might have a kernel of truth to it?" he asked. He was leaning so close that his forearm brushed against my leg, and I didn't think it was an accident.

I took another drink from the tray and knocked back that one, too. Vodka and club soda. "Not really," I answered after coughing a bit from the carbonation. "Not unless you believe that our jewel thief occasionally dresses as a woman and steals purses from people's strollers. I heard that one yesterday from my own grandmother."

He chuckled. "Has anyone besides you and our friend Shari actually seen that private investigator again? He's never showed up here."

"Judging from what I've heard—which is, of course, completely unreliable—I think he talked to several people the day he stopped in the post office, but it's hard to tell. Everyone says they talked to him, but no one can quite recall where they were or what was said, and not one single person has reported anything to my father, including the investigator himself." I shook my head as the rest of the council continued with a round of *did you hear* . . .

"Did you hear he used to be an acrobat with Cirque du Soleil? That's how he's so good at climbing in through second-story windows," said Maggie Webster.

"Did you hear that he speaks seven different languages? He must be an *international* jewel thief!" That from Olivia Bostwick, because just your ordinary, run-of-the-mill jewel thief wasn't nearly exotic enough for her cosmopolitan tastes.

"I heard he's an identical twin, and that's why he always has an alibi. He and his brother work as a team," Vera said. "Of course, anyone with a discerning eye, such as myself, would be able to tell them apart."

"You know what you need?" Leo asked, glancing around the table and keeping his voice low and husky in my ear.

"A bullhorn and a Taser?"

His laugh reminded me that this was actually kind of funny. I guess. "You need a nice dinner off the island. How about you and I take the ferry over to Manitou tonight. I heard there was a nice Italian place over there. When's the last time you ate on the mainland?"

"Me? Um, it's been a while, I guess." Actually, I'd had lunch with my sister in Manitou just a few days before, but I wasn't about to tell him that and diminish his apparent eagerness to whisk me away.

"Then you need a change of scenery." He kept his voice low so no one else could hear, giving the whole invitation a sexy, risqué feel. "How about you meet me at the boat dock at six p.m.?"

He stood up before I had much time to ponder, so I just gave him a quick nod, then tried not to stare at him as he delivered the other drinks from the tray. My temperature jumped ten degrees when he winked at me from the doorway, as if we had a secret. But we sort of did have a secret, didn't we?

"Hey, kid!" Dmitri called after him as Leo stepped out of the room. "Where's my gin and tonic?"

"Ask the mayor," Leo called back over his shoulder.

Chapter 10

The boat dock was busy with day workers heading home, but I easily spotted Leo standing near a T-shirt shop. It was colder tonight than it had been earlier in the week, and he was wearing a soft gray sweater under a leather jacket, and a pair of jeans. Like I had before our first dinner, I'd spent far too much time staring into my closet searching for something that said *you can kiss me if you want to* but didn't say *please, please kiss me*. I'd settled on jeans and a light blue sweater, and a scarf that Dmitri said flattered my complexion. Of course, he'd been peering at me through the veil of his beekeeping hat when he said that, so who's to say if the scarf actually did anything for me at all.

"Tiny dilemma," I said to Leo as I reached his side. "It's already six o'clock, and the last boat comes back to the island at eight. So dinner will have to be fast. I would've told you that earlier but I didn't get a chance."

A flash of disappointment touched his face. "The last boat is at eight? I checked the schedule, and it said the last ferry's at nine."

"It's at nine during the tourist season, but from November until April, the last boat is at eight."

He seemed flustered by the error and gazed over at the mainland as if it were calling to him. Some people got a little stir-crazy from being stuck on the island, and he was clearly one of those people. That did not bode well for any potential long-term connection, but I decided to not overthink that at this particular moment.

"Well, that's no good," he said finally. "That only gives us two hours."

"How about pizza?" I asked. "I know a great pizza place over there where the service is fast. We can definitely get back to the boat in time if we eat there."

He chuckled and ran a hand through his hair. "You realize I'm from Chicago, right? Pizza is a bit of a religion there. You think this Northern Michigan place can compete?"

"Probably not, but when in Rome. Or in this case, when in Manitou . . ."

He smiled. "Okay, pizza it is. There's a line for the ferry. Do you think we'll make this one?"

"No problem. Follow me." We wound our way over to the little shed where boat workers waited in inclement weather, and I found just the man I was looking for. "Hey, Stanley. Can we catch a ride?"

Stanley Burrows was another longtime resident and, for as long as I could remember, he'd worked on this dock—and lucky for us, he owed me a favor.

"Why, if it isn't Brooke Callaghan. How are you, toots? How's life as the mayor? June Mahoney giving you trouble?"

"She is. So are Vera and Olivia Bostwick, but that's to be expected."

He nodded sagely and hooked a thumb in the red suspender of his pants. "Yep, it is. You need a lift, you say?"

"Yes, please. This is Leo Walker, by the way. A friend of mine."

As they shook hands, Stanley said, "Any friend of Brooke's is a friend of mine. If it weren't for her, my son would never have graduated from high school."

"Is that so?" Leo looked at me with approval in his eyes.

"Sure is. She tutored my boy every week until he passed all his final exams. Now he's in college and doing just fine. Come right around here." I blushed under the praise and realized that, although not often, *sometimes* a parent did thank me. Stanley led us to the spot where the workers stood at the edge of the dock waiting to catch the lines and let us board on the front of the ferry. We found seats next to the window because it would be far too cold sitting on the top.

"Thanks, Stanley!" I called out and waved as we left the dock.

"That's pretty nice of you to tutor somebody. Do you do that often?" Leo asked. We were sitting close, and I liked the feel of him pressed against my side. He didn't really need to be that close, but I wasn't going to ask him to move. That would just be rude.

"I usually have a couple of kids each year who need a bit of extra help. I don't mind. All in a day's work, and hey, it scored me front-of-the-line ferry service for life. Or at least until Stanley retires. Then it's back to the end of the line, I guess. After that I'll have to pay money like a regular customer."

"Something tells me you didn't tutor those kids for the financial perks."

That made me smile. "No one becomes a teacher for the financial perks because there are no financial perks. But I do love working with the kids. I love seeing their transformation as they learn things. That moment of realization when they finally understand something that didn't make sense to them before, and you can see it on their face and you know that you helped make that happen."

He smiled, and I suddenly felt self-conscious, talking about my job, my old job, as if it were something miraculous. It wasn't. It was just me doing my part, but his expression was earnest. Leo Walker had a way of looking at me that made me want to open up, to spill my few secrets and give him all my credit card numbers. How did he do that?

"Sounds like you enjoyed teaching."

"I did. Very much."

"I'm glad. I'd be a terrible teacher. I'd never have the patience for it. I'd rather be in boot camp."

"Does that mean you didn't enjoy school?"

He appeared introspective for a moment. "I suppose I enjoyed it as much as I could. I mean, we moved around so often that I didn't have a solid group of friends, so school wasn't always my favorite place. But those times when I got on a team, a team for just about any sport, then I was happy. And I must say, I had a couple of teachers who went out of their way to help me a few times, and I still remember them. I have a ton of respect for teachers, and I probably owe an apology to a few of them. If my memory is accurate, I was an obnoxious teenager."

"Some might argue that's redundant," I said. "But I've found, for the most part, that students want to learn, and if it seems otherwise, there's probably a reason."

Leo nodded with understanding. "So I guess the big question then is why did you stop teaching and run for mayor?"

That was a hard question to answer because sometimes I still wasn't sure. I'm not a spontaneous person, so the compulsion to enter that race was sort of a personal mystery, but I gave Leo the most honest answer I could. "I guess after thirteen years of teaching I just needed a change, you know? I wanted to challenge myself while still helping out the community. Our principal isn't going anywhere any time soon, so there weren't a lot of career path options. And honestly, I didn't really think I'd win."

The conversation moved on to other things, and the twenty-minute boat ride seemed to pass in an instant. Before I knew it, we were walking into Stella's Pizzeria. It was warm and smelled of fresh crust and melted cheese. My stomach rumbled so loudly that Leo burst out laughing. So much for being ladylike.

"Pizza choice says a lot about a person," Leo stated as we stared up at the wall-size blackboard covered with menu choices.

"How so?"

"Well, plain cheese says you have no imagination and boring taste buds. Sausage, garlic, and onions indicate a selfish disregard for the people around you, because you don't care about your breath." He smiled over at me, as if gauging my interest. "Pineapple says you didn't really want pizza in the first place, and meat lover's says you're a dumbass who thinks the rules of cardiac disease do not apply to you."

I chuckled at his assumptions. "That all sounds very scientific. How about a veggie supreme?"

He rolled his eyes. "That says you're on a diet and feel guilty about eating pizza, which is just going to ruin everyone's evening."

I liked veggie pizza but I sure wasn't going to admit that now. "I see. So just out of curiosity, what kind of pizza do you usually get?"

"Me? I'm a purist. Pepperoni because, come on, what's a pizza without pepperoni? And black olives because I'm exotic that way." He laughed at his own humor, and I laughed along with him.

"Well, now I feel a lot of pressure to make the right decision because you're going to analyze me. See, I like pepperoni but prefer green olives. What does that tell you?"

He pondered this for a millisecond. "Green olives. Hmm. It tells me you don't care about feeling bloated with all that salt. I like a woman who doesn't agonize over that."

My hand went to my stomach, and I sucked in my gut out of pure reflex. "Well, I didn't, but I will now."

Leo laughed again. "How about we go crazy and get both black and green olives. I'm ready for an adventure like that."

"Okay, but don't judge me if this pizza doesn't live up to your Chicago standards."

Leo placed our order and got us a couple of beers to drink while we waited. Speaking of bloating. Nothing said *I don't feel sexy right now* like the aftermath of having pizza and beer—not that I had plans for trying to look sexy later, but in the rare event that I had hoped to look sexy, the pizza-beer combo was probably going to ruin it. Plus, I should have suggested someplace nicer, more, dare I say—romantic? But the time constraint had thrown me, and I'd defaulted to comfort food.

Stella's was small and without much ambiance, more of a place for locals rather than one designed to lure in tourists. A few tattered posters of Italy adorned the walls, along with a sign that said employees should wash their hands. That was reassuring. All this went through my head in the time it took for the first sip of beer to travel down my esophagus.

"Is this stuff really cheese?" Leo asked, picking up the container of ground parmesan.

"You have a lot of judgments about pizza and the accoutrements," I teased. "Is that the Chicago thing again, or do you have some real underlying issues?"

Leo laughed in return and set down the canister. "You have no idea. So many issues, but let's not get into that. Let's talk about something else. How about that jewel thief, huh?"

"Oh, not you, too. Why is everyone so fascinated by this?"

"Because it's unusual. If Trillium Bay is like most small towns, something out of the ordinary like that is a welcome diversion. I don't imagine you have much of a crime problem, do you?"

"Not really. My father likes to think it's because the police force is so exemplary, but I imagine it has a lot more to do with a lack of efficient getaway options."

"True. It wouldn't be much of a high-speed chase if everyone is riding a Schwinn."

"Probably not, but if you ride your bike down the hill near the Imperial Hotel, you can build up some pretty good momentum. We have a radar gun, and sometimes people get tickets."

Leo choked a little on his beer. "Speeding tickets on a bike?"

"Yes. During the summer there are tons of pedestrians, and horses, and other people on bikes. We get tourists on the island who haven't ridden in fifteen years—and sure, riding a bike is just like, you know, riding a bike—but if you go flying down that hill and somebody doesn't get out of your way, it can be kind of dangerous."

"I guess I hadn't thought of that." He sounded sincere, but as I spoke the words, I realized his experiences were far different from mine, and his notion of danger was probably a little more intense. I felt the blush stealing up my neck and over my cheeks, and added, "Okay, well, not as dangerous as, say, being in Iraq, but if you got hit by a two-hundred-and-fifty-pound dude on a metal bike going twenty-five miles an hour, you'd get hurt. Probably not *dead* hurt, but you might end up with a broken leg." There. That made my point.

"No question. That would suck." His tone was agreeable and not at all patronizing, which I appreciated. "What else do the cops do around the island, besides wait in the bushes to trap speeding bikers? Maybe I can use something that's happened for my book."

"The book that's supposed to be about an old fort?"

He shrugged. "The book is a blank page at this point. I figure the more stuff I learn about the island, and the people who live here, the more ideas I'll have, so tell me what the police do on Wenniway Island. Any legendary crimes committed there?"

"Well, there's one police chief—who is, of course, my father."

Leo nodded. "Harlan Callaghan. What's he like? So far, all I can tell is that he doesn't say much."

"That's an accurate assessment. My father is not the most effusive guy, but if you get him talking about the island, he'll go on for days. Honestly, if you want good stories to inspire your book, take him out for a beer, and he'll never stop talking."

"Really? Okay, I think I'll do that."

That might have been an error, sending Leo toward my father. In the event that anything ever did happen between us, I'd like Leo and my father to remain complete strangers.

"Take Judge Murphy and Father O'Reilly along, too, and you'll get three different versions of the same story, and a lot of arguing about which of them is telling the truth. Those guys grew up together and have been friends since they were toddlers. Legend has it they raised a lot of hell before they became pillars of our community."

Leo chuckled. "I guess that means none of them are newcomers."

"Nope."

"You said there were the types who only stay a year or so, and people who never leave Trillium Bay. What kind of people move here to stay?"

"Hmm, I'd have to think about that. Even some of the newer families have been here for as long as I've been around. Sudsy Robertson and his wife moved here when I was a kid. I remember there being a lot of fuss about that because there were so many rumors about them."

"Rumors? Like what?"

"Like he'd swindled his previous business partners out of thousands of dollars and used that money to buy the Bay View Hotel. Or that his very young wife, Marilyn, was actually a mobster's girlfriend when she met Sudsy. I think I heard something once about them getting their money by winning a personal injury lawsuit. That sounds like the most reasonable scenario to me. Sudsy seems like the *slip and fall and sue* kind of guy."

"Hmm, interesting. Who else is new?"

My response was delayed as our waitress arrived with the pizza on a wooden tray. My mouth watered as she set it down on the red-and-white checked tablecloth, and I folded my hands in my lap to keep from grabbing some.

"Here you go," she said. "Can I bring you anything else? Two more beers?"

"Sure," Leo answered. "Thanks."

We each took an oversize slice of pizza, and I crooked an eyebrow at Leo as he sprinkled a liberal amount of the *is-it-really-cheese* parmesan crumbles.

"When in Manitou," he answered, passing the jar to me. He smiled after his first bite, and I felt a sense of personal satisfaction for no reason other than I wanted this Michigan pizza to be as good as Chicago's. Not sure why that mattered, but it's human nature to cheer for the home team, I guess.

"Like it?" I couldn't resist asking.

He nodded. "It's excellent. This might even be my new favorite pizza place."

Quite possibly an overstatement, but I appreciated his willingness to give our local joint the benefit of the doubt.

"Brenden Garcia and Xavier Price moved here about fifteen years ago," I told Leo a few minutes later, adding to the list of newcomers. "They own the Dragonfly Inn, and my grandmother was so eager to make them feel welcome that she took them a coffee cake and a gay pride flag. They weren't quite sure what to make of her at first, but after a couple of martinis, everyone was friends. Now they come to our house for Thanksgiving, and every year Xavier tries to tell Gigi how to make gravy."

"That's bold. Even I know not to mess with the cook's gravy." Leo smiled and took another bite.

"Exactly." I took a bite of my own slice, silently cursing the salt-retaining green olives and wondering if anything I was telling him would be useful for his book. Probably not, but at least it was giving him some idea of the types of people who chose to live on Wenniway. I listed a handful of others. Becky and Turner Thompson, who came with their five kids. She homeschooled, while he worked as a manager at the Clairmont Hotel. Dai and Lien Nguyen, who owned a flower shop. Malik Washington, the newest head chef at the Imperial Hotel.

"And of course, Dmitri moved to the island when he was about twenty-three."

"Twenty-three?" Leo wiped his hands on a red cloth napkin. "Where did he move from?"

"Pittsburgh. His story is kind of sad, really. He had a rough time growing up. Apparently, his mom had pretty lousy taste in boyfriends.

Then she died when he was about twenty. His sister took off with her own boyfriend, and Dmitri bummed around for a couple of years, spent time living with a few relatives, but no one really wanted him. He told me he wasn't that easy to get along with at the time, and I can understand why."

"So, how did he end up here?"

"His aunt found an ad in a local newspaper for people to come work on the island for the summer. He figured it'd be worth the bus fare to give it a try, but one season here and he was hooked. He got a job helping maintain the gardens at the Imperial Hotel, and he did that for years."

"What about in the winter?"

"He's done different stuff. Tended bar. Construction. Snow removal. Working at the stables. There's plenty to be done around here in the off-season, especially if you don't mind getting your hands dirty or don't mind being outside in the cold."

Leo looked speculative for a moment. "He invited me to go fishing tomorrow morning, but I'm not sure about getting into a boat with a guy wearing a beekeeper's hat."

I chuckled with understanding. "Oh, he's harmless, and not nearly as strange as he seems. Once you get past the hat, he's quite intelligent. He and I have had some very spirited debates over the years, and I'm always surprised at the stuff he knows. He volunteers at school all the time, and the kids love him."

"So, why the hat, though?"

I shook my head. "You know, I'm not sure. I'm just so used to seeing it that I don't much notice it. He keeps bees, obviously. I think he told me once that he was getting a little bald spot, and it bothered him."

"Yeah, and a bald spot is way more embarrassing than walking around all over the place with a beekeeping hat."

The conversation meandered to and around other topics. Leo told a few stories about growing up on army bases, and all the trouble he and his younger brother got into.

"We were Irish twins," he said. "Eleven months apart and super-competitive with each other, but since we were always moving around, we learned early on to stick together. Nothing quite like being the new kid in school all the time. Like I said before, if I was on some kind of sports team, that helped me let off some steam and then I did okay, but other times it was just Shawn and I egging each other on to see who could make the stupidest decisions. My poor mom was constantly getting called by teachers or principals or neighbors."

The waitress set down the two beers that Leo had ordered for us. "Pizza good?" she asked, then moved on to the next table as we nodded.

"What about your dad? What's he like?" I asked, picking up the fresh drink.

Leo's expression dimmed momentarily before going neutral. "He's okay. He was gone a lot when we were younger, and we missed him. Then he retired and was home all the time, and I realized he's kind of an asshole." He took a gulp of beer. "Not a huge asshole, but I think after life in the army, the monotony of suburban life sort of grated on his nerves. My parents split up when I was fifteen. My mother never admitted as much, but I think she thought he was having an affair. A new girlfriend showed up pretty soon after he moved out."

His tone was matter-of-fact, but it obviously still affected him, as anyone might expect. It tugged at my heart in unexpected ways.

"I'm sorry you had to go through that. Did you ever ask him about it?"

Leo shook his head. "He wasn't the sort to invite those kinds of conversations. You didn't question my father. Anyway, it was a long time ago. We've all moved on."

We sat in silence for the briefest moment before Leo added, "As much as I hate to admit it, I do understand some of what he felt. That transition to civilian life after being overseas can be a little rocky. You get used to the adrenaline. Even if you're bored off your ass on a base, there's always that potential for something big to happen. Maybe that's why I like doing security. Most of the time it's pretty textbook stuff, but every now and again something out of the ordinary happens. And I like being on the move. I'm not sure I could handle an office job, sitting at a desk for hours on end. I need fresh air. I need to be on my feet."

I couldn't help but chuckle at that. "You do realize you're trying to write a book, right? I think that's going to require some desk time."

He laughed along with me, and the weight of the conversation lightened again. "Sure, it will, but I'll be doing something I'm interested in. Don't get me wrong. I can sit for hours playing a video game, it's just that I prefer being active and keeping things moving. Variety being the spice of life and all that."

I could sense that about him. On the surface he seemed all relaxation and charm, but underneath that was an energy, an incessant state of motion, like he was constantly taking in our surroundings. Maybe that was the security training in action. Or maybe it was just his nature. Either way, it made him seem exciting . . . but it also made him a very poor candidate for any sort of romantic entanglement. He would not be a long-termer on this island. He had just all but admitted he wasn't the stay-put kind of guy, and if he craved adrenaline, he wasn't going to find it anywhere near Trillium Bay.

Too bad for me because I liked Leo. I'd started this evening with a chest full of nervous anticipation, yet as we talked, I'd relaxed. My defenses had lowered as my optimism rose. I was enjoying myself, and something about him seemed . . . trustworthy, and that wasn't something I automatically attributed to someone. But none of that mattered because his visit here was a short-term gig. I made a note of that and stuck it to my heart as a reminder.

We finished our second round of beers, and as Leo paid the bill, I realized I'd been paying very close attention to him and zero attention to the time. When we left Stella's, it was already eight o'clock, and as we speed-walked toward the dock, the horn sounded, indicating the ferry was about to pull away.

"Uh-oh. I think we'd better sprint," Leo said. He glanced down at my shoes, and although I was wearing a pair of relatively practical boots, they were not made for running. "Here, jump on." He halted in front of me and bent forward.

"Oh hell no. I am not riding on your back. I'm too full for that. Plus, I'm the mayor, for goodness' sake!"

"If you don't, we're going to miss that boat, and as much as I'd like an excuse for us to rent a hotel room over here, I'm guessing you won't go for that. Hop on."

If I'd had a moment to ponder his comment, I would have surely enjoyed the suggestion, but given that we were about to miss our ride, I was just going to have to tuck that comment away in my memory bank to pull out later. The boat horn blew again, spurring me to chuck my embarrassment, and dignity, and leap onto his back. Leo caught my legs behind my knees, and my embarrassment quickly gave way to a serious case of the giggles as he started to jog.

"You know, for such a little thing, you're kind of hard to carry if you won't hold on," he said, his breath coming out in short puffs of exertion.

No one had ever called me a little thing. I wasn't big. I was totally and completely average. And normal, apparently, because bouncing along with my vahooch rubbing up and down his back was triggering all sorts of delicious tingles along every nerve ending in my body. Clinging to his shoulders wasn't doing my self-restraint any favors, either. So much for trying to remain immune to his charm/muscles/personality/ chivalry etcetera. Damn it.

With seconds to spare, Leo sprinted over the short metal plank and onto the ferry, where we collapsed onto a leather-cushioned bench inside and laughed like idiots all the way back to the island.

Chapter 11

"So . . . this is your place?" Leo asked as I strolled from the sidewalk and up the little gravel path that led to my porch. Our walk from the ferry dock had taken us just a few minutes, and now we were right in front of my home.

"Yep, all mine." I reached the steps and halted, turning back to face him. It was already dark, but the sounds of downtown still echoed all around. The general murmur of people talking on the street, the clip-clop of horses on their way back to the barns for the night, and the ever-present caress of waves on the shore. This was my favorite time of day, as the business of the island quieted down to the hushed sounds of evening.

"You live here by yourself?" Leo asked, eyeing my blue two-story house before setting a foot on the bottom step.

"Yep, just me." I hid my smile. I knew where this was going.

"Living alone is nice," he said slowly. "All that peace and quiet, but sometimes there are some distinct disadvantages."

"Such as?" I crossed my arms and leaned back against the post.

"Well," he said, tapping his foot, "I mean it's nice for when you feel like being alone, but sometimes there's stuff you want to do that, you know, requires two people."

"Such as?" I asked again, as if I didn't know.

"Parcheesi."

My laugh echoed into the air, and he smiled.

"I mean, sure, you'll win, but it's just no fun playing Parcheesi by yourself." He moved closer. "Ping-Pong. Synchronized swimming. Arguing. You definitely need another person for that."

Oh, I don't know. There was a pretty feisty argument going on inside of me right then between my head and my heart. Well, maybe not so much my heart as my long-dormant libido.

"And kissing," he said as his gaze dropped pointedly to my mouth. "You need two people for that."

"At least two," I said, and was rewarded with a throaty laugh from him.

"At least two." He stepped even closer, close enough that I had to look up at him. "You know, my plan was to take you out for a nice dinner, maybe have a few cocktails, listen to some soft music, impress you with my excellent table manners. All that seductive-type stuff to show you what a great guy I am. Pizza and beer is usually more for a fifth or sixth date, when the outcome is, you know, more of a sure thing."

His acknowledgment of trying to play me with a predetermined schedule held the potential for insult, but his smile was full of mischief and humor and optimistic honesty. No one had tried to woo me into bed in a very long time, and quite frankly, I appreciated even the suggestion of his effort. Nonetheless, Leo was the type of guy who should come with a warning label. *Contents may be addictive.* Whatever he had to offer, I wasn't ready to partake.

"Thanks for sharing your playbook with me. I'm not sure where that leaves us." I uncrossed my arms and let them drop.

"It leaves me wanting to kiss you very much."

My breath hitched at the words and the lusty way he said them. The teasing had evaporated, and heaven knew I wanted to be kissed. Kissed by him and to kiss him back. Every part of me felt pulled forward, like the universe was urging us closer, until his lips were just a breath away. All signs pointed to there not being much hope of a future for us, but maybe I could just worry about that little detail tomorrow. Tonight, I'd have just one little kiss. I looked into Leo's ocean-blue eyes until mine fluttered shut and he'd closed that tiny distance between us.

His lips were warm on mine, the kiss soft at first but quickly intensifying. Probably because I'd wrapped my arms around his shoulders as if he were the only thing holding me upright, and maybe he was. My knees turned to liquid along with the rest of me as he pressed closer. His hands moved around my waist as if he were molding me, pulling me tight against him. As the kiss deepened, my mind registered the texture of his hair as I wove my fingers through it, the pressure of his mouth against mine, and the flood of longing that sought to drown me. This was more than just a kiss. More than I was prepared for.

With a gasp, I broke away and laughed nervously, letting my arms drop from his shoulders to his biceps. Not sure that was the best route to take, because feeling the bulk of his arms only made me want to jump back into them. Leo looked at me, a half-confused smile touching his features. Then he offered up a rueful little chuckle.

"Wow, Mayor Callaghan. That was . . . wow. You should probably invite me in."

Oh, how I wanted to, and why couldn't I? We were responsible adults. I was a vibrant woman. It was practically the healthy thing to do. But I wasn't reckless that way. My body wanted him, and my mind was halfway there, but I'd been burned before by handsome guys just passing through. So, as handsome and charming and sexy as Leo Walker was, I needed to be more certain of him before taking this step.

"That's very tempting, but in spite of the pizza-and-beer-themed evening, I am not a sure thing." If he persisted in the slightest, I could almost certainly change my tune on that, but he didn't. Through sheer force of will, I dropped my hands from his arms. He took a tiny step backward and let his hands drop from my waist. Not without a little extra squeeze, though.

"I know you aren't. That's why I like you." He kissed me gently once more, a kiss of patience and promise that made my heart thump hard.

"Thanks for having dinner with me, and thanks for telling me all that stuff about the island," he said. "Maybe I'll go back to my place and start writing that book."

"That's a great idea." *Not as good of an idea as sweeping me off my feet and carrying me to bed . . .*

"Sure." He nodded. "I'll get to it ASAP. Right after that cold shower."

His smile was so sweet as he turned to walk away that I very nearly called him back. I didn't. But I sure as hell wanted to.

Chapter 12

"I can't believe I'm hosting Drunk Puzzle Night when I can't even drink," Gloria said as she set a red plastic pitcher of margaritas down on her kitchen table. "Did any of you ever imagine I'd be the sober one?"

"Nope. Not ever. No way," various women chorused.

There were seven of us squeezed around a wooden table inside Gloria's turquoise-painted kitchen. We assembled about once a month for what was aptly named Drunk Puzzle Night. We used to call it book club, but eventually we came to terms with the fact that none of us ever read the assigned book, and we always just sat around drinking and doing puzzles.

"So, Brooke," Gloria said as she settled into a chair. "How is it going with that sexy new bartender from the Palomino? What's his name?"

"Leo. There's nothing to report."

"Oh, really?" Eva Culpepper said. "Because I heard someone saw the two of you doing it on your front porch."

My gasp was justifiably loud. "We were not doing it! Is that what people are saying?"

Eva giggled. "No, not really, but Percy told Collette that his sister saw you and the bartender standing very, very close on your front porch and that there appeared to be some lip-locking and some potential groping."

My sister turned in her chair to gape at me. "Is that true? Did you kiss Leo the bartender? Without telling me?"

"It was one little kiss. I didn't tell you because there wasn't much to tell."

Actually, there were all sorts of things to tell, but all of them had to do with my messy, inexplicable emotions, my fears, my doubts. My need to keep this delicious secret to myself. Whatever Leo and I had started, I didn't want to share it with the rest of the community. I just wanted to enjoy it a bit before it became part of the island conversation.

"But I'm your sister, and I have to find out about this on the street?"

"Well, since it's out there," Marnie White said, "I saw you two getting off the ferry, and you looked rather cozy."

Emily frowned. "What were you doing on the ferry?"

"We went out to dinner in Manitou."

She made a noise that was part harrumph and part *well-well-well*. She'd be grilling me for details on our walk home.

"So how was the kiss? Did he spend the night?" Marnie asked.

"No, of course he didn't spend the night. I told you, it was just one little kiss."

"Oh, sure," Gloria giggled, running a hand over her belly. "One little kiss is how it starts, and before you know it you've got a meatloaf in the oven and you're marrying Tiny Kloosterman. Well, not Tiny, because he's all mine, but you get what I mean."

"I do get what you mean, Gloria, but I am a long way away from anyone putting a meatloaf in my oven. It was a harmless little kiss, and besides, he's not staying around here for long. The bartending thing is short-term."

"He's sticking around long enough to write a book. How long does that take? Seems like it could take a pretty long time. Almost as long as it takes to read one," Eva said.

"How did you hear about his book?" I asked.

"Shari from the post office told me. She'd heard it from Clancy. Did you know she's making pasties for strippers now?"

"I heard she's made seven hundred dollars so far," Gloria said. "I think I need to get myself a glue gun."

"Who cares about the pasties? I want to hear about the bartender. Is he a good kisser?" Marnie asked.

The back of my neck started to prickle, and I felt my palms growing damp. Talking about this made me uncomfortable because it forced me to label whatever it was that was going on. And at the moment, I didn't really know what was going on. I knew I liked Leo, and he seemed to like me, too. But it was already obvious that he was not a "stay on the island forever" kind of guy.

"He was a fine kisser, but could we move on, please?"

"His kiss was fine as in *meh*, fine? Or fine as in *fiiiiinnnnne*?" Eva punctuated that last word with a little shoulder shimmy. I felt myself blushing, which was sure to fan the flames.

"It was very enjoyable. He was quite . . . adept, but how much can you really tell from one kiss?"

The women around the table exchanged amused glances.

"A lot," Emily stated firmly. "If it's all sloppy and wet, or you find out he's a tongue-thrusting uvula plunger, that's pretty much the end of things right there. But if that first kiss is good, it sets the tone for everything else. So, was he a uvula plunger?"

I found myself laughing. "No, he was not, and it wasn't too sloppy or too wet, either, Goldilocks. It was . . . it was perfect." Crap, I hadn't meant to say *perfect*. That gave the whole situation way too much weight, but the word was already out there, floating gently overhead, bouncing like a balloon off everyone else's conversation bubbles, and now they were all repeating it to each other and exchanging meaningful looks.

"'Perfect,' she says."

"Oh, just nothing special. Just a perfect kiss."

"Leo is perfect; have you seen his eyes?" someone said with a sigh.

"And this is why I never tell you people anything," I snapped, irritation flaring. I didn't like being teased, especially about men and my lack of romantic history. "I didn't mean it was, like, you know, *oh, perfection.* I only meant that it was just the way I like it. It was a perfectly acceptable kiss by my standards."

My lame attempt at clarification only served to fuel their teasing, and for the next fifteen minutes they interrogated me on everything from his cologne to the size of his hands. Had he gotten to second base? Was there any ass-grabbing? Did his mouth taste good? When was I going to see him again?

"For goodness' sake, please stop. We didn't make any plans," I said with a groan. "I usually see him at the city council meetings, so I'm sure we'll talk then."

"The city council meetings are on Wednesdays. This is Friday. You have to talk to him before that. You should text him. Right now."

"I'm not texting him. I'll see him when I see him. Could we talk about something else now? You guys are making me perspire."

Emily finally took pity on me, evidently seeing that I was so very over being filleted for information.

"Fine, fine, fine," she said. "Gloria, how goes the wedding planning?"

"Fantabuloso!" Gloria said with a grin, and the talk moved on to everything matrimonial. "Everyone has been so great about pitching in to help. We thought we'd just end up grilling a few burgers in Tiny's backyard and call it good, but it's turning into a real reception. Buddy at the Imperial Hotel is letting us use one of the rooms at the hotel for a bargain price, and they've offered to reuse flowers that will be left over from a banquet the day before. Georgie Reynolds and her band have offered to play for free drinks. Most of the bars in town have donated a bottle or two of liquor, which seems like the least they can do, because

Tiny is a very reliable patron. And believe it or not, April Mahoney offered me a dress that her daughter bought and never wore. Not sure if it's bad luck to wear a dress from a bride who got dumped the week before her wedding, but hey, I tried it on, and if I do say so myself, I look divine in it."

"You're allowed to say that. You're the princess of the day." Marnie reached over and squeezed her hand.

"Tiny makes me feel like a princess every day. I've been so flippin' emotional with these pregnancy hormones, and he just keeps telling me everything will be fine. He's a saint, that man."

"And to think I introduced you. I'm pretty proud of myself for that one." Emily preened.

"You should be. Speaking of that, I've been meaning to ask you something." Gloria's eyes started to well up. "Emily, would you be my maid of honor?"

My sister's surprise was evident from her expression, and from the sudden sparkle of a tear in her own eye. "Oh my goodness. Of course. I'd be honored. I'd be maid of honored!" She laughed as she hopped up from her chair to give Gloria a hug, and everyone yayed and hoorayed and asked more questions about the ceremony.

We were walking home later that evening when Emily asked, "What exactly does a maid of honor do for a wedding that's eight days away and essentially already planned? I guess I should have asked, but she caught me off guard."

"I suppose you'll have to stand up and be her witness at the courthouse," I said.

"Probably. That won't be so bad, but oh my gosh. You don't suppose she's going to pick out a bridesmaid dress for me, do you? She and I do not have the same sense of style!"

"You don't think a lime-green taffeta dress with pink polka dots would suit you?"

"If only it could be that subtle. Maybe I'll just tell her I have the perfect dress in mind and hope she goes for it. Do you think we should throw her a shower? An engagement-slash-wedding-slash-baby shower?"

"Probably, but when?"

"I have no idea. I'm crazy busy right now, and she didn't give us much notice."

"What do you mean *us*? She didn't ask me to be a bridesmaid. This one is all on you." I smiled because of course I'd help, but I wasn't sure when. "Unless maybe you could have it after the wedding? I'm pretty busy with running the town, you know."

Emily chuckled. "Dmitri told me you and June Mahoney had a catfight and were slapping each other across the face."

"I wish. As much as I might enjoy taking a swing at June Mahoney, we did not slap each other. We raised our voices because she didn't want to let Gigi send her husbands off into the sky inside a firework."

Emily's feet stopped moving. "Gigi wants to do what now?"

I filled her in on the latest shenanigans, and then she moved on to the next inevitable topic.

"So, when were you going to tell me about this Leo guy? And the kissing stuff?"

I couldn't contain my sigh. "I wasn't *not* telling you. I just, I don't know. I'm not sure what to even say about it. We've had dinner twice. It was fun. He kissed me. *That* was fun." I shrugged, suddenly at a loss for words and feeling inexplicably emotional.

"I talked to him for a few minutes at Bridget O'Malley's wake. He seems like a pretty nice guy. And not too hard to look at, either."

"That's for sure."

"So, why do you seem so reluctant to pursue something with him? Shoot, why didn't you hop into bed with him after the first dinner?"

I looked around to make sure no one was near enough to hear us, but the streets were virtually deserted. "Because that's not my style.

When it comes to that sort of stuff . . . I'm a little shy. And I haven't had sex in ages. I'm not sure I remember how."

Emily grinned. "It's just like riding a bike, except that the bike is naked, and the seat is a penis."

I chuffed with laughter. "Good to know, but I guess it's not the mechanics I'm so worried about. It's the, you know, the emotional element of it. I like him. But what if we end up in bed and then I start to like him too much? Then he leaves and breaks my heart."

Emily's nod was sympathetic. "Listen, I totally get what you're saying about that. It's exactly how I felt about Ryan, but things are going great for us. Maybe things will go great for you and Leo, too. Don't you think it's worth a shot? I mean, honestly, Brooke, when's the last time you had a boyfriend?"

"Ouch."

"I'm not asking that to be mean. It just seems like you work really hard to keep yourself working really hard, and maybe you use that as kind of an escape, you know? Like, if you keep yourself occupied by worrying about the schoolkids, or the island's government, or even Dad and Gigi, then you won't have time to think about your own needs."

I felt my cheeks heat up as she continued.

"You know, now that I'm a mom, and especially now that Chloe is a teenager," Emily said, "I've realized what an enormous sacrifice you made by taking care of me and Lilly after Mom died. You were there for us all the time, and I owe you so much for that. But I think you got into the habit of stuffing down your own needs and desires all the time, and maybe . . . maybe it's time you stopped doing that."

We walked a few more steps in silence as her words settled in my brain and hot tears prickled in my eyes. My first instinct was to feel defensive, but in truth, my sister had struck upon something that had started to occur to me, too. People kept asking me why I wanted to be the mayor, and I came up with all sorts of reasons. Politically applicable reasons. But deep down, I think the real reason I ran for mayor was because I was so bored with my life, and quite frankly, I was lonely. But unless I wanted to move to a new town, or take a big new job, I was going to stay bored. And stay lonely. I couldn't do much about the lack of datable men around here, so if I wanted to be really honest with myself, I had to acknowledge that running for mayor had been a substitute.

"You think I stuff down my needs and desires?"

"Maybe. There's nothing wrong with being cautious in a new relationship, but you have to be willing to take some risks. I know we didn't talk much when I lived in San Antonio, and I'm sorry about that, but did you date anyone while I was gone?"

"Geez, Emily! You were gone for twelve years. Of course I dated some people. I'm not that pathetic." *Was I?*

"Of course you're not, but what happened with them? I mean, why didn't any of those relationships work out? Wasn't there some guy named Jason? Whatever happened with him?"

I stumbled a bit and decided to blame an uneven spot on the sidewalk. Because . . . Jason. Yes, there was a guy named Jason. I tried not to think about him anymore, but sometimes I would, like at three o'clock in the morning, when I couldn't sleep and the emptiness of my bed was painfully obvious.

We'd reached my house by then, and I could have sent her on to Gigi's house and ended the conversation there, but suddenly I wanted to tell her. I wanted to tell her everything. "You want to hear about Jason? You'd better come in for some wine."

She followed me in, and I got us two glasses of merlot before we settled down on my old comfy sofa.

"You have my full attention," she said, adjusting the pillow behind her.

"Okay, well, I don't know what you remember about him, or what I even told you at that time, but yes, I dated a guy named Jason. He was an electrician, and he'd come here one winter to do some work at the Imperial Hotel. I met him at a party at Marnie's house, and we just clicked. Everything felt right. I fell hard, and everyone could see that I was head over heels." Talking about that part of the relationship, remembering the beginning and all those wonderful feelings, was hard, and I paused to grapple with the sudden regret. I took a sip of wine, and then another.

"And?" Brooke prompted.

"And I thought he was head over heels for me, too. At least, he said he was, and I believed him. I thought, this is it. This is the guy. We talked about getting married."

"You did?" Her eyes went round with surprise.

I nodded. "Yes, we did. A lot. We talked about me moving to Ohio, because that's where he grew up. We kept that talk a secret, though. I didn't really want anyone to know how fast things were moving. You know how it is on the island. People love to gossip, and I didn't want to give them more to talk about. And I didn't want Dad catching wind of it before I was ready to tell him, but we made plans. I got my résumé together so I could apply for teaching jobs. Everything was lining up, and I could see a whole future ahead of us." I paused for another hearty gulp of wine.

"So . . . what happened?" Her voice was hesitant.

This was the part I really hated. I hated telling it, and I sure as hell hated remembering it. "We were having dinner one night, and he got a phone call. I could tell something was very wrong. When he hung up . . . he finally told me the truth. Turns out, he was married."

"Married? And you didn't know?"

"Of course I didn't know. I never would have gotten involved with him if I'd known he was married. And the icing on that cake? The call was from his sister-in-law, because his wife"—I choked on the words a little—"his wife had just gone into labor. With their third child."

Emily's mouth dropped open. She was sufficiently aghast. "Are you serious?"

"So serious."

"Oh my gosh, Brooke. I'm so sorry."

"He tried to convince me that he'd been planning to tell me, of course. You know, when the *time was right*. I told him the right time would've been before he'd hit on me. And then he said he wanted to stay here. That he'd leave his wife and move to Wenniway, but how could I ever be with some guy who'd do that to his family?"

"You couldn't, of course. What an asshole!"

"Such an asshole. I was crushed, of course. And embarrassed. I didn't know who to talk to, so I ended up at Dmitri's house. I told him the whole story. Unbelievably, he has never repeated it to anyone. Or if he has, no one has breathed a word of it to me, and I think I would've heard something. Instead he went around telling everyone that I'd dumped Jason because I'd finally realized he was too stupid for me."

My sister's head dropped into her palms, and when she lifted it, her face was full of sympathy. "Brooke, I am so sorry you had to go through that. I wish you had told me at the time."

I gave a little shrug, but it was only little because I felt the full weight of the memory. "You had your own drama going on. And I just felt so stupid and awful."

"Have you ever spoken to that guy again?"

I shook my head. "Not a once. He was gone the next day. For the longest time I kept thinking he'd come back, because what I'd felt had seemed so real and so special. But even if he had come back, I mean, I could never be with a guy who cheated on his wife and kids. I'd fallen in love with a shadow." I drained my wineglass. "So, yeah, it's been a while since my last boyfriend, and I'm still a little skittish. Not sure I'm ready to trust Leo, and if I'm hiding behind work, then I guess I'm hiding behind work."

She reached over and grabbed my hand. "I'm sorry I said all that. I'm sorry I made you relive this."

"It's okay. Honestly, it's kind of a relief to finally admit it to someone. And anyway, it's been six years. I suppose it's time to get over it. I'm still humiliated, but it is what it is."

She frowned. "I don't mean to invalidate your feelings, but may I suggest that you have no reason to feel humiliated? Just because he lied, that doesn't mean you were stupid to trust him. A normal person wouldn't do that to another person. Sociopaths do that. You were duped."

"Definitely duped. And even though I don't think Leo is hiding a wife and kids in some other town, I'm not sure I want to fall for some guy who's just passing through. Even if he does stick around long enough to write a book, eventually he's going to leave."

She nodded slowly. "Guys can be trolls. Believe me. I've dated my share of horrible men, but I decided to trust Ryan when he came along. It was kind of terrifying to put my heart out there, but if you don't take a risk once in a while, you'll never know what might have been. Maybe a fling with Leo is just the ticket. If he's smitten with you, who knows what could come of it?"

"I guess." I wanted to take her advice. I wanted to fling with Leo.

"And one thing is for sure," she added with a chuckle, "he seems like the kind of guy who could make you forget all about any shitty old boyfriends."

I found myself smiling. "That he does."

A few minutes later, my sister finished her wine, hugged me way too hard, then left. As I lay in bed that night, I felt lighter somehow. I'd hauled that story around with me for so long. It wasn't something I thought about often. I'd moved on, but I carried it with me. The hurt. The disappointment. The embarrassment. But I didn't need to feel that anymore. I felt a sense of relief. Like taking off a bra that's too tight and kind of scratchy. Getting it off you feels so much better. This was kind of like that. Not necessarily good: just an absence of irritation.

But it was also hard not to remember those first days after finding out Jason was married. That was the kind of dark place I never wanted to go to again, and if I fell for Leo, and then he left, it would hurt. So the only way to proceed was with extreme caution. If at all.

Chapter 13

"Thanks for meeting me for lunch," Leo said as I joined him on Monday at a tiny table in the center of Carmen's Café. "I hope I'm not interrupting a busy day."

"All my days are busy. This city never sleeps," I said, then chuckled. "Actually, that's not true, but Gertie and I are determined to sort through every single file and pile of junk in that damn office. You would not believe the kind of crap Harry Blackwell left behind." I latched my purse over the back of my chair and eased out of my tan coat. I was wearing a plum-colored sweater that looked . . . fine, but if I'd known Leo was going to text me, I would have put in a bit more effort. I thought I'd put on mascara this morning. Or had I?

"What kind of crap?" He handed me a plastic-covered menu.

"Like dozens and dozens of nail clippers. He must have had some serious claws. He did stop back in before he left for Florida, but all he wanted was his picture of George Bush, his other picture of the other George Bush, and his Gerald R. Ford commemorative place mat. He informed us that they don't make them anymore, and I have no doubt that's true."

Leo propped an elbow on the table and rested his chin on one hand. His smile was warm and easy, and maybe it was the deep blue of his eyes, or his sincere expression, or the conversation I'd just had with my sister, but something in that moment made me want to share all the tidbits about my work and all the little pieces that made up my day. Leo wasn't Jason. He was nothing like Jason, and I found myself rattling on, even as we ordered our food and ate our lunch.

"One of the things I really want to do is update the community center, but since that is going to cost money, I'm not sure how to convince everyone that it's important."

"Is the community center that old building with the green siding? The one that looks like half of it is about to fall into the lake?"

"Yes, that's the one. Maybe it's the teacher in me, but I have this dream of setting up some classrooms inside and having a computer lab. Too many of the older residents around here have only a rudimentary knowledge of computers, and it's essential for our local businesses that they get with the program. I've been talking to some internet providers about improving our bandwidth, too, and my sister's boyfriend, Ryan, works for a hotel management company, so we've been talking about getting all the hotels and bed-and-breakfast places to start using the same reservation system. That way visitors could just visit our chamber of commerce website and then link to any hotel they want. Or they could just search by dates and see which places have a vacancy. As of right now there is no communication between the hotels, and half of them keep track of their visitors using paper."

"Paper?"

"Yes, like my grandmother. She has six rental properties and keeps track of everything using a spiral notebook. If that notebook got lost or damaged, she'd have no idea who was booked at any of her places."

"That's pretty risky."

"She says using a computer is even riskier because then the government can track your every keystroke. Pretty sure she learned that from my predecessor. The truth is I'm spending a lot of my time just undoing the damage Harry did by convincing our older population to resist every modern convenience, but I think my niece is softening up my grandmother. Gigi is all about Pinterest now, so hopefully, once I show her how easy the reservation website is, she'll get on board. And once the hotels are linked, the other local businesses will join, too. People come from all over just to taste our fudge, and that's a great draw, so I have to wonder what kind of revenue we could drum up for the island during the off-season if people could order some of our products online. Like the fudge, or Dmitri's honey. Or Shari's pasties."

I grinned at him, waiting for that to sink in.

"Shari's what?"

"The woman from our post office makes custom pasties for exotic dancers. Now if that isn't some good old-fashioned capitalism, then I don't know what is."

Leo nodded. "Nothing says God bless America like red, white, and blue tassels."

We laughed in unison. "I'll have you know that Shari has made almost a thousand dollars from this little venture. Although I'm not sure that's the kind of business I want to link to our tourism website."

I looked up to find Leo gazing at me intently.

"What?" I asked, covering my mouth. Did I have food in my teeth? I really hoped I did not have food in my teeth. I should have ordered the soup instead of the salad. "I'm talking too much, aren't I."

"No, of course not. I'm just enjoying your enthusiasm. Seems like you're getting into the groove of your new job."

"I guess I am."

He nodded. "I'm glad. So, speaking of jobs . . ." He wadded up his paper napkin and tossed it onto his now-empty plate. "I actually have an interview scheduled. I fly out this evening." His voice seemed unnaturally light, and he looked down when he said it, rather than looking me in the eye.

My stomach flipped. "A job interview? That's great." Cue fake enthusiasm, feel heart plummeting. "Where is it?"

"Um, Washington, DC."

Too far away. Definitely too far away. "Awesome. For a security job?" My voice was pitchy, and I cleared my throat.

"Sort of. I'll know more after the interview, but it's with one of my old commanding officers."

Some of the air in the room seemed to seep out, creating a pressure that hadn't been there before. He really wasn't staying on this island. I'd known that. I had, but obviously I'd hoped we'd have a little more time. At least enough to see if this spark between us was worth fanning. Try as I might to hide them, my feelings must have shown on my face, because he reached over and traced the top of my hand with his fingertip, and when I looked up at his face, there was intention in his eyes.

"I like you, Brooke."

"Me too. I mean, I like you, too."

"Whatever happens, I'm here for a few more weeks at least. Can I see you when I get back?"

Try as I might to keep things light, I had two choices. Keep things safe and superficial and don't go out on any more dates, or dive in and gather up as much affection and joy as I could in the time that we had. A smart, practical woman would nip this in the bud, and I was a smart, practical woman. However, I was also a woman in desperate need of some love, even the temporary kind.

"Probably," I answered.

♋

"Close your eyes," Gertie said, standing outside my office door. Her cheeks were extra pink this afternoon, and her eyes were shining. "I have a surprise for you."

"What have you got hiding in there?" I asked. "Please tell me it's something good and not Vera with some new grant proposal about bat health."

"It's something good. At least, I think you'll think it's good. I took the liberty of working over the weekend, and I've made some improvements to the state of your office." She clasped her hands in front of her pancakelike chest and bounced a little on her heels. I still couldn't quite get used to hearing it referred to as my office. I'd been the mayor now for two full weeks, and it had yet to sink in.

"Okay," I said. "Let's see it."

She swung the door open and virtually skipped inside before turning around to face me, smile wide.

"Gertie," I breathed out slowly as I stepped over the threshold of the door. "This office looks amazing. What a transformation! How did you manage it?"

My assistant and I had cleared up the first layer of clutter, but this was nothing short of miraculous. The walls had been painted a lovely, soothing shade of pale blue. The tacky old artwork had been removed and replaced with updated, framed photographs of popular Trillium Bay landmarks. There was a shot of Petoskey Bridge with the sun setting behind it, and another of the gardens of the Imperial Hotel with all the flowers in bloom. On another wall were photos of lilacs, several of the most beautiful Victorian cottages, and the lookout tower of Fort Beaumont. My desktop was now clear of loose papers and instead sported a shiny new computer and keyboard; a stackable bamboo in- and out-box; a coordinating pen holder, tape dispenser, and stapler; and even an updated phone. No more curly corded 1980s relics.

I walked around to the other side of the desk while looking around the rest of the room, trying to take it all in at once. All the filing cabinet drawers were closed. No more bent, tattered files trying to escape. The shelves had been dusted, and the books, from what I could tell with just a glance, had been reorganized by category. There were a few smaller framed photos on the shelves, too. Gertie pointed to one.

"I hope you don't mind," she said, her voice still breathy with excitement. "I got some photos from your family because I thought it might be nice to have a few personal touches in here."

I stepped closer and felt tears prickle my eyes. There was a picture of me with my sisters standing in front of the Lilac Festival Parade, taken the summer before Emily ran off to marry Chloe's father. We'd had a good time that day. It was one of my favorite memories. There were a couple of pictures of me giving the graduation speech to my class of nine, and me standing with the other teachers outside Trillium Bay School, and a photo of me and my dad. He was wearing his sunglasses and had about as much of a smile as he ever had in pictures, but we were standing close together, and he had his arm around my shoulders. I was leaning into him. I wasn't sure when that one had been taken, but my smile was wide, and I looked completely comfortable and happy there with him.

"These are fantastic, Gertie. I can't believe you did all this in such a short time." I dashed a little tear away and sniffled. I'm so not a sniffler, but she'd really caught me off guard with this incredible gesture of kindness.

"Dmitri helped me. He did most of the painting and carried the computer in here. We worked on everything else together."

Still in awe, I went back to my desk and lightly traced my fingertips over the fancy new keyboard. "Who paid for this?" I asked.

"I checked with Sudsy Robertson, since he's the city treasurer. He said we had a line item in the budget for technology upgrades, but Harry never took advantage of it, so there was plenty to get all this new stuff. We have a new printer, too. That's sort of for me. Hope you don't mind."

"Of course I don't mind. You deserve a new printer. Shoot, you deserve a medal, a day off, and a raise after all this work. And I guess I owe Dmitri a nice dinner or something, too."

"Oh, he said he was glad to help. You know how he is. Always ready to lend a hand."

"This is just amazing. Oh my gosh, you even got me a new chair? How did you manage to get all this stuff here?"

"The chief and I went over to the office store in Michlimac City and got some of it. They were able to ship the rest."

"My dad? You went with my dad?"

"Yes. Is that a problem?" She adjusted her glasses nervously.

"No, not at all. I'm just surprised. That's not the kind of thing my dad usually does."

Today was proving to be another head-spinny kind of day. Leo leaving for an interview. Dmitri painting my walls. Gertie rearranging my office. My father helping. It was all very surreal. I sank down into my fabulous new chair and adjusted it to the right height. I moved the keyboard closer and tilted the monitor a bit.

"Gertie, you are simply the best. Thank you so much."

My assistant beamed at the well-deserved praise. "It was my pleasure, Madam Mayor. I've got some emails to answer, so I'll let you get to your work. There's a password to log in to your computer, by the way. It's *wonderwoman*, but you can change it if you want to."

I smiled, and answered, "I think *wonderwoman* will do just fine."

Chapter 14

"Oh my." Gloria Persimmons stared into the beveled-glass mirror on the wall of the lady's room of the Trillium Bay Courthouse and belched like a teenage boy who'd just chugged two liters of soda. She covered her shimmering pink lips with the back of her hand.

"This baby makes me burp. I hope I can get through my vows without blowing Cheez Doodle breath right into Tiny's face. Do you have a mint?"

"I do," Emily said, digging her hand into a white satin bag labeled Bridal Emergency Kit. As the maid of honor, it was her job to make sure Gloria's day went as smoothly as possible, and since Gloria's emotional needs were potentially a multi-person job, she'd drafted me to help. I didn't mind. It distracted me from Leo being gone, and so far all I'd had to do was fix a few hairpins in Gloria's mile-high updo and feed her Cheez Doodles so she wouldn't get any orange dust on her white dress.

"I have some antacid, too," Emily said. "Maybe you should take one of those. It might help with the burps."

My sister hadn't escaped getting stuck in a bridesmaid-dress-from-hell and was currently wearing a hot-pink chiffon number with puffy sleeves and a big bow in the back. Given Gloria's fashion sense, it could have been much worse.

"That's a pretty handy bag you've got there," I said, peeking inside. It contained just about everything a bride could need. Mints, floss, deodorant, stain remover, a pair of satin slippers for when your feet gave out. "Looks like it's got everything except a groom."

"It's totes adorbs, isn't it," Gloria said, giggling. "Shari made it for me. She gave me some white sparkly pasties, too. Tiny's going to love them."

"Did I hear my name?" Shari Bartholomew popped her head inside the room. "Can I come in?"

"Absolutely-positutely," Gloria said, waving her inside the stuffy little room. "The more the merrier, as long as Tiny doesn't see me. Don't want any bad luck."

"Hey, me too!" I heard my niece shout. "Can I come in? Oh, Gloria, you look like a princess."

Judging from the oversize tiara, the mounds upon mounds of tulle, and the elbow-length satin gloves, I suspected that's just the look she was going for. Personally, I found it a little much, especially for a courthouse wedding, but then again, the dress was free, and I was certain it looked better on Gloria than it would have looked on April Mahoney's daughter.

Another knock sounded. "Hey, is the bride in there?" I recognized Ryan's voice, and Emily moved as best she could to get to the door. No easy feat with so many of us crammed in there and Gloria's dress exceeding six feet in diameter. My sister opened the door just a crack.

"She's in here. What's up?"

"Tiny is about ready to pass out he's so nervous, and if he falls down, none of us will be able to lift him, so is she about ready?"

Emily leaned back and looked over at Gloria. "You ready, girlfriend?"

"So ready!" She gave Emily two thumbs up. "Let's go get me married."

The ceremony was brief, presided over by local judge Brian Murphy, and although Gloria and Tiny hadn't expected many people to show at the courthouse, a crowd of nearly forty people tossed rice and birdseed and blew tiny bubbles as the bride and groom walked through the door and descended the short staircase.

"Oh, is that for us?" Gloria gasped as she spotted the white carriage covered with tulle and white roses. Two glossy black horses pranced with energy. One was wearing a top hat just like the driver, while the other sported a sassy bridal veil.

Pete the driver tipped his own hat. "Climb aboard, Mr. and Mrs. Kloosterman," he said. "The buggy is compliments of Taggert Construction."

I turned to Ryan, part owner of Taggert Construction. "Did you do that?"

He nodded. "I'm the best man. It seemed like it was the least I could do."

Emily gazed up at him from his other side. "You sentimental fool. You didn't tell me you were going to do that."

He grinned and put an arm around her waist. "I don't tell you everything, woman. Sometimes a guy likes to prove he still has a surprise or two up his sleeve."

"So romantic," Chloe sighed from her spot next to me. "I can't wait to get married."

I stole a glance at my niece and wondered if she'd make it down the aisle before I ever did.

The crowd watched and cheered as Tiny tried to assist Gloria and all that tulle into the coach. He finally just put both hands on her ample butt and pushed. She nearly flew out the other side, but after some readjusting and a lot of giggling, they were finally settled into the buggy, and off it went. The bride and groom turned around and waved, and I felt myself getting a little misty. They really were cute, and they really were going to be happy.

"Okay, that's done. Let's get drunk," Ryan said, rubbing his hands together as the sound of the horse's hooves began to fade and the group moved in unison toward the Imperial Hotel to start the reception.

I spotted Gigi from the corner of my eye, strolling arm in arm with Gus Mahoney. He was wearing a corduroy sport coat with leather patches on the elbows, and his normally messy hair was neatly combed. No sign of the X-rated tattoos.

"Hello there!" She waved and steered him closer.

I knew Gus because our community was so small, but I couldn't say I actually *knew* him. He traveled in different circles, and besides that, he was a Mahoney, and until the recent cease-fire in the Callaghan-Mahoney feud, there had been no reason to deepen the acquaintance. The two families didn't really mingle, but I guess when Gigi had decided to break down that barrier, she'd decided to really break it down.

"Afternoon, ladies. Young man," Gus said politely, extending his hand to Ryan first, then to me and Emily. We'd all stopped walking as the rest of the crowd continued on.

"This is my great-granddaughter," Gigi said, patting Chloe on the head like a puppy. "Isn't she beautiful?"

Gus gave a slight bow. "A pleasure to make your acquaintance, Miss Chloe. I've heard so many things about you. About all of you," he added, looking at each of us once more. "I'm looking forward to getting to know you better, and rest assured, I hold your Gigi in the highest esteem."

I'd never heard anyone proclaim to hold Gigi in high esteem before. Generally, people liked her, but she wasn't the sort to be . . . esteemed. Maybe Gus saw something I didn't. I mean, I loved her, but that's because she was family. I was morally obligated to love her.

"Such a lovely ceremony, wasn't it?" he added. "So wonderful to see two young people in love."

He was soft-spoken and so polite it was hard to believe he was related to the table-pounding June Mahoney. Maybe Gigi wasn't so crazy after all.

"It's good to meet you, Gus," Ryan said. "Are you two heading to the reception?"

"Of course we are," Gigi answered. "We wouldn't miss a chance to kick up our heels and party a little, would we, Gus?"

"No, we would not."

"Well, let's get a mosey on, then."

The reception room at the hotel was fully decked out, with white satin ribbons twirled around all the posts and light fixtures. They fluttered as people walked by, as if they were waving hello. Linen-draped dining tables were set up on one side of the room, and even the day-old flowers looked sweet and welcoming. The Reynolds band, normally dressed in torn black tees and banging out hard rock, was today dressed in pale colors, and my surprise quadrupled as Georgie Reynolds stood at the microphone and sang one beautiful love song followed by another.

"I had no idea she could actually sing," Emily confided to me. "At work all I ever hear her do is screech at her brother and complain about her cramps."

There was a bar off to one side, and I found my eyes going to it again and again. Clancy McArthur from the Palomino was mixing drinks, and somewhere deep down, I guess I was hoping Leo might be there, too. I hadn't heard from him since we'd had lunch. I knew he'd left for Washington that evening, but he hadn't said when he'd be coming back. Maybe he wouldn't come back at all. It wasn't as if he owed me anything. He really didn't even owe me a phone call. Still, a text might have been nice, that bastard.

Damn. I needed to get some food. I was starting to feel hangry.

I got some cheese and crackers from the snack table and ate them while I stood in line at the bar. As the sun lowered outside, casting golden beams around the room, the reception grew louder, and when Tiny and Gloria arrived, the cheers were deafening. The room was full of happy, celebrating people who ate, drank, and grew merry over marriage. Booze flowed, people shouted their congratulations, and I tried my best to get into the mood of it all. Missing Leo was kind of a waste of time, and I desperately wanted to shake it off, but the glum was sticking to me like saltwater taffy.

Dinner was served, toasts were made, laughter was abundant. After the food was cleared away, the Reynolds band switched from romancey ballads to up-tempo reception classics. Gigi danced with Gus, while the Mahoney sisters sat at a table and glared at them. Dmitri danced with Shari from the post office. Emily danced cheek to cheek with Ryan, and even Chloe got out on the floor with a couple of cute local boys. No one asked me to dance. Not that I would have said yes. I could've just gone out on the floor if I'd wanted to. There was an entire gaggle of women dancing with no partners. Mrs. O'Doul, Vera VonMeisterburger, my pals from Drunk Puzzle Night. But pangs of longing tapped at my ribs, and dancing wasn't going to help. Instead, I tried to drown those pangs with rum and Coke. It always sucked to be the single girl at a wedding, but this was more than that. I would've been fine if this event had happened weeks ago, before Leo had showed up. Rather than filling me with hope, all he'd done was remind me of all that I was missing.

What I was not missing was another rum and Coke.

Standing at the bar (again) an hour later, I saw my sister and Ryan returning from the garden outside. They were both flushed and giggling and leaning into each other as they walked. Looked like someone might have just gotten some action among the rosebushes. I took a hearty swig from my cup as they walked directly toward my father. I took another hearty swig when Harlan hugged my sister and then shook Ryan's hand. Something in my life was about to shift. Big-time. I could feel the seismic rumble all the way from across the room. I walked to where they stood, their smiles stretching from ear to ear.

Emily all but bounced. "Oh, I was just coming to find you. Look!" She held up her left hand, and there it was. A diamond engagement ring. I'd suspected that was coming, but seeing it on her finger made it official. My heart did a triple-flip with emotions I couldn't name. My joy for them was sincere. It really was, but there was so much more.

Too much more, and I wasn't sure what to do with it. The one thing I did know, though, was that I shouldn't, couldn't, and wouldn't let this moment be tarnished by anything as pointless as envy.

"Oh my gosh, you guys! I'm so happy for you!" I hugged them both and dashed away tears easily attributed to joy.

Chloe scampered over, giggling and bouncing as much as her mother. "I knew before you did, Mom." She grinned. "Ryan asked me first if he could marry you, and I said yes for sure."

"You knew?" Emily gasped and hugged her daughter. "You knew and managed to keep it a secret?"

"I managed to keep it a secret, too," Harlan said, his chest puffing out. "But I nearly let it slip last night at dinner."

"You knew, too?" Emily's astonishment showed.

"Of course I knew," he said, looking smug. "Ryan couldn't very well ask for your hand in marriage without my blessing, now, could he? Lucky for you I told him yes."

"Lucky for *him* you told him yes," she said, wrapping her arms around Ryan. Then she looked up at him. "Is there anyone else you talked to about this before bothering to ask me?"

His smile was sheepish. "Well, I guess that depends on how well my own father can keep a secret. I talked to him, and I wouldn't be surprised if Lilly was expecting a phone call from you very soon."

My heart did another twisty thing. It made sense that our father knew, and it even made sense that Chloe had been consulted, but if our sister, Lilly, already knew, I couldn't help but feel that everyone had been in on this wonderful secret except for me. I knew I was just feeling emotional and not being terribly rational, but it just didn't feel good to be left out.

Dmitri wandered by, eyeing us. He had a habit of doing that. Wandering by just when something juicy was happening. His radar for such things was eerily impeccable.

"Do I hear more wedding bells chiming?" he asked, stepping close to my side. I took a hearty gulp from my now nearly empty glass and glanced at my sister. Emily giggled and held up her hand again, setting that big-ass diamond to sparkling.

Dmitri took her hand and bowed over it. "Wowza. I don't know much about diamonds," he said, "but that thing sure is shiny."

"Everything is shiny," she gushed, and turned to kiss Ryan.

Good God. Yes, I was happy for her, but this was going to be a long, painful night. Wasn't this reception nearly over? I glanced at the clock on the wall: 8:15 p.m. *Shhhhhhhit.*

Word of the engagement moved faster than an electric current, and when it was time for Gloria to toss the bouquet, she just walked over and handed it to Emily. *What, so now the rest of us don't even get a frickin' chance?* I reminded myself how very much I loathed the whole *catch the flowers to catch a husband* thing. Then Gloria pulled my sister into a hug so enthusiastic Emily let out an abrupt whoosh of air. She sounded as if she were deflating.

"I'm so happy for you, Peach!" Gloria gushed, using my sister's childhood nickname. "Hurry and get knocked up so our babies can play together!"

I couldn't contain my sigh that time. Because . . . babies. Like love and romance and marriage and happily ever after, they weren't something I let myself think about too often. There was just no point in it. When I was a teacher, I got to spend time with *everyone's* kids. I had the best situation because I could have them during the day when they were fresh and eager, then send them home when they got tired and cranky and needed food. But I wasn't a teacher anymore. I missed my students, and the lack of kid-fix was taking its toll. Gloria's mention of babies sent a dull jab right into my midsection. Like an infant kick that I'd never experience. Of course Ryan and Emily would probably want to have babies. My sister was only thirty-two. She had plenty of time. And good for them, because Harlan Callaghan wanted more grandchildren, and it sure didn't look like he was going to get any from me and my thirty-six-year-old ovaries. Tears threatened me again, and I blinked them away. Was I being ridiculous? Of course I was, but the more buoyant everyone else seemed to get, the further I sank. I was a walking anchor.

Gazing over the happy crowd, I admonished myself for being a drama queen. Just because stupid Leo had a stupid job interview, it wasn't the end of the world. I wasn't any worse off than I had been before he showed up, and I'd been happy enough a few months ago. I needed to focus on what I *did* have. I was the mayor of these people. I should be happy that everyone seemed to be having a good time. But the truth was that, surrounded by so much love and joy, all I could think about was going home, putting on my baggiest pajamas, and binge-watching something on TV. Some good old-fashioned *Game of Thrones* head-lopping should cheer me up.

I looked around, mentally prepping an explanation for why I was leaving early, but then I realized . . . no one would really notice if I left. Everyone was with their people. My friends from Drunk Puzzle Night were currently dancing in a circle around Gloria. Ryan and Emily were slow dancing in a corner, seeming not to care that the tempo of the music was fast. My dad was talking to his poker buddies, and Gigi was telling a very animated story to Gus and Gertie. No one would notice if I slipped away from this fun, rowdy party in exchange for a pity party of one. I glanced at the bar and considered getting another drink, thinking it might flush away my melancholy, but a good night's sleep would probably do the trick better than anything. I'd be fine tomorrow. I was always fine. That's why no one ever worried about me. Because I was always fine. I was Brooke Callaghan. I could take care of anything, and anybody. But that was the problem. Who was taking care of me?

Chapter 15

It was almost nine o'clock when I made my exit from Gloria and Tiny's reception. I'd managed to stick around long enough to watch them cut the cake and smash it into each other's faces, and while everyone was taking pictures of Tiny scooping frosting from his bride's ample cleavage, I strolled out the door without anyone noticing.

Now I was walking down Main Street listening to music coming from the few pubs that were still open. It was chilly, and my black dress coat was insufficient for the weather, and although I was walking as fast as my shoes would allow, I'd been coerced into wearing high heels again. They were Chloe's instead of my sister's, though, and at least they fit. And they had straps, so no danger of stepping out of them. Even so, painful shoes might have been a worthy distraction. Or at least an explanation for the tears puddling in my eyes. What the hell was wrong with me? All this pointless emotion over a guy? A guy I hardly knew?

No, it wasn't about a guy. And it wasn't really about Ryan and Emily, either. It was about me. And my bad luck or my faulty choices or whatever you wanted to call it. I'd thought being mayor might fill the hollow, and maybe it would yet. I just needed to focus on the positive. Time to suck it up, buttercup. I was Brooke Therese Callaghan. I could handle this. I just needed to count my blessings. I had a job, and my health, and my family, and kind of a cute figure . . .

Yeah. It wasn't working. I still felt like crying. I either needed to get home fast and let those tears flow or come up with better blessings.

"Brooke?"

My mind was playing tricks on me. That voice sounded like Leo.

"Brooke!"

I turned, and there he was. It was Leo. *Nice work, universe.*

I stopped walking as he approached, taking a moment to appreciate, and lament, the way his jeans and jacket fit. They fit divinely, and my irritation flared. Why couldn't he have just a little bit of a paunch around that midsection, or a thin spot in that raven-dark hair of his? Why couldn't his teeth be just a little too big or his chin be a little too weak? But no. His abs were rock hard and flat, his hair was thick, his teeth looked like a toothpaste commercial, and his chin was Disney-prince square with just the hint of a dent. What a jerk.

"Hi," I said, clearing the sadness and distress from my voice. "When did you get back?"

He reached my side, and there was a moment's hesitation before he leaned forward to give me a quick and thoroughly unsatisfying hug. "I've been back for a couple of hours, but I was at Clancy's. Where is everyone? I mean, all the regulars? I didn't recognize anyone at the pub. And why are you dressed up? You look very pretty, by the way."

I ignored the compliment. "They're all at Gloria and Tiny's wedding reception up at the Imperial Hotel."

"Oh, that's right." He slapped a hand against his forehead. "I forgot that the giant and his neon bride were getting hitched tonight. But hey, if it's at the hotel, then why are you walking down Main Street in the opposite direction?"

We were standing on the sidewalk not far from O'Doul's grocery store. Not far from the spot where he'd rescued my shoe, and as much as I wanted to be glad that he was there, I couldn't help but wonder why, if he'd been back for a couple of hours, he hadn't tried to call me. Probably because, unlike me, he wasn't wading knee-deep in a swamp of infatuation. Leo had a life far removed from this island. I was just a flicker of a distraction to him. This did not lighten my mood. The fact that he seemed just a little bit drunk didn't cheer me up, either. "Long day. I'm tired. I'm heading home."

"Home? It's like, nine o'clock on a Friday night. How about we stop and have a nightcap, and I'll tell you all about my trip."

He listed to the side a little as he said this.

"I think maybe you've already had some drinks."

"Yeah, but the good news is, I can't drink and drive around here." He laughed at his own joke, but I wasn't in the mood to encourage him. I didn't care that he was tipsy; I just wished those rum and Cokes from the wedding had left me in the same state. Unfortunately, they had not, and I was stone-cold sober. Heavy on the stone and the cold.

This whole grumpy, melancholy mood of mine was catching me off guard. I'm not a pointlessly grumpy person, and I'm not an emotionally indulgent person. I'm sensible. Sensible and intuitive enough to know that the origins of my snarly state of mind could pretty easily be traced back to the fact that this delicious man standing before me was really nothing more than a blip on the timeline of my life. If I chose to, I could throw caution to the wind and have myself a little affair, and it would be thrilling, but then it would be over and my heart would deflate like a balloon. It just wasn't worth it. I wanted what Emily and Ryan had, and what Gloria and Tiny had. Shoot, I'd even take what Gigi and Gus had, but what I didn't want was something that lasted a week or two and then was over. I deserved better than that. If I wanted to get married, if I wanted to have children, maybe it wasn't too late for me, but that wasn't going to happen with Leo because he was temporary.

"Thanks for the offer, Leo," I said patiently, "but I think I'll pass. How was your interview, by the way?" I said that to remind him that I knew he was already halfway out of my life.

"The interview? Oh, it went well. Have a drink with me and I'll tell you all about it."

"Another time, okay? You go enjoy the rest of your evening."

He put his hand on my arm as I started to walk away. "Hey, are you okay? What's wrong?"

I shook my head. "Nothing's wrong. I really am just tired." I really was. I wasn't mad at him. I couldn't be mad at him for not living here. Could I?

"Did something happen?"

Oh, quite the opposite. Nothing had happened. Not to me, at least. And nothing was going to happen to me because I was practically invisible around here. "Nothing happened, so no need to rescue me tonight, Leo. I'm not Cinderella. I have both my shoes. I really just need to get home."

"Before you turn into a pumpkin?"

"Something like that."

"Then how about I walk you home, Mayor Callaghan?" He bowed, tipping again ever so slightly.

"I'm pretty sure I'm in better shape than you, so I think I'll be just fine."

"Okay, then think of me as your security detail."

"That's comical. You do realize you're drunk, right?"

He straightened up. "Hardly at all. Give me two ibuprofen and a big glass of water, and I'll be totally sober."

I chuckled against my will. "That will take care of your hangover tomorrow, but I'm not sure it will do you much good right now. Even so, water. Go drink some water." I started walking down the sidewalk.

He trotted along beside me. "I can't. I'm busy walking you home. Do you have water at your place? Aren't you the mayor? Isn't it your job to keep drunks off the street?"

"Technically that job falls to my father, but trust me, you do not want my father getting involved in this. If you're in the mood for drinks, I suggest you head that way to the Imperial Hotel. Gloria and Tiny's reception was in full swing when I left."

"Then why did you leave?"

I tamped down a sigh. "I'm pretty sure that's where this conversation started. I left because I'm tired and want to go home."

"Excellent. I will walk you."

I didn't have the energy to take this ride again. "Okay, Boy Scout. You may walk me home." With any luck he'd have his bearings by the time we got there, then I could send him off to his own place, which, I suddenly realized, was a mystery to me. "Where do you live?" I asked.

"Over that way." He gestured broadly, indicating he lived somewhere between our present location and the lake.

"Maybe I should walk you home, instead."

"Ohh, I like the way you think, but what would the neighbors say if I brought some woman back to my rental cottage?"

I guessed I was glad to know that he didn't make a habit of doing that. Or so he said. "People will say pretty much the same thing if they see you walking me home. Someone saw us kissing on my porch the other night. I got quite the interrogation from the women at Drunk Puzzle Night."

"Really? What did you tell them?" He looked very eager to hear, but I wasn't about to get into that.

"So, again, how was your interview? Did you get the job?"

He scowled at my redirection, and we walked for a few feet before he finally answered. "It went well. Thanks for asking. As far as the job goes, it's really something that's just being formulated right now. Nothing's official."

"Is it in Washington?"

"Part of the time. There would be a fair amount of travel involved. Lots to still mull over. Tell me about the wedding."

We continued walking, past Tasty Pastries, past Link & Patty's, past the Episcopal church and its tall white steeple. I told him about Tiny pushing Gloria by the ass into the white bridal carriage and about watching Vera VonMeisterburger doing the Macarena on the dance floor.

"What's the latest on your book?" I asked as we turned from Main Street to Ojibwa Boulevard.

"My book? Lots of notes, lots of ideas. Talking to your pal Dmitri was very enlightening. I learned a lot of very useful information from him. And I spent some time at the records office, too."

We fell silent for a few minutes until we got to my place. Light glowed from my front porch as we turned into my yard. Leo seemed to have sobered up a bit as we walked, and now he strolled on up the steps and right to the door. "You're going to invite me in this time, aren't you?"

His company wasn't unwelcome, but all things considered, inviting him in would not be a wise choice. I was feeling utterly vulnerable, and if he hoped to take things to a new level, I wasn't entirely sure I'd put up much of a fuss.

"This wasn't a date, Leo. I'm not sure where in the playbook this might fall, but I'd call it an accidental encounter. Definitely not indicative of a sure thing."

"Call it whatever you want, and I'm not suggesting you're a sure thing"—he smiled—"but I'm an optimist, and I'd like to come inside and talk with you some more."

"Talk?"

"Yes. Maybe if we talk a bit longer, you'll tell me why you left a wedding reception right in the middle of it."

"My sister just got engaged." I hadn't meant to say that. It just popped out.

He turned to face me, the overhead light creating odd shadows and making it hard to read his expression. "That's two weddings and a funeral so far. This is a busy place."

"Yep."

"Is this sister, um . . . Emily?"

"Yep."

"Don't you like the guy?"

"The guy is fine. I mean, the guy is great. I like him a lot, and he adores my sister. And my niece, Chloe, loves him, too, so now she'll have a stepfather, and that's really good news."

"Okay, so why do you sound like it's not good news?"

Why, indeed? Why did my chest feel tight and my eyes feel hot?

"Because everyone is getting married or having babies or taking on lovers. Sorry to be so blunt, but even my grandmother has decided to shack up with some guy, and it's all just a lot to take in at one time. I've spent my entire life worrying about everybody else, and I had one chance at marriage and it all went wrong. I missed my turn and now it's too late."

I somehow managed to sound both annoyed and pathetic, but thankfully Leo's reaction was inquisitive rather than patronizing.

"Missed your turn?" He crossed his arms and leaned against the doorframe. "How old are you, Brooke?"

"How old am I? What? Are you trying to make me feel worse?"

His chuckle was rueful. "No, of course not. Just tell me."

"Thirty-six."

"Okay, well, I'm thirty-five, and I've had my heart stomped on a couple of different times, and I've stomped on a few, but I hardly think that means I've missed my chance."

"Sure, but you're a guy, and you don't live on an island with people you've known your entire life."

"True, but don't you get lots of visitors here? Like . . . me, for instance?"

He didn't even realize what a cruel tease he was. "Sure. Guys like you. Guys who don't live here. Guys who stop by on their way to someplace else, and then they leave. I'm not interested in temporary. I'm looking for forever." This was his chance. His chance to tell me that he was different. That maybe he would stick around. He'd buy a cottage and write that book so we'd have time together and see if what we'd started was worth pursuing.

"You don't have to stay here, you know. You could leave," he said.

Not the response I was hoping for. "I can't leave now. I just became the mayor."

"But you were a teacher before that. Couldn't you go be a teacher someplace else?"

His comments were all very global rather than personal, and it added to the edge in my voice. "You think I should just up and move to some new, random city on the off chance I'll meet someone? That's a bit of a risk, don't you think?"

"I think just about everything in life is a risk. Even standing still and waiting. Sometimes your best bet is to just jump, even if you don't know where you'll land." Still impersonal. He wasn't offering specifics. He wasn't talking about *us*; he was only talking about *me*.

"Jumping without a target seems foolish to me."

He chuckled and let his folded arms drop. "I'm sure it does, but it's worked okay for me so far. See, here I am, standing on the front porch with a beautiful woman, about to be invited in because I took a chance and escorted her home."

He didn't seem so intoxicated now. Just back to charming, self-assured Leo, and I started to wonder if maybe those rum and Cokes were still in my system because suddenly I was the one feeling light-headed. Or maybe that's because he'd stepped closer.

"So, what if some other woman had walked past you? Would you have decided to follow her home, just to see what might happen?"

His gaze locked with mine, and he took another step forward until his jacket brushed against my coat. "No, Brooke. Not just any woman. You. The truth is I asked you out to dinner that first time simply because you were beautiful, and I liked your smile and really wanted to know why you were wearing someone else's shoes. And the next time I asked you out because I'd discovered you're smart and funny as well as beautiful and I really wanted to kiss you. And tonight, I walked you home because the whole time I was away, I kept thinking about getting back here and seeing you again. And I'm not going to lie. I'm really hoping to kiss you again because the truth is, you've got me all kinds of hot and bothered, and I was hoping we could spend a little time together. But if you want me to amble on home, I will. I won't be glad about it, but I also realize you've had a lousy night, and if you're not in the mood for my company, I'll give you some space."

Space. He was offering me space. My entire life was nothing but space. Still, everything else he'd said had disarmed me and warmed me and made me feel like someone special. Not just special, but special to *him*. He'd said "hot and bothered." He'd said he'd thought about me while he was away. That was a good sign, wasn't it? So what should I do now? I could send him on his way and go have that little cry I'd been so looking forward to. Or . . . I could invite him in and let him flirt with me and seduce me and make me feel even *more* special, even if it was only for a little while. Even if it was only for pretend. Leo Walker, with his deep-blue-ocean eyes and linebacker shoulders, could woo me and kiss me and convince me, if only for tonight, that love wasn't really that far out of reach.

I couldn't contain the sigh I'd been holding in since first seeing him on the sidewalk. "You should probably come in, but just for a little while, okay?"

"I will be a complete and total gentleman."

I sincerely hope he doesn't mean that.

I pulled my house key from my purse and reached past him to unlock the door. He smelled like whiskey and cologne. The combination was vintage-sexy and oh-so-appealing. My mind instantly wondered if that whiskey would be on his lips if we kissed, and then the rest of me flushed with anticipation. Because, come on. Who was I kidding? We were absolutely going to kiss.

He followed me inside as I flipped on the lamp.

"How about that water, or some coffee?" I asked, pulling off my coat while simultaneously slipping out of my strappy shoes.

"Mmmm, whichever you want, but I sure wouldn't mind something a little stronger."

"Good, because water sounds boring." I needed a drink to fend off my nerves because I was about to get some action, and in spite of being very happy about that, I was also tied up in emotional knots. I wanted this. I did. And I knew if I suddenly changed my mind, Leo would respect that, but mostly I was nervous because I wanted him to keep wanting me. I didn't want him to change his mind or to realize that whatever he saw in me wasn't really there.

I went to the kitchen and pulled a bottle of white wine from the fridge, and turned to find Leo right behind me, practically in my shadow.

Laughter caught in my throat. "Geez! You're like a ninja."

"Sorry. I thought you could use some help."

"Help opening a bottle of wine?" I reached behind me and pulled the corkscrew from the drawer.

"Sure. I'm trying to be a perfectly helpful gentleman, plus I really need something to do with my hands." His smile was bashful, which ironically made it sinful. I wasn't sure where in the Leo Walker playbook this evening fell, but I didn't really care. He was trying to seduce me, and I was going to let him. I handed him the bottle and the corkscrew, then moved to the cabinet where I kept my wineglasses. I took two from the shelf and held them out to Leo as he deftly pulled the cork and poured a liberal amount into each goblet. We took our drinks to the front room, and Leo took a moment to look around.

The outside of my house was like so many others on the island. Victorian architecture with lots of lacy scrollwork. An oversize front porch with wicker furniture. The inside was more my style, though. I'd had the kitchen remodeled a few years before, changing out old pine cabinets for painted white. I'd splurged on granite countertops and modern stainless-steel appliances. The room Leo and I were in now had a big comfy sofa just perfect for reading and napping. It was ruby red, and everyone had teased me when I'd bought it, saying I'd tire of it soon, but I still loved it. A couple of oversize striped chairs sat on either side of the front window, with built-in bookshelves behind them. On the walls hung a collection of watercolors done by a local artist, and even one done by Shari from the post office. It was one of her more successful attempts from her painting phase.

Leo stepped closer to a large framed picture of me surrounded by a classroom full of kids. "What's this one from?" he asked.

I sat down on the sofa, trying to position myself while wearing a dress that didn't really allow for reclining. The skirt was straight, and there wasn't much give to it. Leo was going to have to work for it. "That picture was taken on my last day of teaching. All the kids wanted me to remember them, so those are their notes on the matting."

"Dear Miss Callaghan," he read aloud. "You're the best teacher ever. Go be a great mare, M-A-R-E." He chuckled at the misspelling. "Dear Miss C. We will miss you. Thanks for teaching me to whistle." He turned to look at me. "You taught them to whistle? What class was that for?"

"No class. I used to whistle when I was trying to get them to quiet down and listen. Maybe I should try that at a city council meeting?"

He crossed the room and sat down next to me. Not too close, but not so far that he couldn't reach me if he wanted to.

"Whistling might work. Or you could wear that smokin' hot dress. That would get their attention."

I sipped my wine while taking a moment to enjoy that compliment. He had a bit of facial scruff tonight, and it looked as if I might be able to solve the mystery of whether it was soft or scratchy. "I don't think June Mahoney cares what I wear."

"Mmmm, probably not." He leaned back against the cushion and repositioned himself so he was turned toward me. "So, tell me about your sister getting engaged. When did that happen?"

"Tonight, at the reception. She's very excited and Ryan is great. Anyone willing to move here and take on our whole family is pretty brave and dedicated. I am happy for them."

He looked at me as if to gauge my sincerity. "Well, I guess that's good to hear, but you don't really think you've missed your chance, do you?"

A flush of embarrassment heated my skin, and I took a sip (gulp) of wine. "Feel free to forget I said that. I was just feeling emotional, I guess. Honestly, marriage really isn't something I obsess over. I mean, I have a big family and a great job. It's all good."

It was all good, but it wasn't necessarily *enough*.

He shook his head slowly, never taking his eyes off my face. "And how is it that you say you only had one chance? The guys on this island must be morons to not be lining up at your door."

That prompted an unexpected smile. "That's nice of you to say, but I think you're forgetting again that I'm fishing in a very small pond. There's just not that many guys around here, and the ones who did pay attention when I was younger were not much of a catch. One of them used to eat chalk when we were little kids, and I'm not sure he ever stopped. The other guy got kicked in the head by a horse when he was about twelve, and he never was quite the same after that. He moved away. I think he's in politics now. Then there were a few college guys. One of them liked to brag about being a feminist, but all he meant by that was he expected me to pay for everything. I think he was less about female empowerment and more about being a cheapskate." I wasn't going to tell him about Jason. That would simply be too much.

Leo shook his head. "Guys are jerks."

I smiled. "Some guys are, but you seem pretty nice so far. It makes me very suspicious. So, what's your secret flaw? Please tell me now and save me some time." *Wife and kids back home, by chance?*

Leo laughed. "Hopefully my flaws are pretty standard issue. I drive too fast, I can waste an entire day watching *Star Wars* movies, I think poop jokes are funny. But I gave up eating chalk a while ago because it tastes terrible, and I'm more than willing to pick up the tab while still believing in equal pay for women."

"There's one other flaw you haven't mentioned. A pretty big one."

His gaze shuttered for a moment. "Which is?"

"You don't live here."

He visibly relaxed, and reached a hand toward me, stroking my arm. "No, I don't live here, but I'm here now. I can't offer you forever, Brooke, because I just don't know where my job will take me, but I'm pretty glad to be here with you tonight. Can't that be enough? For now?" He set his glass on the table.

"I don't know," I answered honestly.

"Maybe if we kissed, it would help you decide." He took my glass and set it next to his.

The ploy was so obvious I had to smile. "You don't think kissing might just confuse the issue?"

"Not for me." Now he smiled, too, and my heart gave a little lurch, like that feeling you get when you miss the bottom step and nearly fall. He made it sound so simple, and maybe it was. Maybe I should just let him kiss me and confuse the hell out of me. Maybe I should let him unzip my too-tight dress and remind me of all the ways I was glad to be a woman. Maybe the biggest risk *was* doing nothing at all.

"I guess a little kissing wouldn't hurt."

He sighed, comically, with his whole body, before pulling me closer. "Thank God. If you'd sent me away with no kisses, I'd have to go find that oversexed librarian and see if she was busy tonight."

I laughed as he pressed his face against my neck, and I felt the warmth of his own laughter caressing my skin. The scruff was the perfect combo of not too scratchy, not too soft. His hand came up to cup my jaw in his palm, and suddenly he was looking into my eyes. His smile faded, and my breath hitched. His thumb traced over my cheek as his gaze traveled down to my mouth and then back up again.

"You really are beautiful, you know," he whispered, sending shivers along every nerve in my body.

"Am I?" I couldn't help asking.

"Very, very." His lips were nearly on mine as he spoke, and I slanted upward, eager to make that final contact. He met me halfway and his kiss melted my resistance, my doubts. I kissed him back, arching and shifting until we were reclining on the sofa. In that moment, I decided Leo Walker was a risk worth taking.

Time lost its meaning as the kisses and caresses continued, and Leo's motions grew more bold, more insistent, more irresistible. His hand pressed at my waist and moved up slowly, ever so slowly over my breast, the sensations delicious, with my constrictive clothes just adding to the anticipation. My hemline had been nudged a few inches up my thighs, my neckline lowered. His shirt was untucked (I might have done that), and several pillows had been tossed to the floor to give us more access to each other. His back was smooth and warm and taut under my eager fingertips. Everything inside me wanted to explore his body as our legs tangled.

"This dress would look so good on the floor," he murmured. "Are you sure you want to keep it on?"

I chuckled deep down in my throat and caught his hand as it moved toward my zipper. He lifted his head and gazed down at me, looking outlandishly sexy with his hair slightly mussed. (I might have done that, too.)

"Maybe we should go upstairs." I hardly recognized the sultry tone of my own voice, and his responding smile was more intoxicating than all the rum and Cokes in the world. This was actually going to happen, and I was as excited as I was relieved. He lowered his head for another deep kiss just as the front door to my house rattled for a long second and then swung open, banging against the interior wall.

"What the fu—?" I gasped as Leo twisted and I arched to see who the hell had just broken into my house. "Dad?"

Harlan's face went from calm to shocked to mortified in less than one millisecond, and he turned his back to us while I tugged down my hem. Leo tried to sit up and accidentally knocked me to the floor with a *ka-thunk* as I bashed my elbow against the coffee table.

"Dad, what are you doing here?" I demanded, heat of an entirely different origin coursing through me.

The chief kept his back turned. "Um, I wanted to check on you. You left the reception so early I thought something must be wrong. Looks like you've got everything under control, though." He peeked over his shoulder to where I still sat on the floor. Leo stood and reached down to help me up. Then he extended a not-all-that-steady hand to my father.

"Good to see you, sir."

Harlan turned around, with his *take-no-nonsense, I'm-a-policeman-and-you're-not* expression back in place. He took Leo's hand with an obvious death grip in a show of machismo, and I sighed from the depths of my toes to the top of my head. How was this possible? How was this happening? I hadn't gotten any action in nearly six years, and the night I'm finally going to get laid, my dad shows up? *Screw you, universe.*

"Aren't you the bartender?" my father asked with the same tone someone might use when asking, *are you the asshole who just rear-ended my car?*

Leo nodded. "Yes, sir. Leo Walker."

Another pump of the handshake. "*Chief* Callaghan," my dad said.

"Oh, for God's sake, Dad. Thanks for stopping by, but as you can see, I'm just fine."

I wasn't, of course. I was horrified on so many levels, but that was for me to sort out after he left.

He dropped Leo's hand. "Yep, I see that. Is this why you left without telling anyone? Your sister was worried."

"She could have texted me. She didn't have to send the cops."

"Um, maybe I should go," Leo said, reaching for his jacket. Harlan looked at him as if to say, *yeah, you should.*

"No, Leo, it's fine. Dad? Was there anything you needed to talk to me about, or were you really just checking in?"

"Just checking in, so . . . I guess I'll be on my way, then."

My father had checked in on me less than a dozen times since I'd moved into my own house. Once when I'd left the light on in my attic by accident. Once when I'd left my bike near Potter's Pointe because I'd gotten a flat tire. Once when I'd accidentally butt dialed him and left no message. But for him to pop in unannounced like this was virtually unheard of. Times when I could have used his help, he was a vapor, but not tonight.

"Good night, Dad. See you later."

Leo looked at me, guilty as a teenager caught stealing beer from his parents' bar, as my father hesitated, then stepped back out onto my front porch. "Don't forget to lock up," he said before closing the door firmly behind him.

"That was . . . unfortunate." Leo held tight to his jacket, and I had a sinking sensation that our night of wild abandon had just been abandoned. I could hardly blame him. My dad was a lust-kill. Fuuuuuuuuck.

"I'm really sorry, Leo. He never checks on me." I started picking up pillows from the floor and tossing them back on the couch.

"It's cute," he said, without much conviction. "At least he didn't arrest me."

We stood there awkwardly for another minute. "Maybe we could pick this up another time," I finally said. I still wanted to hit the sheets with Leo, but quite frankly, I wanted it to be memorable for the right reasons, not because my dad had burst in unannounced.

Leo chuckled. "I think that's probably a good idea. My playbook is all screwed up, but I still owe you the nice relaxing dinner. I work for the next couple of nights, but how about Tuesday?"

"That sounds good. Really good. Sorry about tonight."

He stepped closer, running his hands down my arms until he wove his fingers with mine. He kissed me softly, with a nuzzle and a sigh. "I'm sorry that it ended here, but I'm very glad I followed you home. I'll call you tomorrow, okay?"

I walked him to the door and scored another slow, sweet kiss before he finally stepped outside. He looked around, clutching the lapels of his jacket together against the breeze.

"Your dad's not going to be hiding in the bushes to arrest me for jaywalking, is he?"

"Not sure, but if he does, call me. I'll bail you out. And just say no to the strip search."

Chapter 16

My phone rang at eight o'clock Saturday morning, rousing me from a deliciously wicked dream starring Leo and me and, strangely enough, unicorns. I didn't have time to ponder the meaning of that, though, because my sister was calling.

"Hello?" My voice was rough with sleep.

"Hey, what happened to you last night?"

I nearly got laid. "Nothing, why? What did you hear?"

"I didn't hear anything, but all of a sudden you were just gone. Dad went looking for you."

"Oh, he found me."

"Where did you go?"

I could hear all kinds of voices in the background of her call. She must be out and about town.

"I just came home. I was tired, and everybody was dancing, and my shoes were killing me, and my dress was too tight."

"You should have just taken your shoes off. You missed a great reception." She sounded personally wounded by my lack of fun-sense.

"I was there for a lot of it, but like I said, I was exhausted. Besides, I have to start planning your wedding shower." I knew bringing that up would steer the conversation away from me running into Leo. I'm not sure why I didn't want to tell her what had happened. I guess I wanted to keep it my happy little secret for as long as I could. Of course, that was assuming my father wouldn't spill the beans to her or my grand-mother. For once his monosyllabic personality might come in handy.

"Oh, we've got plenty of time to talk about showers and such. Did you know Leo was back?"

I rubbed my eyes. "Um, I did know that. How did you know?"

"I just saw him getting coffee at Joe's Cuppa Joe. He's gone now, but I'm still here. Want to come have a latte with me?"

"I'm still in bed. How about you get me a latte and come here?"

"Done. I'll be there in ten minutes."

She was there in nine, which gave me just enough time to brush my teeth, wash my face, and coax my big, wild hair into a ponytail. I opened the door and she all but scowled at me.

"What the hell are you wearing?" She stepped inside with a whoosh of cold air.

I looked down to see my fuzzy gorilla slippers and my favorite pajamas, which were mint green and covered with dalmatian puppies playing cards and roller-skating. "Pajamas. I told you I was still in bed."

She set the drinks on the table near the front door and shrugged out of her jacket, tossing it to the nearby chair. "You know, whenever I'm at the store and I see those types of pajamas with the goofy stuff all over them, I always wonder who buys them. Now I know."

I picked up a cup with one hand, managing to flip her off at the same time. "I love these pajamas. They're soft, and Gigi gave them to me for Christmas."

"What year?"

"Shut up. Did you just come over here to insult me? Shouldn't you be in a better mood than this? You just got engaged."

A smile split her face and she hugged me, nearly spilling my latte.

"I am engaged. Isn't it wonderful? Can you believe it? See, I told you that things work out sometimes. If you'd told me last summer that Ryan and I would be in this place, I never would have believed it." She grabbed her own coffee and plopped down on my sofa.

I pulled a throw blanket from the back of a striped chair and wrapped it around my shoulders before settling in next to her. "I could see it coming from a mile away. You two are nauseatingly adorable together." In spite of my left-handed compliment, I was feeling happy for them. In the light of day, with the memory of Leo's kisses still on my lips, I was free to fully embrace their joy. "I think he's perfect for you, and I love how much he loves you and Chloe."

She reached over and squeezed my hand with the sparkle of a happy tear in her eye. "I know. I'm so lucky, and Chloe is over the moon. Ryan is going to be such a good dad to her. They get along so well, and God knows her own father was never any good." Chloe's father was Emily's first husband, a guy who should have had *I'm a mistake* tattooed across his forehead.

"Have you set a date?"

"In the spring, probably. And of course, we'll have it on the island. Ryan's family will have to fly in from Sacramento, but they can afford it. It might be kind of awkward, though." Her expression dimmed.

"Awkward? Why?"

She kicked off her shoes and pulled the edge of my blanket over to cover her feet. "I talked to Lilly last night," she said.

Lilly was our twenty-seven-year-old sister, who was currently shacking up with Ryan's father. Handsome and fit, he was a young sixty, but I admit it was a relationship I didn't begin to understand.

"I think she and Tag may be having trouble," Emily added. "I'm not sure, but something about her seemed odd on the phone."

"Maybe she's thinking it's time Tag proposed to her?" That would be weird in so many ways, not to mention making me truly and completely the spinster Callaghan sister.

But Emily shook her head. "No. I asked Ryan about it, but he said that everything was fine, as far as he knew. If they were having trouble, I guess I wouldn't be surprised. I mean, we all kind of figured that relationship had an expiration date on it. I just hope it doesn't make things strange at my wedding."

"I'll give her a call today and see if I can find out anything. I haven't talked to her in a couple of weeks, anyway. She did send me some pictures of her and Tag riding camels in Morocco. They looked pretty happy to me, but I guess it's easy to be happy if you're on vacation all the time. Maybe he's getting tired of traveling."

"Hmm, maybe," Emily mused, then lit up again. "Hey, guess who was at the coffee shop besides Leo."

"Ryan Reynolds? Ryan Gosling? Oprah?"

"Unfortunately, no, no, and no. But that creepy little private investigator was there. You were not wrong about him. He's gross."

"Bill Smith of B.S. Investigations? That guy?"

"How many private investigators do you think we have wandering around here? Of course it was Bill Smith. But the weird thing was that he wasn't asking anyone any questions. He was just sitting there drinking his coffee."

"Really? All by himself?"

"Yeah. I thought at first he might be waiting to meet somebody, but I was there for almost fifteen minutes and he didn't approach anyone. Then I got distracted by seeing Leo. He is maximus hottimus, by the way. You should seriously consider giving that a try."

I tried to hide behind my cup but felt my telltale blush stealing over my cheeks. My sister pounced.

"Wait a second! Do you have something you need to tell me?"

"I would've had a hell of a lot more to tell you if Dad hadn't come busting in here last night." I couldn't stop myself from laughing, even as my skin flushed with embarrassment over the whole debacle.

"Oh no! What happened?"

I filled her in, leaving nothing out, not even the fact that my dress had been halfway to my waist when Harlan arrived. She laughed far more than she should have, but in the end, I joined her. It was funny. Mostly funny.

"So I assume you'll be seeing him again?"

"He's taking me out to dinner in a couple of days," I said, feeling a sudden wave of shyness overtake me. "But honestly, Emily, I'm just not sure how far to take this. He just had a job interview in Washington, DC, which means he might only be here another couple of weeks. If that job falls through, there will be another. He could end up on the other side of the country. I know I need to be less guarded, and learn to trust guys who've earned it, but if I'm going to take that risk, if I'm going to invest my time and emotions into someone, shouldn't it be with somebody who at least has the *potential* to be permanent?"

"I suppose, but you like him, right?"

"Of course I like him. I wouldn't bother thinking about this if I didn't like him. That's half the problem. I like him too much. If I just wanted a fling, fine. I'd have a fling. But the more time I spend with him, the harder it will be when he leaves."

My sister gazed over at me, her expression gentle. "Brooke, you and I are not exactly wired the same way, and I can't say that jumping into bed with Chloe's dad before we got married was a great idea. But jumping into bed with Ryan was a huge risk, too, and now look at us. Engaged!"

Her grin returned and she flashed her ring at me, making us both laugh.

"That rock is gloriously ostentatious. You could direct freighters through the fog with that thing. How many carats is it, anyway?"

She held her hand out and gazed at the ring, rotating her wrist to make the stone catch the sunlight. "I don't know. Seems like it might sound a little mercenary to ask Ryan how much he shelled out for this bauble."

"Aren't you curious?" I was certainly curious.

"Oh hell yes, but once we're married I'm sure I can find the receipt!" We laughed again.

"What if you find out it's a cubic zirconia?" I teased.

"I'm pretty sure it's not. Ryan told me it was designed by the guy his mother got all her jewelry from, and my impression is that she had pretty expensive taste."

"So, no off-the-rack ring for you, huh? You'd better not lose it. Or let the jewel thief swipe it."

"No kidding, and speaking of off the rack, we need to get Lilly back here so we can all go wedding-dress shopping. Oh, and since we're talking weddings, I should make this official. Will you be my maid of honor?"

"Me?" I felt a swell of tenderness and sisterly affection. I thought for sure she'd ask Lilly, or one of her friends from the island. But I was the chosen one. It felt overwhelmingly good. It made up for the fact that my dad, and Chloe, and Tag, and Lilly had all known about the engagement before me. "Of course I will. I'd be thrilled." I leaned over for a clumsy hug, but the blanket and the lattes in our hands did not cooperate.

"Hug me later," she said, pushing me away as I nearly dumped my latte in her lap. "But tell me now, what are you going to do about Leo?"

I leaned back against the cushion, tucking the blanket back in around my very stylish pajamas. "I have no idea."

"Well, I say go for it. What have you got to lose?"

"Um . . . my heart. Like I said, what if I start to really care about him and then he leaves?"

"Is that worse than ending it now and never knowing what might have been? I know you, Brooke. You're going to overthink this. Don't think about it. Just *feel* it. Trust your gut. If you want to roll around with Leo, then roll around with Leo. For God's sake, if Gigi can take a lover, you should, too."

I smiled. "Leo says sometimes you have to just jump without knowing where you'll land."

Emily smiled. "Exactly, but I bet if you jump right now, you'll land on him. How bad could that be? Now get dressed, because you and I are heading over to Manitou for mani-pedis and maybe a little shopping. I want to buy some bridal magazines, and you need a nice outfit for your next date. And for gosh sakes, let's find a Victoria's Secret over there so we can get you some pretty underwear and some new pajamas!"

"Why are you so certain I don't already have pretty underwear and sexy pajamas?"

Her expression said it all.

"Okay." I nodded. "You're right. We'd better go shopping."

⁓

"I've never actually been to Victoria's Secret before," I admitted to Emily as we walked into the store full of pink walls and glimmering chandeliers. She stopped in her tracks and looked at me like I'd just admitted to an alien abduction.

"Never? Where do you get your lingerie? Oh, wait. I've seen your pajamas. You get your sleepwear at the Disney Store. But what about your bras and underwear?"

"Target."

I could almost feel the effort it took for her to resist a snarky remark. She patted my shoulder instead.

"Well, that's very practical of you . . . however, some events call for a little something special."

"Can I get a package of ten panties for ten dollars here? Because I can at Target." Now I was just messing with her. My underwear wasn't *that* bad, but I did enjoy watching her lips press into a straight line.

"Probably not, but you're just going to have to trust me on this, okay? Time to splurge a little."

A perky brunette salesgirl with even perkier breasts popped up beside me, waving a bottle of perfume at my face.

"Spritz?" she asked, and then spritzed before I had a chance to answer. I coughed my way through the cloud, waving my hand.

Another salesgirl popped up beside Emily. Actually, she didn't pop so much as she materialized. Her skin was dark, her hair was natural, and she wore sparkly gold eyeliner that made her look like a princess. Her breasts were perky, too. I suspect that is a job requirement, but really, hers were remarkable. If she could sell me a bra that did that to my girls, count me in.

"Are you shopping for anything in particular, ladies?" Her voice had a husky quality and she exuded sex appeal, even though her outfit of jeans and a formfitting pink T-shirt was very modest. How did women do that? Send out that *I'm powerful yet utterly feminine* vibe? The only thing I'd ever exuded was something that attracted mosquitoes.

"She's going to need to get measured," Emily said, pushing my shoulder. Then her voice lowered as she leaned toward the beautiful salesgirl. "She's been buying her bras at Target."

They exchanged a glance, prompting me to straighten my shoulders and stick out my boobs. My Target bras were fine, but the salesgirl's sympathetic smile was all *oh, honey!* She pulled a tape measure from her pocket and had it wrapped about my torso faster than I could say 34B. I started to perspire. It wasn't at all awkward standing in the middle of the crowded store with my arms up as she adjusted the tape around my breasts. I'd had pelvic exams that were less invasive, but I felt slightly better when she murmured that I was a 34C instead of a B.

She showed us around after that, telling me the difference between lined and unlined (which was pretty obvious) and the difference between push-up and demi and full-coverage. There were wireless, and underwire, and T-shirt bras, and strapless, front-close, and racerback, and something called a bralette. Then she talked about thongs, and briefs, and hipsters, and bikinis, and something called boy-shorts. So many variations. Seriously. I was thirty-six years old and I had no idea. There was a whole underworld of unmentionables that no one had ever mentioned to me.

"How have you never heard of boy-shorts?" Emily asked as we stepped into the dressing room, which very much resembled the lobby of a 1920s brothel. Or so I imagined. I set my purse down on the furry white bench next to the huge gilded mirror and slipped out of my jacket.

"I don't know," I answered. "I guess it's because I learned all about bra shopping from Gigi. After Mom died, if I needed that kind of thing, she took me to Target."

"She took me to Target and Walmart and Kmart, too, but I still figured out to shop for nice underwear at a nice underwear store."

"Well, I don't know what to tell you, Emily. I guess pretty underwear always seemed like an extravagance to me. We didn't have that much money, and I didn't have all sorts of guys trying to get a look at mine like you did."

She set her purse down and frowned. "I'm not sure if that was a compliment or an insult."

"It was a compliment. Guys notice you. They don't notice me. Not usually."

She stared at me for a second. "See, here's the thing, Brooke. They do notice you. You just don't notice them noticing you, and so you assume they're not interested. The good news is, this pretty underwear isn't for them, anyway. It's for you. Even if you're the only one who sees it. You deserve it. Now, let's get you out of that very serviceable Maidenform brassiere and into something a little sexier."

We left the store an hour later, and I had more than doubled my bra collection. I could hardly wait to get home and throw away all my old stuff. The old panties were going, too, because now I had stuff that was lacy, silky, and even beribboned. I'd gotten some practical colors, like white and beige, but Emily had also talked me into stuff that was hot pink, red, black, and patterned with flowers and stripes and polka dots. She'd even managed to talk me into buying a silky little nightie and matching robe that I was pretty sure I'd never wear. The quasi-feminist in me thought push-up bras and lacy underpants perpetuated a sexist agenda. But then I tried them on, and damn if they didn't make me feel pretty. And maybe, just maybe, even a little sexy. It felt wonderful to splurge, to indulge myself this way, because I virtually never did. It wasn't that I was a martyr or something. It just never occurred to me to spend time and money on these kinds of things. I spent my money on school supplies and stuff for my house. Today, all that changed. I was officially now the kind of woman who wore pretty underwear. But I drew the line at the garter belt Emily and the salesgirl had tried to talk me into. Yes, I was feeling about ten times sexier than I'd felt yesterday, but there was simply no way I'd be able to pull that off, metaphorically speaking.

After Victoria's Secret we visited a handful of clothing stores, where my sister continued to pile item after item into my arms.

"Are you working on commission?" I finally asked.

She ignored that. "The stuff you have is fine for teaching, and it's even fine for city council meetings, but you need some stuff that shows off your assets, now that your new bras have moved your assets up where they need to be," Emily said instead, tossing five more shirts into my dressing room at the trendy boutique we'd discovered right behind Stella's Pizzeria.

By the end of the day, I had new jeans, several cute tops, a collection of belts, scarves, and jewelry, and two pairs of new shoes. Shoes that actually fit. My debit card was sizzling, I was exhausted, and I also felt happier than I had in ages. I think I finally understood what people meant by *retail therapy*.

Chapter 17

Church on Sunday was particularly awkward.

As Delores Crenshaw pounded out an uneven version of "How Great Thou Art," April, May, and June Mahoney threw poison eye-darts at my grandmother because Gus had mustered the stones to come sit with us instead of them. And everyone in the congregation noticed, because there was no way not to. The seating chart at Saint Bartholomew's was essentially carved into a stone tablet, so we were in our usual Callaghan spots, fifth row back on the right, but then Gus arrived at our pew, knit cap in hand, and an entire row of people had to shift. We managed, but there was much rustling of coats, then whispers of parishioners, as everyone realized that Gus had left his sisters for Gigi.

Three rows in front of the Mahoney sisters was an open spot where Bridget O'Malley used to sit. Gloria Persimmons-Kloosterman waved at me as she walked down the aisle, Tiny in tow, and blew a little kiss to the empty spot before sitting there. It was only right that she have it, since she'd been the one to bring Mrs. O'Malley to church for the last several years. Emily, Ryan, and Chloe were right in front of us, and I caught my sister moving her left hand ever so slightly so that the sun coming in the window might set her diamond engagement ring to sparkling. She accidentally flashed me in the eye with it, so I flicked her in the back of the head, which made Gigi pinch me.

This all paled in comparison, however, to the awkwardness of having to sit next to my dad after what had happened the other night. I always sat next to my dad, per the stone-tablet seating chart, but today he could hardly make eye contact. I guess something about seeing me on my red sofa, arms and legs twisted around Leo Walker like a tantric pretzel, was a little more than he could handle. Quite frankly, the idea of him seeing us that way was pretty hard for me to take, too. Maybe I was the one avoiding eye contact.

I'd felt pretty good as I got dressed this morning. Under my brand-new sage-green cashmere sweater, I was wearing a new bra and *matching* panties. I'd gone for a pale pink set because it was, after all, Sunday and I was in church, but I still felt . . . sassy? Sexy? Pretty? Sinful? No, I didn't feel sinful. For one thing, I hadn't done anything wrong. I was thirty-six, for goodness' sake, and if I wanted to roll around on my couch with a consenting adult, that was okay. Then my father cleared his throat, and the whole scene played out in my head again, and I wondered if I should talk to him about this or, per family history, just ignore the entire situation.

"How goes it in the world of politics, Brooke?" Judge Murphy asked me after the service as everyone was strolling out. "Think you'll be running for governor one day?"

"Not a chance, Judge," I answered. "But I appreciate you even thinking that was a possibility."

He dashed away the compliment with his follow-up. "Well, anyone can run."

I decided to not take that personally.

"Say," he mentioned a second later, "I had a nice afternoon with that writer friend of yours. Len? Lenny?"

"Leo?"

He snapped his fingers. "That's the one. Nice guy. Interesting background. Told me he was in Iraq, then he did security, now he's a bartender and writing a book? Wow. Kid's got his poker in a lot of fires."

My father cast a droll glance over his shoulder at the judge. "You have no idea, Brian," he muttered.

Awesome.

"Excuse me, Judge. I just remembered I need to have a word with my future brother-in-law." I turned back to find Emily, Ryan, and Chloe stuck by their pew talking to Vera VonMeisterburger. This posed a dilemma. Few people willingly approached the batty librarian, but I did want to avoid my father, and I really did have something I needed to talk to Ryan about. I took a deep breath and shook off my resistance.

"Hey, Aunt Brooke," Chloe said as she dashed toward me for a hug. Her eyes were wide, and as we embraced she whispered in my ear, "Get me away from the batshit crazy bat lady."

I chuckled against my better judgment. "Don't swear in church."

"Sorry, but that's what Ryan always calls her. And she is, you know."

"Yes, I know." We linked arms and walked toward the others. "So, what do you think about this getting-married business?"

"I'm legit excited. I told Ryan I'd only give him my permission to ask my mom if he promised to get me my own horse." She giggled and leaned in against me. "I think he thought I was kidding."

"I'm sure he thought you were kidding, but you could get a job at Colette's Riding Stable in the summer, and then you could ride for free."

"That's not nearly as awesome as having my own horse."

"Maybe not, but it's a hell of a lot cheaper."

"Aunt Brooke!" she gasped with feigned shock. "Don't swear in church."

We stopped a few feet from my sister, Ryan, and Vera. "Make a break for it, kid. I'll cover for you." She scampered away with a grateful wave.

"Hello, Vera," I said. "I hate to interrupt, but I have pressing governmental matters that I need to discuss with my sister and her fiancé."

"What matters?"

"Oh, nothing you need to concern yourself with."

Her eyes narrowed to even slittier slits. "Democracy will crumble without transparency, Brooke. I should think as the mayor you'd realize that."

"I understand your point, Vera. I'll have a report for the council next week. But for now, I need to pull these two away."

I reached forward to pull Ryan and my sister by the coat sleeves down to the other end of the pew, just to make a full break from the cone of Vera's presence.

"'Pressing governmental matters'?" Ryan asked.

"Yeah, not really, but actually, sort of. I was wondering if you'd check out the old community center with me this afternoon. I'm urging the council to approve some renovations, but I want to know what it might cost before I approach them about it. Is that something you think the Taggert companies might be interested in?"

"A bid on a government job? Can I triple all my prices?" He pulled some gloves from the pockets of his wool coat.

"No, but you can give us a ten percent discount if you want. Let's call it the Callaghan family discount. Emily will make it worth your while." I winked at my sister.

"What? What do I have to do with this? I'm not the mayor."

"No, but maybe if you're helpful, then the city will hire you to do the interior design work."

She smiled. "Awesome. Can I triple my prices?"

"No, but Ryan will make it worth your while. See how I did that there?"

"Clever. You're getting good at this politician stuff," Emily said. "Hey, on a completely unrelated topic, did you ever talk to Lilly?"

"Shoot. No, I never called her. I was so tired from having you spend all my money yesterday that I went to bed early last night."

"Alone?"

Her question prompted Ryan to look at her in surprise. Then at me. Then at her. "Is there something going on I haven't heard about?"

I shook my head and tried to flick her again, but she expertly dodged my hand and laughed. "Brooke has a little somethin' somethin' going on with the new bartender at the Palomino."

"Emily!" I scolded. "That's a secret. And anyway, I did go to bed alone last night. Stop spreading gossip." I chuckled and looked around to make sure no one could hear us. I could feel the blush stealing over my cheeks, even though I didn't mind that Ryan knew. It actually felt a little fun to be teased. And to have something so delicious to be teased about.

"I'm not spreading gossip because it's true. And besides, we're in church. You're not supposed to lie in church." She stuck her tongue out at me because we were that mature.

"I think you're not supposed to punch your sister in the face in church, either, but I'm feeling rebellious." I raised my fist, but that only made her laugh again.

"Ladies, ladies, ladies." Ryan took both of us by the shoulder and turned us toward the front door. "Let's head on over to the community center. I think the cold air and the walk will do you both good."

❧

"I'd consider this a midsize overhaul," Ryan said as we stood on the third floor of the community center. "It's very doable. The bones of this place are good, and the electrical isn't in too bad of shape, from what I can tell. I see a lot of potential. What's your timeframe on wanting it completed?"

"As soon as possible and under budget," I answered with a chuckle. "But I guess my question is, if I get the financing approved, how long do you think the project would take? And how much would it cost?"

"I'll need a little time to give you an estimate on cost. I'd have to do more inspections, check the plumbing and a few other things, but assuming there's no huge defect that I just don't see right now, I think we could be in and out in six to eight weeks. Maybe faster if I move some of my crew in here from other projects."

"That's awesome. Do you think if I got the council's approval right away, you could start immediately? Maybe even have the main floor functional by Christmas?"

"Hold your horses, there, Mayor Callaghan," my sister said. "I still need my crew working on the Blueberry Lane Bed-and-Breakfast."

"I know. I was just thinking how fun it would be to have a big holiday party here. They used to do that when we were kids. Do you remember?"

Emily looked around, maybe trying to jog a memory. "Sort of. But Christmas isn't that far off. Thanksgiving is next week."

That caught my attention. "Thanksgiving is next week? Where the hell did November go?" I'd been so busy and distracted by work and Leo and more Leo and more work lately that the time was flying by. I couldn't help but wonder if Leo would still be around at Christmas. Or New Year's Eve. It sure would be nice to have someone to kiss under the mistletoe. And someone to kiss as the clock struck midnight. But just as a lot had happened in the past few weeks, a lot could happen in the upcoming weeks as well.

"Definitely not by Christmas," Ryan answered, bringing me back to the moment. "Sorry, but there's just no way to make that happen. Maybe by Valentine's Day?"

Valentine's Day? My mind wandered again. It sure would be nice to have someone to kiss on Valentine's Day . . .

Chapter 18

I was nervous to the point of hyperventilating as I waited for Leo to come pick me up. I'd offered to just meet him at the Pier Lounge, since we'd agreed to have dinner at the Imperial Hotel, but he insisted on picking me up. And I wasn't entirely sure what he even meant when he'd said "I'll pick you up," because his choices were horse taxi, tandem bike, or perhaps me riding on his back again. None of these options were good, so I was mildly relieved and a little amused when he pulled up in front of my place in a rented carriage—with him holding the reins. The sight of him sitting in the front of the carriage muttering *whoa, whoa, whoa* at Old Barney was definitely laughable. Many of our five hundred horses were moved to warm, cushy stables in Manitou in October and returned to the island in April, but Old Barney stuck around all year. He was known as a reliable, easygoing horse but, like most of the equine population, if you didn't know how to guide him, he'd inevitably take you back to the stable.

"You sure you know how to drive that thing?" I asked from my spot on the front porch.

"I'm a natural. Practically a horse whisperer, but please don't make me climb down and help you with your coat because I'm afraid to let go of the reins."

I chuckled as I stepped back inside, grabbed my coat and purse, and took a moment to check my reflection in the mirror by the door. Thanks to my wallet-busting shopping spree, I was sporting not only cute new jeans but also a pale blue, silky V-neck blouse that did wonders for my cleavage, and a black lacy push-up bra that did even more wonders for my cleavage. Matching black lace panties? Check. New lipstick and mascara, and freshly painted fingers and toes? Check, and check. I'd exfoliated, plucked, and waxed. I was even wearing perfume for the first time since my old bottle of J'adore had run out two years before. This girl was ready for some action. Probably.

Leo reached out a hand to help me as I clambered up into the carriage. Old Barney turned around and looked at me blandly, as if to say, *I see you're all dressed up, but I'm a horse, so I don't care.*

"Mind your own business, Barney," I said without thinking.

"What?"

"Oh, nothing. Just talking to your one-horsepower engine up there. His name is Barney. What on earth possessed you to rent a carriage, anyway?" I couldn't help but laugh again as Leo inexpertly shook the reins and Barney stood stock-still. Other than a tiny flick of his horsey left ear, he could have been a statue.

"I have no idea, but I'm starting to regret it. I'm feeling decidedly Amish, which is not what I was going for at all. And this guy doesn't know how to drive." Leo gestured toward Barney.

I reached over and jostled the reins, giving the horse's rump a little thwack. "Git up, Barney." He nickered softly and started to amble away from my house.

"Impressive, Mayor Callaghan."

"Yeah, I don't mean to be a back-seat driver, but I have had a little practice with this sort of thing."

"I imagine. I would like to point out, however, that I did manage to get this buggy all the way from the stable to your house. Not without some mishaps, I might add, but I did get here. It only took me about four tries to get him to turn onto your street."

It was chilly outside, and my black coat was more stylish than warm, so I pulled the wool blanket from under the seat and spread it over my legs. Leo moved a bit closer, which warmed me up faster than any blanket could. He had his brown leather jacket on with a darker brown sweater underneath, and a tan-and-white-striped collared shirt. His dark hair was a little messy from the wind and he was clean-shaven again. No scruff today, which was good because I'd gotten a little scratched up the last time.

"I've been looking forward to this," he said.

"Me too," I answered, and my shiver had nothing to do with the temperature outside.

The ride from Ojibwa Boulevard to the impressive front entrance of the Imperial Hotel took us past the turquoise-painted library, the butterfly garden that was now brown with frost, and the tall white stockade fence surrounding historic Fort Beaumont.

"Have you been to the fort yet?" I asked while trying very hard not to reach over and take the reins.

"I have. I went about a week ago. Pretty interesting stuff."

"Does that mean that your book is still going to be about an old fort? Or did your conversation with Judge Murphy give you ideas for something else?"

Leo smiled. "If the judge had his way, my book would be about a small-town judge who metes out justice along with bits of homespun wisdom. Nice guy, though. I enjoyed talking with him very much."

"So, what is the book about? You're very cagey about it."

He clucked at the horse, which had no impact at all. Barney had only two speeds. Walking and standing. "I'm not trying to be cagey, honestly. It's just that right now, I have about a hundred pages that don't really go together. I can't quite figure out where to start, or what happens in the middle." He chuckled and shook his head. "And I'm not sure how it ends. I'm beginning to suspect that writing a book is a lot harder than it seems."

His leg was pressed against mine, and the jostling of the buggy caused our shoulders to tap. I wove my arm around his and snuggled a little closer. You know, because it was chilly.

"I'm sure you're right about that," I said, resisting the urge to rest my head on his shoulder. "I always thought that writing a book would be pretty hard. Especially fiction."

His face turned toward me. "You don't like fiction?"

"Oh, I love fiction. I'm just not sure I could make stuff up like that. I'm a science teacher, remember? I like facts and figures and stuff that's tangible. I could probably muddle my way through writing a nonfiction paper about something, but my imagination just doesn't work that way."

It's true that I wasn't good at fiction and my imagination was lame, but over the past few weeks, my fantasy life had blossomed. For every time I reminded myself that Leo Walker was *just passing through*, I spent equal time on all the *what-ifs* and picturing long, elaborate montages in my head. What if he stuck around? What if tonight was the start of something really fabulous? What if he fell in love with me?

Oh, but what if I fell in love with him? There was so much uncertainty, and I didn't like uncertainty. I liked predictability. But I also liked Leo. It was time to jump. Leo Walker was an opportunity I didn't want to miss. He might not turn out to be my kind of forever, but he was most certainly my kind of right now.

We arrived at the hotel, and Chester the English doorman took hold of Old Barney's bridle as we climbed down. My feet hit the ground, and I wondered if I should've waited for Leo to come around on my side and help me. Too late now. Missed my chance.

Leo stepped up to the uniformed doorman. "Um, can you do whatever it is you do with horses while we have dinner?" he asked.

Chester was 130 pounds of stiff upper lip and wore white riding pants with a red jacket bedecked with gold fringes. "Very good, sir. If you'd be so good as to have the hostess notify me upon the completion of your meal, I shall have the carriage ready for your return home."

Leo straightened in reaction to the prim and proper Brit. "Jolly good," he said, and his head gave a little shake as if he wasn't at all sure why he'd said that. I laughed and took his hand as we walked up the red-carpeted steps to the front door. The lobby of the Imperial Hotel was huge, full of gilt-framed oil paintings of hounds chasing foxes, boldly floral upholstered furniture, plush, pine-green carpeting, and gleaming chandeliers. There was nothing subtle about any of it. The décor was intended to look, well . . . *imperial.*

The Pier Lounge was a bit more subdued, with a decidedly nautical theme. Pictures of sailboats, lighthouses, anchors, and signal flags adorned robin's-egg-blue walls, and brass fixtures gleamed from doors, windows, and the multiple beer taps at the mahogany bar. Tonight, the place was all but empty, no doubt because it was seven o'clock on a Tuesday evening just a few days before Thanksgiving. Still, the hostess led us to a corner booth with tall backs and navy-blue velvet upholstery. I was glad for the cozy ambiance. A crystal votive candle adorned our table, and the walls surrounding us were nearly all window, giving us a magnificent view over the bay. Darkness was fast approaching, giving everything a soft glow and making the lights of the marina seem particularly festive.

Leo ordered a Red Label scotch on the rocks. I ordered an old-fashioned. Small, but powerful. That's what I needed.

When the drinks arrived, Leo raised his glass to clink against mine. "To?" he asked.

"Um . . ." I didn't know what to toast to. To our first time? To taking a leap of faith? To my new push-up bra and matching panties?

He smiled at my hesitation. "To getting to know you," he said, filling in the blank.

"To getting to know you," I echoed, taking a much bigger swig than I should've. The bourbon burned a path down my throat that made my eyes water. It was only by sheer force of will that I didn't cough.

Nice. Real smooth, Brooke.

His gaze was direct after our toast, and I knew I should say something, anything, but I was suddenly tongue-tied and nervous. Tonight had expectation written all over it, and I didn't know how to proceed. I mean, honestly, how were you supposed to act when you both knew you were going to have sex later? Did you talk about it? Or did you just ignore the elephant? I decided to take said elephant by the horns. Or tusks. Whatever.

"So, what's the plan?" I asked, setting my drink down on a red paper napkin.

"The plan?" He took another sip of his scotch.

I felt my cheeks get warm. Did I have to spell it out?

"Yeah, you know. You. Me. Us. Tonight." Geez, one sip of alcohol and I'd lost the ability to form complete sentences.

Leo chuckled, a soft, sexy laugh that tripled my sense of vulnerability. His smile was sincere instead of seductive, which, ironically, made it twice as seductive.

"What happens is that you stop analyzing things and just enjoy however the evening unfolds."

Okay. "That's not the answer I expected from the guy with the playbook."

He reached across the table and twined his fingers with mine. "Here's a secret, Brooke. There's no playbook. I just said that to make you laugh. And even if I had a playbook, I'd toss it out now because everything with you feels like brand-new territory."

My breath hitched in my chest because *that* was a really sexy thing to say.

"New territory?"

"Uh-huh. While I can't deny I'd like to end up back at your place," he added with a chuckle, "I want you to know that I'd never assume that's a given. So let's just relax and have a nice meal and a drink or two and just . . . follow our feelings."

Wow. He was good. And we hadn't even gotten to the good stuff yet. If I followed my feelings right now, I'd scramble over the top of this table and start pulling his clothes off in the corner of the Pier Lounge. Probably shouldn't do that.

"Okay," I said breathlessly. "That sounds good."

"Good," he said, and picked up his menu.

We lingered over a delicious dinner of filet mignon and whitefish, shared a decadent chocolate mousse for dessert, and had a few more cocktails. We talked about everything from what I hoped to accomplish as mayor to what board games we played as kids. We laughed while comparing which movies we loved and hated and talked in depth about our favorite authors. And while, as the evening progressed, I didn't feel the pressure of expectation, I did feel a building sense of anticipation. Because I'd already made up my mind. Brooke Therese Callaghan was about to take a lover.

~∾~

"Did you know that the Imperial Hotel has the widest front porch of any hotel in the world?" I asked as we exited the lobby to walk outside. Now that dinner was over and we were headed back to my place, my nerves were kicking in again, and I'd been spouting off random hotel facts.

"I did know that," he answered. "I read the back of the menu while you were in the ladies' room. And now, as we're standing here, I just realized a slight flaw in my plans."

"What's that?" I buttoned my coat against the wind. Winter was definitely on its way. The temperature had dropped about twenty degrees while we were at dinner, and the wind had picked up considerably.

"Well, I have to get the carriage back to the barn. So I guess I'll drop you off at your place and then go return it, but . . . um . . . I guess my question to you is, will that be the end of our evening?" He looked so worried that I might say it was, I couldn't help myself from laughing.

"I hope not. It's only nine thirty." I grabbed ahold of his jacket and lowered my voice. "How about you drop me off, return the buggy, then run like the wind over to my place?"

"Done," he said, kissing me hard and fast.

English Chester cleared his throat.

The ride back to my house was quiet, not because we'd run out of things to say, but rather because conversation didn't feel necessary. I'd wrapped the blanket over both of our laps and took the opportunity to rest my hand on Leo's warm thigh. Old Barney was in a much bigger hurry to get to the barn where his oats were waiting than he'd been to get to the hotel, so he kept up a steady clip.

"I'll see you in fifteen minutes," Leo promised as I hopped out at my place.

I knew it would take him a bit longer, and that was just fine because I had some primping to do. I raced to my bedroom and lit a few candles. Then blew them out because candles seemed kind of cheesy, but then I lit them again because now my room smelled like recently extinguished candles. The flames did lend a nice glow to the room, and heaven knew I could benefit from dim lighting.

I took all the decorative pillows from the bed and stacked them neatly near the wall, then pondered whether or not to turn down the bed linens. I went with yes, mostly so he wouldn't see that my comforter had a big stain on one side from when I'd spilled coffee all over it. That's what all those damn decorative pillows were for. To cover up the stain.

I brushed my teeth and spritzed another round of perfume on myself. I took off my shoes and tossed them in the closet and caught a glimpse of my new nightgown folded on a shelf. I halted and stared.

Oh, should I?

I could put on that new nightie. What would Leo think if he showed up and I was wearing that little number? I giggled and tapped my fingers against my lips. He'd probably like it. No, not probably. He'd definitely like it. But it seemed awfully forward . . . Then again, I'd rarely heard of a circumstance where a man complained about a woman being too eager for sex. But . . . I wasn't really the kind of woman who opened the door of her house in nothing but a bit of lingerie . . .

Oh, there was a matching robe. Problem solved.

I stripped down and put on the slinky ensemble. Then I quickly took it off and pulled my jeans back on. Then I stared at the nightie on the floor. Debating.

"Oh, what the hell," I finally said to myself, and pulled off the jeans once more.

Leo tapped on my front door not long after. I was barefoot, wearing the robe and nightie and had changed twice more before he arrived. But now it was go time. I opened the door, and his expression as he took in my apparel made me certain I'd made the right call.

"Well, all right then," he said, stepping inside and pulling me into his arms. He kissed away all my doubts before he'd even taken off his coat.

"How about some wine?" I asked when he finally stepped away to remove a few layers of his own. He dropped his coat in the chair and kicked off his shoes while pulling his sweater off over his head. Now he had the striped shirt and his jeans still to go.

"Wine sounds great," he said, but then grabbed me and kissed me some more, and in the back of my mind I commended my nightgown decision.

"Sorry," he breathed against my lips. "I just needed to kiss you again."

"I'm not complaining."

My fingers were in his hair, pulling him closer. His hands moved to my backside, lifting and pressing me against him until I was dizzy with longing. No regrets. I wanted Leo as much as he wanted me. And that was a lot. He walked me backward until I bumped up against the door, and he reached down and turned the dead bolt.

"I'm not letting your dad in here tonight," he said, his voice low and husky.

I might have laughed except I didn't think he was joking. This Leo was all business. I could feel the length of him pressed against me and I lost awareness of anything but him. Wine was forgotten as I pulled him up the stairs and into my room. He took a moment to notice the candles and the turned-down sheet, and the sexiest of his smiles made my legs turn to noodles.

"Too presumptuous?" I asked, already knowing the answer.

"Very, very presumptuous," he said, slowly pulling me back into his embrace, "and very, very appreciated." He kissed my cheek, nuzzling along the line of my jaw until his lips were pressed against the curve of my neck and his hands were splayed across my back, slipping over the silky material.

I leaned back and started working on the buttons of his shirt. I grew impatient after the first three and just started pulling it up and over his head. His arms rose and then dropped along with the fabric, and his chest was bare to me. I put my hands on him, wondering if this was how sculptors felt as they molded a piece of art, for surely that's what Leo was. He was all angles and planes, taut skin over smooth muscles. Just a sprinkling of chest hair above a flat belly.

His breath hitched as my fingers traveled over him and down to the waistband of his jeans.

He lifted his head and gazed down at me.

"Are you sure?" he whispered, and I had to chuckle. The nightie and the candles and the turned-down bed linens hadn't been obvious enough? I smiled up into his ocean-blue eyes.

"Very sure."

His low chuckle was sexy times infinity, and I suddenly found myself wrapped in an embrace so strong it stole my breath away. Or maybe it was his kisses doing that? Or his hands on my body? Did it matter? Whatever it was, I was dizzy and breathless—and liking it. The robe slid from my arms as he kissed my shoulder. I popped the button of his jeans and had the momentary wherewithal to wonder if my new black lace underwear had granted me superpowers of seduction. I'd taken the bra off earlier but still had on the panties. I had thought about taking those off, too, but realized I might be feeling bold, but not *that* bold.

Minutes later, those panties were on the floor anyway, along with the nightie and Leo's jeans and boxers, and we were on the bed. I couldn't seem to keep my hands in one place. I wanted to explore all of him all at once. His shoulders and back and hips . . . and all the rest of him. Leo's mouth and fingertips seemed to be doing the same over my body, exploring. A heated kiss here, a soft caress there, a squeeze, a nuzzle, a not-so-gentle bite that sent sensations tumbling over themselves as they raced from my core to the tips of my limbs. Our breath mingled as our torsos pressed together.

Leo teased his lips against the corner of my mouth, then lifted his head to gaze down at me. His eyes were dark and intense in the candlelight, his voice husky as he whispered, "I like you, Brooke."

Such a simple declaration, yet it made my heart hammer in my chest, because I understood what he meant. It was easy to *want* someone, easy to be infatuated with a smile, but far more complicated to actually *like* someone. And Leo Walker liked me.

"I like you, too," I said, and then I showed him just how much.

Chapter 19

"Where do you think we're going to find money in the budget to fix up the community center?" Vera VonMeisterburger had her white hair up in a bun today, which accentuated the beaklike quality of her nose, which, in turn, matched remarkably well with the screechy, crowlike quality of her voice. "If we can't afford a simple bat sanctuary, I don't see how we can afford to redesign the community center."

It was Wednesday, and that meant another city council meeting. My reluctant reentry into reality after a glorious night spent rolling in the sheets with Leo had been tough to take, and now I was sitting at the Palomino Pub, torn between arguing my point or just staring over at the bar to watch Leo wash and dry glasses. He was *so* good at it. Washing and drying glasses, I meant. Although he was damn fine at everything he'd done last night, too. I didn't have a long list of partners to compare him to, but just like I don't know how to ballroom dance, I could still recognize a master at work.

He'd stayed until almost two in the morning, and we'd made the most of that time together. We'd even briefly discussed him staying until morning, but the idea of Leo doing the walk of shame and encountering my father on his morning sojourn through town made us think better of it. After Leo had left, I'd pulled the blankets up and pressed my face against the pillow just to capture the last tiny vestiges of his cologne.

"I like the idea of updating the community center," Dmitri said. "I think we should have a section devoted to all the UFO sightings we've had on the island."

It took a second for that to register. I turned to look at Dmitri, as did everyone else, but he was smiling directly at me. "Just kidding," he said with a grin. "Just trying to make sure the mayor here is actually paying attention."

Damn it. He'd caught me staring at Leo. "Of course I'm paying attention," I said, turning my chair a bit to the side so I was facing the rest of the council members. Fortunately, my father had skipped this meeting. I had nothing to be ashamed of, but other than church, I'd been avoiding him. I even skipped Sunday evening dinner at Gigi's house, claiming an upset stomach.

"I think we can all agree that the visitors' center is looking a little dingy these days, too," I added. "And my thought is, if we merged the two together, we could tap into that budget. We could add a little gallery to display some of our local artists' work, maybe add a coffee shop. The revenue from that could help offset the costs, and Taggert Property Management has agreed to do the reconstruction at a very reasonable rate."

"Oh, I see how it is," Olivia Bostwick piped up. "You just want to create business for your sister and her fiancé."

"Now it's all making sense!" June Mahoney scoffed.

"That's not true, Olivia. The Taggerts would barely be breaking even on this job, but Ryan has offered his services because he's become a member of the community. We would not get such a great deal from any other contractor, and you've seen the quality of their work from the projects they've already done around here. Of course, we can certainly get some bids from other remodeling companies if the council wants to do that."

"I hope you're not blaming me for the visitors' center looking dingy," Maggie Webster interjected. She'd been the director for several years, and I knew she'd done the best she could with what she'd had to work with. "I pestered Harry Blackwell since the day I started that job for an increase to my budget so I could make some improvements."

I shook my head. "I'm not blaming you in the least, Maggie. You've done a fabulous job, and I know you never had much budget to work with. Now, just imagine how amazing the visitors' center would be if we moved it to the first floor of the community center. It could be twice as large as it is now, and it would be even closer to the boat docks. Everybody wins."

"Especially Taggert Property Management," June muttered.

I ignored her, as I often did, and looked around at everyone else instead. "Think about it, everybody. If we consolidate the community center and the visitors' center, we'd have so many options for other things. We could have reenactors from the fort hang around and tell tourists about the day's activities. Fran Foster could bring in some Petoskey stones and talk about them with the kids. Little kids are fascinated by rocks. And we could simplify a bunch of the stuff that's currently being duplicated by the staff in both places. Anything we can do to streamline things will save us money in the long run."

"I'm with the mayor on this one," Sudsy said. "Sometimes you have to spend money to make money."

I offered him a grateful smile. One down, nine to go. "As I said, I was thinking the main floor could be the visitors' center, the second floor could be classrooms, and the third floor could be office space for the town government." This would be the perfect time to say I'd want to shift our meetings from this beer-soaked bar to a nice, freshly painted conference room, but they were just barely nibbling at the hook. Too much too soon and I'd lose them again. Besides, if we changed locations, I'd have less opportunity to ogle the cute bartender.

"And for the locals," I said with enthusiasm, hoping to reel them in further, "the community center could become a great gathering place again. Dmitri, remember when we used to have dances there in the winter? You love to dance. June, if I recall correctly, you and your sisters used to sing, didn't you? Wouldn't it be fun to host events there again? And I'm thinking free computer classes for anyone who lives here year-round. Ben, you could learn to Skype with your grandkids, and Olivia, you could teach a scrapbooking class."

My attempts to appeal to each of them on a personal level were beyond overt, but they either didn't see it, or they didn't mind. Interest was beginning to tap at their brains. I could see it in their eyes. I was getting to them. At last.

"I could teach a knitting class," Gertie offered. "Or we could invite the Nguyens to teach a class on flower arranging. Maybe we could get a chef from the Imperial Hotel to do a cooking class?"

Gertie and I had discussed the new community center at length, and she was fully on board. She'd become a true ally over the past few weeks as we bonded over paper shredding. She'd told me story after story of how frustrating it had been to work with Harry, and how appreciative she was of me for giving her a chance. Each time I'd reminded her that she was doing *me* a favor. If she'd ever thought to run against Harry on her own, she probably would've won, and she would've done a great job.

"What about a class on origami?" asked Monty Price, the town lawyer. "I've always wanted to learn origami. And I could teach a class about setting up a will. No one ever wants to talk about their wills, but eventually everybody dies."

"Thankfully," added Ben Hawthorne—the director of the cemetery board.

The ideas started rolling in, and at last we had a real conversation going. If I could get them emotionally invested in this project, then we'd find the money somehow.

"Don't forget, we still need money to build my bat sanctuary." Vera pulled a tissue from the sleeve of her purple cardigan and dabbed at her perpetually runny nose.

"We could have a bat display," I said, thinking fast on my feet. "You could help design it, Vera, and we could include all the information about white-nose syndrome and your efforts to combat it."

She stopped dabbing to stare at me. "I could have a display?"

I'm sure she was thinking something huge and interactive with big, attention-grabbing lights and audio. I was thinking more along the lines of a cardboard poster or two and maybe a few pictures, but those were details we could work out after I had her on my side. I was starting to catch on to how this whole politician thing worked.

"There could absolutely be some kind of display," I said.

"We need a new gate at the South Shore Cemetery. If there's money for the community center, there should be money for that, too," Ben added.

"We can absolutely look into that, Ben, but we'll have to prioritize things. How about if you get some bids on repair costs, and we'll take it from there? And Vera, you give some thought to that display."

I turned toward Sudsy as the rest of the group continued talking about all the things they wanted this potential community center to include. I guess they were all on board now. At least until we figured out how much it was really going to cost.

"You're the council treasurer, Sudsy," I said quietly. "How much shuffling around of stuff do we need to do in order to have money for a remodel?"

"I guess it depends on what the total cost is going to be, but I'm pretty good at finding money." He took a sip of his drink. "And hey, if I can't find it, I can always steal it."

I reached over and patted his hand. "Let's not resort to that just yet, but could you and I meet next week and crunch some numbers? Ryan will have some estimates by then, and we can decide if this is at all feasible."

Sudsy nodded, but his gaze shifted from me to some movement out in the bar. I looked out, too, and saw a tall, slender woman with jet-black hair who'd obviously just entered. She was striking and hard to miss with her sleek pixie-cut hair and dramatic eyeshadow. She slid onto a barstool at the far end and shrugged out of a black leather jacket. Leo turned, and my gut did a half flip with a kick and jab at his expression. It came and went so fast, I might have missed it, but I didn't. The woman had his full attention for a split second, then he turned away from her, busying himself with some bottles on a shelf. Another blink or two, and then he turned back. This time he was the same old Leo. Smiling, charming Leo.

My Leo.

Or was he?

Oh, get a grip, Brooke.

I mentally slapped myself. She really was attractive, and any guy would notice her. She had the angelic profile of a cameo, but her clingy black T-shirt scooped low in the front, and I could barely make out the hint of a tattoo on her collarbone, so although her features said angel, everything else about her said sexy badass. I glanced at Sudsy to find his skinny green cocktail straw dangling from his open mouth, even though his drink was nowhere near it.

See? Standard dude reaction. No matter how evolved we become as a species, a residual reptilian portion of a man's brain could easily be triggered by an attractive female.

The truth is I asked you out to dinner that first time simply because you were beautiful, Leo had said to me. At the time, I'd found it flattering. Endearing, even. What if he thought the same of her?

Oh my God, Brooke! Seriously. Get a grip.

I observed surreptitiously as Leo got her a shot of Patrón. Naturally. She couldn't order a dorky piña colada or some kind of froufrou drink, and I was tempted to go introduce myself. Not because I wanted to remind Leo that he'd just had sex with me not twelve hours ago, but because she was not our typical tourist. I was the mayor, after all. It was my job to make new visitors feel welcome.

We finished up our meeting, and the woman was still sitting at the bar. She and Leo seemed to be chatting, he'd gotten her a beer, and every now and again, he'd glance my way and give me a subtle smile. I smiled back, hoping my overreactive jealousy wasn't like a neon sign over my head. She caught my eye once, too, so I smiled at her. She didn't smile back.

Dmitri helped me gather up all the agendas that everyone had left on the table because no one read them anyway. It really was a waste of paper. He stacked them up and handed them to me as everybody shuffled out.

"What's going on with you and the kid?" he whispered.

"What? Nothing." I looked around, guilty as a teenager trying to sneak in after curfew.

"Liar. You've got a hickey on your neck."

My hand flew to my throat. "Seriously?"

His laughter was a slow rumble under his breath. "No, not really, but if nothing is going on with you and the kid, then you would have known I was kidding." Dmitri glanced over at Leo and then back at me. "We went fishing. Seems like a nice enough guy. Is he married?"

I restacked the papers in my hands. "Of course not. I mean, I didn't ask specifically, but I'm sure he's single. I've heard his whole life story, and there was no mention of a wife."

"There never is."

I looked up at Dmitri. His face was shadowed by his beekeeping hat. "You don't think he's married, do you? I couldn't possibly make that same mistake twice."

He patted me on the shoulder. "I don't think he's married. Just be careful. You bringing him to Thanksgiving dinner tomorrow?"

My mind had been on the spin cycle lately and could not seem to grasp the reality that tomorrow was Thanksgiving. I hadn't invited Leo to Gigi's house for dinner, of course. It was way too early in our relationship, or whatever it was that we had. I couldn't have him passing the mashed potatoes between my father and Gus, my grandmother's lover. I couldn't have him sitting there while we talked endlessly about wedding details with Emily and Ryan. And I couldn't have him interrogated by Dmitri about his past indiscretions or his future intentions. "No, I didn't invite him."

"Maybe you should. What's he going to do otherwise? Clancy's is closed."

"I don't know. Maybe he'll work on his book?"

Dmitri shrugged and adjusted his hat. "Up to you, I guess. Just seems like it might be nice for the kid to have someplace to go."

I stuffed the papers into my bag. "Why do you care if he has someplace to go?"

"I don't, I guess . . . I just, you know. Wish you'd find a nice young man."

His eyes were soft as he spoke, and I remembered why I cared for Dmitri so much. He was one of the few, maybe the only one, who made a point of wondering how I was doing. I knew my dad cared, and my family and friends cared. It's just that Dmitri actually took the time to ask. And although he usually couldn't keep a secret if his life depended on it, he'd kept mine. He knew all about Jason and had never told a soul.

I gave his arm a quick squeeze. "I wish I'd find one, too. Currently Leo is on the 'catch and release' plan, so we'll see how that goes. I'll see you tomorrow."

I walked from the meeting room and over to the bar. Leo was leaning on his elbows on the surface and reading the latest book by Lee Child. Badass Tequila Girl was gone.

"Where's your friend?" I asked, hoping I sounded like I was teasing.

"My friend?"

"Yeah, Biker-Chick Barbie. Where'd she go?"

He chuckled and folded the corner of his page before closing the book. "I have no idea. She wasn't very chatty."

"She's not our typical tourist."

He nodded. "Yes, I picked up on that. She said she was headed to the Upper Peninsula."

"She realizes this is an island and not connected to the UP, right?"

He stared down at me for a moment, and I realized I sounded kind of bitchy, but he smiled and leaned over toward me again.

"We didn't really get into it," he said. "I was too busy watching you run the city council like a boss. Sounds like they were excited about the community center."

My tension eased. "I think so. Now we just have to find the money." I stared at him a moment longer, unable to tear my eyes away. A moment of sentimentality overtook me. Because the holidays are apt to do that to a woman. Especially a woman who'd just had some delicious naked-wrangling with a new fella. "Hey, by any chance are you busy tomorrow? And before you answer, let me tell you why I'm asking. We do a big Thanksgiving shindig at Gigi's every year. It's not just family. Dmitri comes, and Brenden and Xavier come. They're the two guys I told you about who own the bed-and-breakfast. Gus Mahoney will be there, and my sister and Ryan. My dad. Not sure who else. Anyway, it's a big crowd, and there's tons of food, and it's, you know, Thanksgiving, but I totally understand if you don't want to come."

He didn't hesitate at all. "Why would I not want to come?"

"Because it's my *family*. I don't . . . I don't want you to think I'm making assumptions about stuff just because of . . . because of . . . you know."

"Do you think your dad still wants to arrest me?"

"Arrest you? No. Toss you off the Petoskey Bridge? Maybe. The jury is still out on that. But if you come for dinner, maybe you can use your nice table manners and show him what a stand-up guy you are. Unless the idea of spending the day with my family weirds you out. I'd totally understand. And I'm sure you could go to Vera's for dinner."

He chuckled and ran a hand through his hair. Hair that I now knew was incredibly soft. "That's a hard no on spending the day with Vera, but I think it would be nice to come to your grandmother's house."

"Really?" My heart did a flippity-flop.

"Sure. What time should I be there?"

"We eat the meal around five, but everybody shows up around three. I'll let you decide how much Trillium Bay ambiance you're prepared to handle."

He gazed up at the ceiling as if to ponder. "I can handle quite a bit. Speaking of handling things," he said, holding up his hands and wiggling his fingers, "I wish I was handling something in particular right now."

I flushed at the memory of his expert handling. "Me too. Do you work tonight?"

"Yeah, until midnight. What would happen if I stood in your yard at midnight-o-five and threw pebbles at your window?"

"I'd probably invite you in, even though in the playbook, that is totally a booty call."

"I told you, there's no playbook. There is only new territory to be explored."

I wanted to say yes because, well, because I wanted to! Leo and I might not have much time together. He could get a job offer any second, so I really needed to make the most of this.

"Text me when your shift ends. I'll leave the front door unlocked."

Chapter 20

It was Thanksgiving Day but felt more like Christmas morning simply because I'd woken up with Leo in my bed. How was he able to make me so giddy? Had I just missed sex that much without realizing it, or was it something more? My heart squeezed in my chest as I felt him moving beside me. It was still dark out, and chilly in my room, but so warm under the covers with his arm draped over my hip. Tears threatened my eyes. I wasn't sure if they were caused by worry over what might come next, of what I might lose, or my gratitude that we'd had these hours together.

I snuggled back against his chest, and he mumbled something in his sleep before tightening his arm around me. I could get used to this. I wanted to get used to this. I let my mind wander in that half haze between sleep and wakefulness where I couldn't tell which visions were dreams and which were my sleepy mind formulating wishes for a future. There was Leo, smiling at me from the kitchen, offering me a cup of coffee. Leo on bended knee holding out a tiny black box with a diamond ring inside. A vision, more potent than the others, of the two of us on a plaid blanket in the backyard with a curly-headed toddler sitting on my lap. I sighed, and tears welled up again. I wasn't going to be all doomsday-negative and say that it would never happen. Leo cared for me. I knew he did, and maybe that would be enough to convince him to move here and keep writing. But wanting that, and getting that, were worlds apart.

I kissed him goodbye a few hours later as he stood at my front door, looking sleepy but satisfied. Still dark, and now raining. I wanted him to stay but needed him away from my house before the sun rose. It's not as if we were a big secret, but discretion was still in order. If anyone saw him coming out of my house at that time of day, there'd be no question that a full-blown scandal was going on.

"Make sure you take Woodland Avenue instead of Main," I told him. "Nobody will be around there this morning."

"I don't know where Woodland Avenue is," he said with a yawn. "But whatever way I take to get from here to my place is along the backside of town. Not Main Street."

"It just occurred to me that I still don't know where you're staying. What's the address?"

"It's a rental house on Cahill Road. The yellow one with blue shutters."

"Oh, I know that place. It's one of Sudsy Robertson's rentals. If you go straight from here to there, you should be okay. Still up for Thanksgiving with my family?"

He leaned over and gave me a kiss on the cheek. "Wouldn't miss it. See you in a couple of hours."

I shut the door and watched him walk away through the glass panel, feeling bad that he had to trudge through the nasty weather, and also feeling happy but wistful, tired yet energized. It's like my mind and body couldn't decide or agree on which emotion to land on. After a minute, fatigue overruled the rest and I climbed back into bed, turning a pillow lengthwise down the middle so I could press against it and pretend it was him.

I got up a bit later and texted my dad. I didn't want to face the whole day wondering how he felt about the other night. Especially since

Leo was coming to Gigi's. My dad wouldn't volunteer that information, so I was going to have to ask. I pulled my phone from my purse.

HAPPY THANKSGIVING. WHAT TIME R U GOING TO GIGI'S HOUSE TODAY?

His response was almost instantaneous.

HALF AN HOUR

COULD YOU SWING BY MY PLACE ON YOUR WAY?

YEP

Texting with my father was not unlike trying to have a conversation with him, but when he got to my place exactly thirty minutes later, I was ready.

"Hi, Dad. Thanks for stopping by. Want a cup of coffee?" It was still drizzling out, and he shook out the water from his coat on the front porch before stepping inside.

"Sure, I guess."

I poured one for each of us, and we sat down at my kitchen table.

"So . . . I guess I wondered if we needed to talk about the other night."

"Do you need to talk about the other night?" He sounded more bemused than angry. Not that he had a right to be angry. He was the one who'd burst in through my front door unannounced, but he was still my father; no matter your age, getting caught by a parent while in a semi-reclined, semi-undressed, semi-aroused state probably required some kind of acknowledgment. And maybe some kind of apology from either side.

"I just don't want things to be awkward today," I said. "Leo and I have been, um . . . getting acquainted, and we've gone out a few times.

I guess I just don't want you thinking I bring random bartenders home with me all the time."

The chief actually chuckled, which was not the reaction I was expecting. "I never thought for a second that you were doing that all the time. I just didn't expect you to be doing it that night."

"Well, it was a bit of a surprise to me, too. I left the reception and ran into Leo and, like I said, we've kind of, sort of been seeing each other, so . . ."

"Okay."

"That's it? Just okay?" I thought there might be some lecture or something, but my dad just took a sip of coffee, casual as on any given morning.

"What do you want me to say, Brooke? You have a right to a private life. I mean, if you want to know if I think that he's good enough for you, then I'd say no. He's not. But I'm not sure I'm very objective about these types of things."

Huh. That nearly sounded paternal. And sweet. He looked uncomfortable for a moment, but then he looked over at me, and I could see some undisguised sentimentality in his eyes, followed by a hesitant smile.

I offered back a smile of my own and couldn't help but chuckle. "What possessed you to come over to my place anyway, Dad? You never check up on me."

He took a swallow of coffee before answering. "Look," he said with a sigh. "No one ever accuses me of being an insightful parent, but I couldn't help but notice the other night that when your sister got engaged, you seemed a little . . . knocked off-kilter by it."

I thought I'd been far more discreet. Had everyone noticed? "I was just really tired."

"You didn't seem tired when I saw you on the couch." Oh boy. Something told me I was never going to hear the end of this. Maybe I should have left us both operating under the invisibility cloak of denial.

"Okay, in that case, let's just say I was . . . bored."

"If you say so, then fine. I'll believe you. I just thought that maybe your sister getting married, again, and Lilly off traveling the continents with old what's-his-name, I thought maybe you might be feeling a little bit left out. I know better than anyone it's not always easy being the one who's alone."

Alone. I tried not to focus on the fact that I was *alone*. I tried to focus on all the good stuff I had going in my life, but there was no denying my father's words. Or word. Alone.

"I'm really happy for Emily and Ryan." The pause was unavoidable. "But you're not wrong. I want what they have."

"Is that why you brought the bartender home? You think he's the answer?"

"No, of course not. I mean, sort of. Maybe? I was feeling kind of blue after I left the reception, and he did show up at a very opportune moment, but I want you to know, Dad, Leo is a gentleman. It's not like he took advantage of me."

My father started looking uncomfortable again. People's sex lives were not something he was interested in discussing, but he was the one who was pressing the issue.

"Clancy told me he's only around for a few months. He's writing a book or something?"

I nodded. "That's the plan, to stay for a few months, but, you know . . . plans change."

"Not everyone is cut out for living on Wenniway, you know."

"I know. I'm not thinking very far out into the future right now, Dad. But I haven't dated anyone in a while, and Emily pointed out that maybe I was shutting myself off too much. She said I take care of other people so I don't have to think about what my own life is missing."

"Ouch."

"I know, right? But I can see what she means. Maybe I do that."

My phone pinged, and I picked it up off the table. "It's a text from Chloe. It says 'WHERE THE HELL ARE YOU? POTATOES DON'T PEEL THEMSELVES.' SIGNED GIGI WHO IS LEARNING TO SEND NOTES WITH CHLOE'S PHONE."

I looked over at my father. "Well, I guess we'll have to pick up this conversation another time. Gigi wants me to peel potatoes. But before you leave, there's something you should know."

He kind of blanched, clearly thinking I was going to say something far more incendiary than what I had to say. "Leo is coming for Thanksgiving. Can you handle it?"

He downed the last of his coffee and thumped the cup on the table. "I can handle it."

"Will you be nice to him?"

"I'll be as nice to him as I am to anyone else." Then he smiled.

Chapter 21

Chloe and I stood at the sink in Gigi's kitchen, peeling about three hundred pounds of spuds.

"Are you sure this is enough?" Chloe said with a giggle. "I've never seen so many potatoes."

"You can never have too many mashed potatoes," I answered. "Although it does seem like we've been peeling for an hour."

"You have been peeling for an hour. What's taking you so darn long?" Gigi demanded from the table, where she was chopping celery.

"If you don't like the way we're doing it, maybe next year you could assign someone else?"

"This seems like a good job for Ryan and my mom," Chloe said, winking at me. I love my niece. She's sassy without being a smart aleck, and I'd spent enough time with teenagers to know that was a very fine line.

"So, Gigi," I said, changing the subject, "I hope you don't mind that I invited a friend to join us. He's a man, but don't start getting all Gigi on him and asking him all sorts of questions, okay?"

"Well," she huffed, "I'm not sure what you mean by that, but it doesn't sound like a compliment." She was wearing a sweatshirt with a big turkey on it. The turkey was drinking a martini. No wonder she liked that shirt.

"It's not meant to be an insult, but, you know, he's new to the island, and sometimes you can come on a little strong. I'd rather we didn't discuss your sex life with Gus or your dead husbands being sent into space."

"They're not being sent into space. Why does everyone keep saying that? They're just taking a little ride and then drifting back to earth. And anyway, their souls are already up there."

The door to the kitchen opened, letting in a gust of cold air, and Chloe let out a squeal of glee that had nothing to do with the wind. "Aunt Lilly!" She dropped the potato and the peeler into the sink, just as I turned to see my sister coming through the door.

"Lilly?" I said, instant joy coursing through me. I dropped my own potato and peeler and joined in on the sudden group hug between Lilly, Chloe, Gigi, and myself. "I had no idea you were coming," I said a minute later as we all untangled. My sister was as beautiful as ever, with her dark hair twisted into a messy bun and the hint of a suntan on her face. She took off her brown parka and hung it on the hooks near Gigi's front door.

"I know. I wanted it to be a surprise. That's why I didn't return your call last week. Sorry about that. Where's Emily?"

Our other sister came bounding down the stairs and let out a squeal before flinging her arms around Lilly. "Oh my gosh! I'm so glad you're here!"

"Of course I'm here. As soon as Ryan told Tag he was going to propose, I booked myself a plane ticket. Let's see the rock."

Emily held out her hand so that Lilly could demonstrate proper reverence for its luster and size. "Very impressive. Now tell me every detail. How did he ask you?"

I watched as Lilly pulled Emily to the sofa and they settled down on it, giggling like sorority sisters. I felt a pang of something I didn't want to name. Because if I had to name it, I might have to acknowledge some resentment that I didn't want to acknowledge. Sure, I'd been the one to virtually raise Lilly. She'd only been five years old when our mother died, and I'd been the one to help her learn how to read, and how to make her bed, and how to tie her shoes. I'd been the one to make sure she had breakfast every morning, and got her homework done in the evenings. And I'd been the one she'd cried to when she'd fallen from a tree and broken her arm. I was the one who stayed after Emily ran away.

But Emily was her hero. Emily was the exotic, worldly sister who'd run off at nineteen to get married and blown back into our lives last summer. It was wrong of me to be jealous of them. So wrong. But the two of them were more alike. I was the other. The bossy, rule-setting sister. I'd never had any adventures of my own to compare to theirs. I was the one who'd come back to the island right after college, and now Lilly was a world-traveling jet-setter in her own right, which widened the gap between us, both physically and emotionally. It wasn't really fair or productive for me to feel this way, but that didn't make it untrue.

But then Lilly turned to me and held out her hand. "Come sit with us, Brooke. I've missed you so much," and the world started to right itself again.

The potatoes were finished, although I'm not sure who did them. We all pitched in to make stuffing and green-bean casserole. The house warmed up and the noise increased exponentially as people arrived. Dmitri, wearing a knit beanie today instead of his beekeeping hat. Lovebirds Xavier and Brenden bearing a platter of cheese and olives and crackers and dips.

"That's a tapenade," Xavier said, pointing to one of the spreads. "I hate olives, but I love saying the word *tapenade*."

Ryan arrived with six bottles of wine, two of which he offered to share, and finally, Leo.

"Should I have brought something?" he whispered to me as I took his coat.

"We'll have enough food and drinks for about seventy people, so no. You're good."

Most everyone had already met him, so introductions were more of a *hey, everybody knows Leo, right?* And I breathed a sigh of relief as the chief shook his hand.

"Don't let Gigi talk you into making her a martini," I told Leo a moment later. "She knows you're a bartender so she's sure to ask, but Chloe is martini monitor today."

"Martini monitor?"

"Yes, we try to keep track of how many she's had because if we leave it up to her, she'll have a dozen, and then the turkey will never get finished and she'll start singing show tunes. That happened one year. She put the turkey in the oven and never turned the oven on. So each year we designate a martini monitor to keep count. Chloe drew the short straw, which is good because she's only thirteen and won't end up drunk herself."

∽

"Come sit on the porch with me. I need some fresh air," Lilly said, tugging on my sleeve.

Dinner was in the oven, and the only thing left to do was set the table, which Chloe and Brenden were doing right now. I glanced over at Leo, who seemed to be deep in conversation with Dmitri and Ryan. The chief was watching football, and there'd been no dark looks or snarky comments from him, so it was probably safe to leave them alone for a few minutes. I grabbed a blanket off the back of the couch to wrap around us outside. It was rainy and windy today. Not hospitable, but sitting outside in rough weather was something we'd always loved to do as kids: a habit we'd learned from our mother. She'd take us outside for rain and thunderstorms and blizzards. We'd have blankets and hot chocolate, and all snuggle together on a long outdoor sofa. I couldn't ever hear thunder without thinking of my mom.

"Leo seems nice," Lilly said as we sat down on the wicker sofa, which resembled the one from our childhood. She scooched closer and tucked the blanket edges in around us.

"He is."

She laughed at my brief response. "Sometimes talking to you is just as bad as talking to Dad. How about a few details? Where's he from? Where's he going? What's his story?"

"What are you doing out here?" Emily interrupted, stepping out onto the porch and rubbing her arms for warmth. She had on a pink-and-gray plaid flannel shirt with a pink tank top underneath.

"Just chatting," I said.

"The smell of that turkey was starting to get to me," Lilly answered. "I needed some fresh air."

Emily looked at her quizzically. "The smell of the turkey?"

Lilly nodded. "Yeah, Gigi uses so many spices, it just smells a little strong."

Emily continued staring at Lilly, until Lilly finally said, "What?"

"Lilly, are you pregnant?"

My head swiveled toward her so fast I heard wind whooshing by my ears.

"What? No, of course not."

"Are you sure? Because when I was pregnant with Chloe, the smell of meat cooking was enough to make me hurl."

Lilly shook her head, the messy bun wiggling from side to side. "No. I mean, yes. Yes, I'm sure, and no, I'm not pregnant. I couldn't be." She stopped to look at the porch ceiling and started counting on her fingers. My guess was she was tabulating her period and the calendar. She shook her head again, leveling a gaze at Emily. "Yeah, no. I could not be pregnant. Especially since Tag had a vasectomy years ago."

Emily sat down on a chair across from us. "Sometimes those things don't take."

Ryan opened the door and extended his arm outside, Emily's charcoal-gray wool jacket dangling from his fingers. "Want your coat? It's cold out."

She accepted it, slipping it on and blowing him a kiss. "Thanks, babe. Want to come sit out here with us?"

He shook his head. "Nope, have some girl time. Chloe is about to whip my ass in some Xbox game."

"What's Leo doing in there?" I asked. If he wasn't talking to Ryan, he could be fair game for my father.

"He's fine. He's watching the game with the chief."

I nearly jumped up but resisted. "He's sitting with Dad? Are they talking or just watching?"

Ryan looked at me as if the question was a dumb one, but it wasn't. It was a perfectly logical and reasonable question.

"Um, I think they're talking about football. While they watch football."

"Okay," I said, when what I really wanted to say was *please go sit with them and run interference*. Ryan went back inside, Emily wiggled in between Lilly and me, and the blanket was tucked once more.

"Okay," Emily said. "So you're not pregnant, but what else is going on? What's the latest with Tag?"

Lilly fiddled with the tassel on the sofa pillow for a second. "It's good. Pretty good. You know."

"Hmm, not sure I do. What do you mean?"

"We're just having fun. We've been to some amazing places, and I love being with him. I love *him*, but . . . he's got kind of a retirement frame of mind. I think I'm starting to realize what everyone was saying about the age difference. It's not that we don't fit together well, because we get along about virtually everything, but he's leaving his career in the past, and I haven't even had one yet. As much as I love the traveling and the fabulous restaurants and the galleries, being perpetually on vacation can get kind of monotonous. I realize that's a super first-world problem to have, so I feel bad about complaining, but I just always expected my life to have a bit more substance to it. I need to spend some of my life doing something useful."

"Have you talked to Tag about this?" Emily asked.

"Sort of. I think he understands, but he thinks I should try volunteering for something. He thinks that will make me feel more validated, and maybe he's right, but I can't shake the feeling that I should have a job. A real job. But when I told him that, he said he was sure he could find something for me to do at Taggert Property Management. We actually had a huge fight about it because I told him I didn't just want to be handed some job designed to keep me occupied. It's not that I'm *bored*, it's that I want to do my share. I want to do something that matters."

That made perfect sense to me. I could totally relate. I reached around Emily and squeezed Lilly's shoulder. "I understand that feeling," I said.

"Me too." Emily nodded.

"I know when I worked here at the preschool on the island it wasn't some big, significant job, but I was good for those kids. They learned stuff from me. And I could see how relieved the parents were to drop them off in the morning, and then how happy they were to see them again at the end of the day. I served a purpose, and not to toot my own horn, but I was a damn good caregiver. Those kids loved me."

"That's true. Kids have always loved you," I said. Realistically, everybody loved Lilly. She was sweet and good-natured and generous to a fault. Bubbly and beautiful, so it's no wonder John Taggert had fallen for her. But also, no wonder that the relationship was starting to struggle. I saw Lilly dash a tear from her cheek.

"And I'd better not be pregnant because Tag doesn't want more kids." I felt the stab of her words, the pain behind them. Kids loved Lilly, and Lilly loved kids. I couldn't imagine her going through life without having any of her own.

"I don't blame him," she said, her voice trembling ever so slightly. "His kids are in their thirties, and he doesn't want to go through all the baby stuff and toddler phases again. But I do. I want kids of my own."

"Oh, honey. I'm sorry," Emily said, leaning her head on Lilly's shoulder. "What do you think that means for you and Tag, then?"

Lilly took a big, breathy sigh that shook the whole couch. "I think I have to break up with him. But I don't really want to. And anyhow, how am I supposed to do that when you and Ryan just got engaged?"

"Ryan and I will figure out our own stuff. You take care of you. Maybe if you end things with him right now, there will be time for the dust to settle before the wedding?"

"Maybe, but I'm not ready. I still love him, and Christmas is coming, and Tag and I have plans to go to the Caribbean in the middle of December. He wanted to come with me for this trip, but something came up with some work project that he had to take care of."

"I thought he'd retired?" I asked.

"He has, but there are a handful of jobs that he still has to sign off on. Plus I think he sensed that I wanted a little space. It just doesn't make sense. I mean, love is the simplest, most natural thing in the world to feel, so why does it always end up being so frickin' complicated?"

Why, indeed.

Chapter 22

"Brooke, I'm so glad you're here." Shari motioned to me from behind the counter of the post office. It was Monday, and I'd stopped by to get my mail. And, yes, to get some baked goods.

"I have something I have to show you," she said, her voice low, her eyes darting around. She almost seemed nervous, but why on earth would she be nervous? Maybe she had some particularly naughty pasties to show me, but judging from her demeanor it was something more significant than that.

I'd spent the morning in my office going over budget spreadsheets. My eyes were sore, and so was my brain. No one had warned me that being the mayor would involve so much math. I was good at math, but I didn't love doing it, and this wasn't really math so much as it was accounting. Sudsy was supposed to check in with me later this week. Maybe I'd make him do the crunching.

"Come in the back here with me," Shari said, gesturing for me to follow as she walked toward the back. I'd never been in the back room of the post office before. Was I even allowed back there? Did my new status as mayor give me security clearance? I glanced around furtively, as if federal postal agents were going to pop out and arrest me. Maybe that's why she seemed nervous. My curiosity doubled.

"What are you hiding back here? Is it chocolate chip cookies, because I hope it is."

She led me over to the corner, where tall unvarnished pine shelves sat full of old, dusty banker's boxes. Around the room were various post office items. A copy machine, a package scale, rolls of bubble wrap, and wide packing tape. Posters on the wall advertised collector stamps with pictures of bald eagles, the Liberty Bell, fish, flowers, bridges. Typical stamp stuff. In the center of the room was a white Formica worktable. Going to the corner, Shari rearranged a few of the boxes and pulled one from the back. She set it on the table and solemnly placed her hands on the top.

"I have been debating what to do about this for days, Brooke. I discovered something. Something big, and I just didn't know who to tell."

My curiosity tripled.

She lifted the lid and took out a stack of a dozen or so letters held together with a rubber band. They were yellowed with age and tattered at the corners.

"You've got my full attention, Shari." My heart was starting to skitter about just from her behavior.

"Every once in a while," she said, "we get a letter addressed to someone I don't know. Usually it's for somebody working here for the summer who never bothered to set up a post office box, so I just keep it in here, figuring eventually someone will come and claim it. The other day, I got to thinking about what that private investigator said, and it niggled at me until I finally figured out why. He said the jewel thief went by the name of James Novak, remember?"

I nodded, feeling my breath grow shallow. Shari tilted the letters in my direction, and ho-ho-holy shit. They were addressed to Jimmy Novak, Wenniway Island.

"You've got to be kidding me," I said, taking the letters gingerly into my hands. "They're letters to the frickin' jewel thief? He was here?"

"Sort of," Shari answered. "I know it's a federal offense to open someone else's mail, and I could certainly lose my job over this, but if you look at the postmarks, you'll see they're all from the 1980s. With them being so old and everything, I just couldn't help myself. I opened them, and read the letters, and now I wish I hadn't."

I looked up at her. "Why?"

"Because of what I learned. Will you promise me you won't tell anyone about these until you and I can agree on what to do about them?"

"Geez, Shari. You're kind of freaking me out right now."

"I'm a little freaked out myself. Do you promise?"

"Yes, of course."

"Okay, then. Here, let me show you."

She took the envelopes back and pulled off the rubber band. She flipped through until she found the one she wanted. She pulled out a sheet of yellowed notebook paper covered with big loopy writing, just like the handwriting on the envelopes. Then she pulled out a handful of photos and handed one to me. Sure enough, it looked like the same guy that Bill Smith of Skeevy Guy Investigations had been looking for. His hair was bushy in this picture, and his mustache went across his upper lip and down both sides of his chin—although I can't imagine why. The woman in the photo was the same, too. Just like in the Polaroid from the PI, only this time she looked younger, with her hair hanging down in two thick braids. Shari handed me another photo. Same woman, same guy, but his hair was cut short and he was clean-shaven. She was kissing his cheek and he was smiling. Big. Exposing a significant gap between his two front teeth.

A gasp escaped me, and my eyes darted back to her. "What the fuck, Shari? That looks just like Dmitri."

She nodded slowly, her ever-present smile nowhere in sight. "That's what I thought, and there's more." She pulled out a few more pictures: various shots of the couple posing near a flower garden, in front of a brick building, and at a bar. The resemblance was too strong to ignore. It was Dmitri's smile, and his eyes, and his nose, and his forehead. But that just made no sense. My brain was virtually crackling, overloaded by a sense of doom. I suddenly understood how an insect felt the moment it flew into a bug zapper.

"Look at these." She opened another envelope and gently set down a few more photos. Photos of the woman pregnant, and then with a baby girl. But the man wasn't in those pictures. I glanced at Shari.

"What do the letters say?" I asked quietly, as if whispering might keep this from being such momentous news.

"They're all letters from someone named Alice Williams to Jimmy Novak. She says she understands why he had to leave but she hopes he'll come back. She talks about someone named Mick going to prison. She tells him about the baby, who she's named Amelia, after his mother." Shari sighed, and a tear ran down her cheek. "And then in the last letter, she says she has to move on with her life. She says she's met someone wonderful who wants to be a father to Amelia, and they're going to get married. It's obvious that Jimmy . . . or Dmitri . . . it's obvious he never responded to her, but how could he? He never got these."

The pressure inside the tiny back room nearly gave me the bends, and I doubled over, bracing one hand on the table to keep from toppling over completely. "This just doesn't make any sense, Shari. This guy cannot be Dmitri." I was flummoxed, astounded, dumbfounded, and flabbergasted. I was flabberstounded. I was . . . well, I didn't really know what I was because these were simply feelings I had never experienced before.

"That's what I kept telling myself, too," Shari said, her brow creased with distress. "I've been wrestling with it for days. But think about it. Dmitri moved here in the late eighties. The woman talks about a trial and that other guy going to jail. Maybe Dmitri has been hiding from the law."

"All this time? In Trillium Bay? You think Dmitri is actually a jewel thief? That's absurd. He might be the man in the photos, and he might be this Jimmy Novak, but that doesn't make him a criminal."

"Then why would he move here and change his name? Besides, if you read the letters, you'll be as convinced as I am."

Did I want to read the letters? Did I want to find out my dear friend was a liar and a thief? "This is crazy, Shari. Maybe we should just give the letters to my dad."

Her hand shot over as she grabbed my wrist. "No, we can't do that. Harlan would be obligated to turn Dmitri in to the authorities, and whatever he might have done in the past, we know him. He's a good man. He should have a chance to explain."

The brass bell over the front door jingled, and we both jumped as if someone had fired the cannon right through the post office wall.

"Helloooooo? Share-bear? Are you here?" It was Gloria Persimmons-Kloosterman. Definitely not a person we wanted to draw into this moment of drama.

"I'll be right there, Gloria!" Shari called out, her voice thin and shaky.

"Take your time. I'll just help myself to these macaroons out here while I wait. This baby loves macaroons!" Gloria called back.

I leaned toward Shari to whisper. "Can I take the letters with me? So I can read them tonight?"

Shari hesitated for a moment, then nodded and stuffed the pictures back in one of the envelopes. She wrapped the rubber band around the stack, and then grabbed a big manila envelope to shove the whole stack inside. She hugged the bundle to her chest.

"I swear I will not discuss this with anyone. Do you?" she whispered, holding up a manicured pinky.

I wrapped my pinky around hers and we shook on it, and everyone knows a pinky-swear is legally binding. "Of course. I won't tell a soul. I'll come back tomorrow, and we can talk about this more."

We walked together to the front lobby, probably looking guilty. It's why I never tried to keep secrets. I felt as if there was a big neon arrow pointing at me that said *she's up to something!*

"Well, hey, hello, and hi, Brooke," Gloria said, giving me a quick hug. "What have you got there? You're holding on to that envelope like it's trying to get away."

I loosened my grip. "This? Oh, nothing important. Just some boring government papers. Nothing even remotely interesting. Goodbye."

"Wait!" she said. "Do you want to have lunch?"

"I'd love to," I answered, "but I'm late for a meeting. We'll have to do it another day."

I left the post office and walked straight to my office, clutching that manila envelope with all my strength and constantly looking behind me to make sure I hadn't dropped anything. I would rather read these letters at home, but my office was closer and the curiosity was killing me. Gertie was away for the afternoon getting her bangs trimmed, so I locked the door behind me. I didn't want someone wandering in and finding me with old pictures of Dmitri Krushnic all over my desk with no explanation as to why. I even closed the blinds and turned the bust of Ronald Reagan around. I didn't want him staring at me while I read.

Then I sat down and rolled my new chair toward the desk, took a big, deep breath, and opened the manila envelope.

Chapter 23

A wet, drizzly snow was falling from an overcast sky as I stood on Dmitri's front porch. My canvas tennis shoes had gotten soaked as I walked from my house to his, and now I was shivering, both from the chill and from my own nervousness over what I was about to do.

Shari had been right. After reading those letters, there was no question that Jimmy Novak was running from the law, and the photos left little doubt in my mind that Jimmy Novak and Dmitri Krushnic were one and the same. I knew with certainty that taking the letters to my father would be the right thing to do, but I just couldn't. Dmitri was his friend, too, and my father would be shocked and embarrassed, and he'd feel betrayed. I couldn't let that happen, so Shari and I had agreed that I'd talk to Dmitri. Jimmy. And hear his side before taking any further steps.

My hand shook as I lifted it in front of his cheery red door. His house was small. Instead of one of the Victorian cottages, he lived in an area of the island called Southville, where the woods were thick, and the homes looked more like log cabins. I could hear him whistling inside, and I thought about turning around and going back home. I didn't want to know the details of his life before he came here. I didn't want to know if he was a criminal. That wasn't the man I knew. Then again, it seemed maybe I didn't really know him at all.

I swallowed down my anxiousness and rapped on the door with one knuckle. The whistling stopped, and seconds later the door opened. No beekeeping hat. I guess he didn't wear it at home. His hair was loose, and he was wearing cargo pants and a dark green shirt with a mosquito embroidered on it. Underneath the bug were the words BITE ME. Typical Dmitri.

"Brooke? Hello. Come in. What are you doing out in this dismal weather?"

I gave him a wan smile and stepped inside onto a well-worn rug. A few dozen jars of honey sat on his counter, with some labels next to them, and a small television sitting on a tiny entertainment center was turned to the home and garden channel. I'd been here before, lots of times, but had never paid much attention to the décor. Surely a jewel thief would have expensive tastes, but as I surveyed the room with a critical eye, nothing I saw looked remotely expensive. The couch was beat-up leather and had a hollow in one cushion where he must normally sit. The artwork, if I could even call it that, was faded prints of ducks and moose and snowcapped mountains. His watch was an old Timex, and his boots were standard issue. The same kind just about every other guy on the island wore. If he was rich, he sure knew how not to flaunt it.

"Hi, Dmitri," I said as I peeled off my wet wool coat. He took it from me and hung it on a hook near the door. I had a canvas bag with me, too, with the letters inside, and fortunately I'd had the forethought to put them inside a plastic bag. That's all I needed: to present Dmitri with a bunch of wet, smeared letters that he couldn't read and some ruined photographs.

"Sorry to drop in on you unannounced, but I've got something pretty heavy on my mind, and I was hoping you had time for a chat."

He nodded at me knowingly and patted my shoulder. "Is this about the kid?"

"The kid?" I gasped. *Had Shari told him?*

"Yeah, the bartender. Leo. Is he not behaving himself?"

Oh. The stress of this made me giggle, then giggle some more. If I didn't get control of myself, I'd be hysterical in a second.

"No, Dmitri, this isn't about Leo. It's about . . . something else. Can we sit down?"

"Sure. I just made some coffee. You want some?"

"Coffee would be great."

We sat down a few minutes later, each with a hot mug. I took a sip then set mine on the pine coffee table.

"Okay, let's have it. What's on your mind?" he said, stretching out his legs. He looked so casual and comfortable. Dmitri was like *home* to me, and I was about to take everything and throw it into an emotional blender.

"You know I consider you one of my closest friends, right?"

"Sure."

"And I'd never do anything that might hurt you or get you into trouble."

A frown creased his forehead. "Is this about the pie I took from Gigi's house after Thanksgiving? I know I should've asked her, but she was knee-deep in a conversation with Gus, and I knew she'd tell me I could have it."

"No, Dmitri, this is not about you stealing a pie." I sighed. "It's about you stealing . . . jewelry."

His face turned white and then just as quickly flushed pink. He half coughed, half laughed. "Jewelry? I'm not much of a jewelry wearer, honey. I'm not sure what you're getting at."

"Are you Jimmy Novak?"

He seemed to grip his cup more tightly even while his gaze remained steady. I knew him well enough to know I'd struck a nerve.

"Who is Jimmy Novak?" he said.

I'd kind of hoped he'd spill the beans right off the bat. It hurt to have him staring right at me while being deceitful. I wanted to give him the benefit of the doubt, but the letters were too convincing.

"Jimmy Novak used to be in a relationship with a woman named Alice Williams, and in 1988, Alice Williams had a baby girl who she named Amelia, after Jimmy's mother."

The color in his cheeks drained away again, and the cup in his hands wobbled, splashing coffee on the table as he sat forward to set it down. He rubbed both hands over his knees as he stared down at the floor for a minute. Then he looked back up at me.

"Where would you hear such a thing?" The pain in his voice shot straight through my heart.

"Alice wrote you letters," I said softly, and pulled the banded stack of envelopes from my bag. "Shari and I are the only two people on the island who know about these. We haven't told anyone, and I want to give them to you, but first, please tell me the truth. Who are you, and what did you do?"

He stared at the letters like a desert wanderer desperate for a glass of cool water. Longingly, and with disbelief. Maybe it was cruel of me to make him wait, but if I was to keep his secret, if I was to become complicit in his deception, then I had to know exactly what he'd done.

"I'm going to need something stronger than coffee," he said after a pause. He stood up slowly, as if all his bones suddenly ached, and he walked into the kitchen to pull a dusty bottle of whiskey from a tall cupboard. "You want some?" he asked. It was only about two o'clock in the afternoon, but he was right. This conversation called for something other than coffee.

"Sure, but put some water in mine. I'm not much of a whiskey drinker." Judging from the dust on the bottle, neither was he. He got a couple of glasses, added some ice, then filled his glass nearly to the brim. Mine had a healthy shot, too, but he topped it off from the faucet. I watched him as he moved, wondering what could possibly be going on inside his head. I hoped he'd tell me.

He came back to the sofa and handed me my glass, then he sat in his chair, fast and clumsily, as if all the strength had suddenly left his legs. His head turned as he gazed out the window. Then he started talking, slowly, carefully, as if pulling fragile old keepsakes out of a box.

"I guess I ought to start at the beginning."

I leaned forward, breathless.

"Remember how I told you I'd grown up dirt-poor in a rough part of Philadelphia?"

"Yes."

"Well, that part was true enough. All the stuff I've shared about my childhood was true, and my mother did pass away when I was twenty. My sister took off with a boyfriend, and my stepfather was only interested in his two best pals, Jack Daniel's and Johnnie Walker. He didn't much care what happened to me. I guess I didn't care that much, either."

He took a slow sip from his glass, his hand still not entirely steady.

"So, when my buddy Mick suggested we head down to Florida, maybe hit Daytona Beach, get a tan, it sounded pretty good to me. At the time, we had about sixty bucks between the two of us, and no hotel reservations, but we just figured we'd drive down there, sleep on the beach or in the car." He got lost in a memory for a second before coming back to me.

"For some reason, not sure why, we ended up going all the way to Miami, and after a few days we found a beach full of kids our age willing to share their weed and their beer. That's about as elaborate as our plan was. Then I spotted Alice Williams. She was a beautiful girl. The love of my life, honestly. Honey-colored hair, big blue eyes, and the tiniest bikini I'd ever seen." He offered up a wistful smile, but it wasn't for me. It was for Alice.

I took a sip of the drink and let him continue, thoroughly fascinated.

"There was a bonfire that night, and she sat next to me. Somebody had a guitar, so we all sang. She had the voice of an angel, and she could kiss like—"

He stopped mid-thought and looked at me as if suddenly remembering I was there. His cheeks turned red. "Well, you get the idea. She was my dream girl, and so far out of my league, but she seemed smitten with me. We spent that night together, and I told Mick I was never going back to Philadelphia. He was fine with that. He didn't want to go home, either."

The wind whistled outside the windows of Dmitri's cozy house. Anyone seeing us would think we were just enjoying a drink on a lazy afternoon, but inside, it was so much more than that. Dmitri was rewriting everything I knew about him.

"Alice was in college at the time, but she lived at home. We kept seeing each other, which her parents were not happy about." He took a gulp of his drink and looked over at me. "They were rich. Not outrageously rich, but certainly well-off, and I was a bum. A moocher. All her father's instincts about me were completely accurate. He should have stopped her from seeing me, but you know how it is. She and I were determined to be together, and I think he figured if he could just wait it out, Alice would realize I wasn't good enough for her and dump me. That was my motivator. I was determined to make as much money as I could, as fast as possible, to prove I could take care of us, but I had no college education. I worked as a busboy and a cook. Not much money in that. Sometimes I'd wait tables, but there wasn't much cash in that, either."

"Where did you live?" I asked. "In your car?"

He shook his head. "No, Mick and I found a couple of guys looking for roommates. The place was a dump. We didn't care, though. We'd swipe leftover food from people's plates from whatever restaurant we were working at. We'd shower at the outdoor beaches because our bathroom was so small. It's surprising what you can put up with when you don't have many options. And I was willing to do all that so I could save as much money as possible. Then one night, Alice tells me she has an idea. She wants to stage a robbery at her parents' house."

He looked at me as if to gauge my reaction. I'm sure I looked surprised, because that's not at all the direction I thought his story was going. Actually, I have no idea what direction I thought his story was going, but all the photos of Alice, and her tearstained letters, made her seem so sweet and innocent. Was she the mastermind behind his life of crime?

"She wanted to rob her own parents?"

He nodded, and a big sigh escaped. He took a hearty swig from his glass, and the ice clinked.

"Naturally, I thought it was a crazy fool idea, but I went along just for the adventure of it. She always wanted to do crazy shit like that. I think her parents were so strict, she just wanted to act out. I didn't realize that at the time. Needless to say, I've had lots of time to reflect on the chain of events. Anyway, a few nights later, when Alice's folks were gone, she packed up a bunch of her mother's jewelry, her dad's cuff links, some sterling-silver candlesticks—all sorts of random things. I stood outside and smashed through a window so it looked like somebody had broken in, and we knocked some things over inside the house, left some drawers open. Then we took all that stuff to a pawnshop for cash."

"And her parents didn't realize it was you two?" That seemed kind of shitty, but I guess him being a burglar was going to have some shitty elements to it.

He shook his head and looked remorseful. "They didn't have a clue, and why would they? I mean, they sure wouldn't have suspected it of her, and even though her dad didn't like me, I don't think he ever thought that I'd pull something so incredibly stupid. Somehow, Alice and I were able to justify it to ourselves. Her father was kind of an asshole, and her mother liked to complain and criticize. What we did wasn't okay, but at the time, we thought it was kind of a joke."

"And you didn't get caught?"

"Nope."

"Okay, so if you didn't get caught, what happened next?"

"Ah, you see, that's the rub. It was supposed to be a one-and-done kind of thing. Steal a few baubles and trinkets. Just enough to have money for beer and maybe go out to dinner. But we discovered there's a rush to stealing something. It was exciting. We felt superhuman. It's like gambling. Like an addiction. We had fun that night, and we didn't get caught, so, like the dumbass kids we were, we decided to try it again."

"You robbed her parents twice?"

Dmitri chuckled. "No, we weren't that stupid. Just stupid enough to rob her friends' parents. Alice knew garage codes and where people kept their keys. She knew people's schedules and whether or not they had a dog or an alarm. She was wickedly good at it. By this time, all her friends had met me, and I was accepted into the group. I had a whole backstory about how I'd ended up in Miami and painted my background as a little more well-to-do. Most of her friends didn't even know where I lived, and no one thought to question me, because why would they?"

As captivating as his story was, I was bothered by it. This was sweet, thoughtful Dmitri talking. A man I'd trusted all my life. A man who came to the island school and talked to the kids about different kinds of geological formations, about how lightning happens, and how butterflies form a chrysalis. He could have just as easily been explaining to them how to pick a lock or outmaneuver an alarm system. It was so incongruous to what I'd always known about him. Well, not known, I guess. It was different from what I'd believed about him.

He continued with his tale, and I continued to listen. Like watching a car crash in slow motion. I had to stay and see what happened next.

"Mick started working with us, and we'd usually hit houses that I'd been inside of. Alice and I would go to a party or hang out with some friends. One of us would make sure to unlatch a window or unlock a service door. We'd wait a few days, and make sure that one of us could be an alibi for the other two. I have to say, despite it being illegal, we really did have an impressive system worked out."

"I'm having trouble wrapping my head around this, Dmitri. I just can't believe you did any of this stuff. I feel bad if I borrow something and forget to return it, so how is it that the guilt didn't eat you up inside?" I sounded judgmental, and there was just no way to avoid it.

"I should have felt guilty, I agree. All I can say in my defense— which really is no defense at all—is that we did it as kind of a lark. We were taking things from people who could well afford to replace whatever was stolen. We convinced ourselves that we weren't hurting anyone. Looking back now, though, I realize how wrong we were. We took more than things. We took away people's sense of security, and that's not okay. If I had my life to do over again, I wouldn't have done it. At least, I'd like to think that."

I'd like to think that, too. "I'm pretty curious, then, if it was all going so well, how did you end up here under an assumed name? In the letters, Alice mentions Mick going to prison."

Dmitri blanched at that, and despite the irony, I felt bad for saying it so casually. Mick had been his friend. He paused for a minute before answering.

"Like most aspiring criminals, we got a little bolder with each successful score. We got comfortable and we got impatient, and those are two things that prove to be the downfall of many a crook."

I thought about downing the rest of my drink and asking for another because I suspected his story was about to get more complicated.

"We'd been playing at burglary for about a year. The rush was still there, but we'd run through just about everyone that Alice could get us access to. Then Mick suggested we all get jobs at this upscale hotel. Miami was a pretty happening place during that time, and lots of celebrities would come and stay. He figured if we could work in maintenance or housekeeping or security, we could take advantage of our clearance to roam around the hotel. And we did. In fact, he got a job in security, I worked in maintenance, and Alice got a job as a housekeeper. She told her parents she was working at the college library. We made some decent scores over the first couple of weeks, worked out some kinks in our system, but then we came up against an opportunity we just couldn't resist. Have you ever heard of Marian Singer Wellington?"

"No."

"She is an heiress. Her grandfather was a lumber baron, and her father invented something huge, like the disposable cigarette lighter or VCR players or something. I can't remember exactly, but whatever it was, it made them rich as hell. She was coming to stay at our hotel for some highbrow charity event, and the temptation was just too much. We started working on a plan. Mick was in security, remember, so he adjusted the cameras in the hallway away from her penthouse suite door. Then he made sure he was working that night, just to keep an eye on things. The plan was that I'd use a housekeeping key to get in the room, stash as much stuff in my toolbox as possible, then stroll away. In and out. Alice had to sit this one out because she was with her parents at the country club, and I was glad. I didn't want anyone to see her at the hotel. This was before cell phones, so Mick had arranged for me to borrow a radio from security so he could keep me up to date in case anyone was in the hall. I didn't need it. Everything went off without a hitch. It was seamless."

"So, what happened?"

"Mrs. Singer Wellington called security the next morning when she realized her jewelry was missing, and because of the extraordinary dollar value, the head of security called the Miami police. The first thing the police did was look at the security footage from the hallway."

"And they saw you?" My heart fell on his behalf. Even though I shouldn't be rooting for Jimmy Novak the common criminal, I couldn't help but feel something for my friend Dmitri.

"No, I was in the clear. They didn't see me because I wasn't on the tape, but Mick wasn't always the sharpest tool in the shed. When he repositioned the cameras right outside her door, he put his damn face right up to them. *He* was on the surveillance tape. The cops could see him as clear as day."

I pressed a palm to my cheek and actually felt sorry for the guy. The poor, dumb guy. I shouldn't because he was a burglar, but so was my dear friend Dmitri, apparently.

"They accused him of taking one of the security radios, so they figured he had an accomplice. I didn't know if he'd keep our names out of it. He and I had agreed beforehand that we'd never rat on each other, and that we'd definitely keep Alice's name out of everything, but we also never figured we'd get caught. So Alice and I were scrambling. We didn't dare take the stuff to the fence we'd formed a relationship with, because the robbery was all over the news, and then Mick's face was all over the news, too. Only a handful of people knew that Mick and I were friends, but all it would take was one tip and we'd be arrested, so Alice and I took off. She dyed her hair brown, I bleached mine blond. Not a good look for me, in case you were wondering."

I caught myself smiling. "I'm going to need a splash more of that whiskey."

"Sure." He freshened our drinks and was back in just a few minutes. "Where was I? Oh yeah. Alice and I were on the run, even though we had no idea if anyone was looking for us. Because we had all the stolen loot with us and we were terrified about being stopped and having the car searched, we did the most logical thing."

"Hid the loot?"

"Sort of. We wrapped it in a towel and then rolled it into a ball and stuffed it under Alice's dress. We figured that way, if we did get stopped, they'd think she was pregnant."

His eyes lost some of their gleam, and his voice went soft. "Sounds like she was. She didn't tell me."

"She tried to. It's all in the letters, and you haven't yet told me how you ended up here."

"We drove north without much of a destination in mind. Then Alice suggested Wenniway Island. She'd heard about it from some Michigan snowbirds who lived at her grandparents' retirement village. Seemed like as good a place as any. Then my name got linked to the crime. Mick had turned me in. I don't really blame him. I might have done the same. And at least he never mentioned Alice. For that I will always be grateful to him. After just a few days on the road, she was done. She missed her parents, and the fear of getting caught had ruined all the fun for her. We were terribly naive."

We sat for a moment, he lost in memory, me still trying to reconcile this story with the man I knew.

"What happened next?" I finally asked.

"I recall having a huge argument. She thought I should go stay on the island, and she'd take a bus back home. I wasn't about to let her do that alone, so I drove her myself. That drive was miserable because we were so certain we'd get caught. And she was just as afraid of facing her parents as she was of facing the police. Even if they never realized she'd been involved in any burglaries, she'd still run away with me, an accused criminal on the lam. When we got to her house, her dad hauled me out of the car and punched me right in the face. He told me to never step foot near her again. I don't blame him, either. If I had a daughter . . ."

He paused and I saw tears glistening in his eyes. He blinked them back and said, "Well, any father would have a right to beat the shit out of a kid who put his daughter in that kind of situation. I actually can't believe he didn't try to keep me there and call the police, but I think he was just so relieved to have Alice back. I took off like a coward, ditched my car, and stole another one. I'd never stolen a car before, but then again, I'd never been running from the law before, either. I guess I panicked. Looking back now, I realize the smartest thing to do would have been to just give back the jewelry, do my time, and start my life over, but I wasn't thinking rationally. All I was thinking about was getting away."

He got the lost look again.

"And a few days after that, I showed up here. By myself. I tried repeatedly to get in touch with Alice, but there were no cell phones in those days. I called their house about fifty times, but her father finally said if I called again, he'd make Alice confess to the police where I was hiding. Not sure if he was serious, but I couldn't take that risk."

"How did you come up with a new identity?"

"I figured if the police ever came here, they'd be looking for a Philly kid named Jimmy Novak, so taking a foreign-sounding name would throw off suspicion. I waited about a year and finally went to the secretary of state over in Manitou and managed to get a state ID. Not sure I'd be able to pull that off now, but record keeping was a little easier to manipulate back then."

A sheepish expression passed over his face. "Did you ever wonder why I was such a gossip? Always telling stories about other people? It was just to keep people talking about other people, and not talking about me. I made up stories about anyone new to the island so they'd look suspicious. Hell, I made up that story about the housekeeper at the Imperial Hotel finding a bag of lockpicks and identification badges. Sorry about that."

"You made that up?"

"Yes. I mean, I have slept with a few housekeepers at the Imperial, but the part about the bag of lockpicks was an embellishment. That's also why I wear the hat."

"The beekeeping hat?"

"Yes. I started wearing it ages ago so I couldn't get caught in some tourist's photograph. Probably a little paranoid of me. Now it's just a habit."

"You are making my head explode right now." I should be angry, probably. Maybe insulted that he'd lied to me, to everyone, for all these years, but I was just drained, and fascinated. I was trying to sort through all the things I knew were true and figure out which things were false.

"The private detective from Florida said he'd talked to one of your associates who'd seen you within the last year or so. How is that possible?"

"I've mentioned my sister who lives in Pensacola, right?"

"Yes, a few times."

"Well, when I go down to visit her, I'll occasionally stop by to see my old friend at the pawnshop, too. The first time I went back to Florida, I'd been living up here for a couple of years. I thought alarms would go off as soon as I crossed the state line, but nothing happened. I went to the pawnshop, then I drove by Alice's parents' house. No sign of her. I stalked their house for a few days, and finally she showed up, with a guy and a couple of kids. She looked good. She looked happy. I couldn't ruin that, so I just drove away."

"I'm so sorry, Dmi . . . Jimmy?"

He shook his head. "Please call me Dmitri. I haven't been Jimmy Novak in what seems a lifetime."

"You've lived here for so long carrying these secrets around. Does anyone know? Does my father know?"

"No one knows, except you and Shari now. There were times I so badly wanted to confide in someone. The community here has been so good to me. Your family has been so good to me. I grew to love my life here, and I just couldn't risk revealing my secret. The statute of limitations has run out on those crimes. I could go back to Florida and shout my name from the rooftops and there'd be nothing the cops could do about it, but what purpose would that serve? That was another life, and I was another person. A person I'm not at all proud of, but Dmitri is an honest, law-abiding citizen. Well, except when I go to Florida and fence stolen goods. I suppose that's still criminal. A technicality, I'd say."

"You still do that?" My heart fell a little.

"Only when it's absolutely necessary. I make enough money to get by on around here, but every now and then I need a bit of cash. The jewels I have left are my retirement fund."

"So you just have, what, diamond necklaces lying around someplace? In a nightstand or something?"

He chuckled. "No, in the base of my bee houses. Ingenious, yes?"

"I suppose, but if the statute of limitations has run out, why would a private detective be looking for you?"

Dmitri heaved a big sigh. "Because I don't think he's a private detective. I think it's Mick."

"Mick, your partner?"

"Yeah. He got sentenced to three years for the burglary at the hotel, but after his release, he tried to rob somebody else, and this time he had a gun, so it was straight back to prison for him. I think he may have just gotten released again, and he may think I owe him some jewels or compensation. If it's not Mick, then I have no idea who it is."

"Well, we have to make sure he doesn't find you!" My concerns were all twisted around. I wanted him to come clean, and yet I wanted to protect him, too.

"Honestly, Brooke, if he did find me, I guess I'd give him what I have left and hope that satisfied him. He went to prison and I didn't, so maybe I do owe him."

"Is he dangerous? Would he try to hurt you or somebody else? Because maybe we should tell my dad."

Dmitri's face fell. "So many times, I've wanted to come clean with Harlan. I've hated lying to him. I've hated lying to everyone, but I've never had the courage to tell the whole truth. At first, I was just too scared about going to prison, but now I'm devoted to this island and to the people. I would hate to lose everyone's respect. Brooke, I won't ask you to lie for me, but I can't deny I hope you'll keep this secret for me."

Dmitri had kept a secret for me. Did I owe him? Maybe, but my secret didn't involve any illegal activity.

"I don't know, Dmitri. It's kind of a big thing. I'll have to think about it, but I promise I won't do anything without telling you first, and now that I know the circumstances, I can understand why you did the things you did. I mean, maybe not the stealing part, but the hiding out part."

"Thank you. I know I'm not in a position to even ask this, but could I ask a favor? If you feel it's essential that Harlan know, could I tell him myself?"

"Of course. Absolutely."

"Thank you," he said again. "Now, do you suppose I could see those letters?"

After all this, I'd practically forgotten about the letters. I pushed the plastic bag toward him. It had been sitting on the table that whole time. He could have just grabbed them at any point, but that wasn't the kind of man he was. I set my empty glass down on the coffee table.

"How about I get out of here so you can read them in private. I'm sorry that Shari and I read them."

His chuckle was rueful. "I think in the grand scheme of things, you had every right to. I'm honestly a little nervous to read them myself, but I'd . . ." His voice choked with emotion, and he cleared his throat. "I'd like to hear about this daughter you mentioned. God, if I'd known about that, nothing on earth could have kept me away from Alice." He sighed again, as if the world was crushing him. "Maybe it's better this way, though. If I'd gone back, I'd have ended up in prison and I would have been such an embarrassment to her. Alice deserved better."

"She loved you. You'll see that when you read the letters." I stood up, a little woozy from the whiskey, and Dmitri helped me into my coat. Then I hugged him tightly. I'd gone there thinking I'd find out he wasn't the man I'd thought he was, but that isn't what I discovered. Yes, he'd lied about his past, but the Dmitri I knew was still standing right there in front of me.

Chapter 24

I left Dmitri's house, and even though the snow was getting thicker and wetter, I walked past my house and found myself standing outside the Palomino Pub. I couldn't tell Leo what I'd learned about the jewel thief, but I still wanted to be near him. His presence somehow calmed me down, even as it electrified me in other ways. Having him at Gigi's on Thanksgiving had turned out to be a mixed blessing. He fit in with my family and friends so seamlessly, it was as if he'd always been there. Been a part of us. But Lilly's words about Tag kept nagging at me.

My sister had been so certain about her relationship with Tag last summer. Even in the face of insurmountable odds, she'd trusted her gut and followed her heart. She'd quit her job and moved her entire life just to be with the man she loved. But where was she now? Feeling confused and disillusioned, knowing that hearts were going to break because sometimes love just wasn't enough. What if whatever Leo and I had—lust, infatuation, maybe the first stirrings of love, whatever it was—what if it turned out to be just not enough? He was never going to want to live on Wenniway Island. I was wasting my time and letting the tentacles of attraction wrap around me. Pretty soon, I'd be helpless and devoured.

But what a way to go.

After Thanksgiving dinner, we'd all played cards and then charades. We drank a little too much, ate some pie, and laughed until I thought my stomach couldn't take it anymore. It was *fun*. Pure and simple, it was just . . . *fun*, and I'd had far too little fun in my life. I was always all about the teaching, and being responsible, and challenging myself to be a better version of Brooke Callaghan today than I was yesterday. It was exhausting, but worse than that, it was boring. It was so fucking boring. I was so boring, but I didn't feel that way with Leo. He made me feel excited. And exciting. He made me laugh and he made me want to try new things. He made me want to open up to the possibility that sometimes you need to jump, even if you don't know where you'll land.

We'd spent the entire weekend together, talking, giggling, exploring each other's turn-ons like a couple of college kids with their first lover. Leo, I discovered, was an expert ear nibbler and had a ticklish spot on either side of his waist. He discovered that under no circumstances should he ever touch my feet without warning me first, and that I had a habit of mumbling in my sleep. Since my dreams had been full of him, I hoped I hadn't said anything too embarrassing. He assured me I had not.

I pushed open the Palomino Pub door and walked inside. It was busy tonight, the wet weather having made everyone eager to be inside. Judge Murphy, Father O'Reilly, and Monty Price were playing darts in the corner. My sister's construction crew was occupying a big table off to one side, with mammoth Tiny Kloosterman animatedly telling a story. I'm sure Emily would be thrilled to know they were at the bar, but it was, after all, happy hour. I recognized Georgie Reynolds, who'd sung so beautifully at Gloria and Tiny's wedding reception, and Yoga Matt, our local fitness instructor who, until Leo had showed up, had carried the title of cutest guy on the island. Fortunately, there was no one there who might expect me to come up and say hi, leaving me free and clear to go sit at the bar, which I did.

Leo came out from a set of double doors that led to the tiny backroom kitchen, and his face lit up when he saw me. It wasn't just his usual *I'm-a-super-friendly-guy* smile, either. It was his *I'm-interested-in-you*

212 / Tracy Brogan

smile. At least, that's what I decided to tell myself in that moment. It's possible the whiskey from Dmitri's house was still churning around inside me, coloring my judgment. Then again, the weekend had been pretty spectacular.

"Hi there. I didn't expect to see you today," Leo said, placing a cardboard coaster down in front of me on the bar. "Having a drink?"

I should have coffee. "A Manhattan, please."

He crooked an eyebrow. "Day drinking. I like it. Just leaving the office?"

No, I'm just busy aiding and abetting everyone's favorite jewel thief. "I was doing some community work. How has your day been so far?"

"Pretty good. I spent some time this morning talking research with a couple of guys Clancy hooked me up with. Took lots of notes."

"Eventually I think you have to take the notes and put them into book format so people can read it." I smiled, even though I was still mad-impressed that he was writing a book.

"Is that the part I keep forgetting? I knew there was something."

He finished making my drink and set it on the little coaster. He leaned forward and said, "This one is on the house."

"Thanks. I owe you."

"I work until seven. Can I collect after that?"

"Yep."

I sipped my drink and chatted with Leo. He took care of other customers, and I took a few minutes to visit with a handful of locals who had come in for dinner. I wanted to be distracted because my afternoon with Dmitri had pretty much rocked my world. I wanted to review all my memories and see if there had been any signs, any signs at all. I wondered if, somehow, my father knew. But I highly doubted that. He wasn't the type who could have sat by and done nothing. Dmitri was his friend, but the law was his true north. It was the moral compass by which Harlan made all his decisions. And he hadn't been the chief of police back in the eighties when Dmitri had first arrived. That's when people might have been suspicious, but no one on the island would question his background now.

"Hey," I said to Leo a bit later, as I finished a second drink, which was really like my fourth drink because I'd had two glasses of whiskey and water at Dmitri's house. "What do you think about me picking up some to-go chow at Carmen's Café and we can eat at my place? Maybe watch a movie?"

That's what I needed. Carmen's macaroni and cheese and a mindlessly entertaining couple of hours in front of my television. Followed by something naughty with Leo that involved nakedness and lots of thrashing.

"That sounds great. Are you sure you don't mind going to get it? It's pretty lousy outside. If you want, I could get it."

He was so sweet, worrying about a little rain. Didn't he realize we Trillium Bay folks were quite accustomed to traversing around in all sorts of weather? I'd be just fine.

"That's okay. It's nearly seven, so I'll go now and you can just come over whenever you're finished here."

"Awesome. Let me give you some money."

I held up my hand to halt him. "I got this."

～⑨～

Drunk-ordering at Carmen's Café had resulted in me arriving at my house with two huge bags full of delicious food. I wasn't sure what Leo was in the mood for and realized, as I'd stood there staring at their menu board, I didn't really even know which things he liked. So I got a little bit of everything.

I set the bags on the coffee table in my living room and trotted upstairs to take a fast shower. My hair was already wet from the snow, and I was chilled to the bone from having walked around in wet shoes. The hot water was relaxing and did a fine job of warming me up. It felt so good I must have been in there longer than I realized, because a soft knock on my bathroom door just about sent me to the ceiling with a yelp.

"Brooke?"

It was Leo, of course. Not a psycho ax murderer. He opened the door just wide enough to stick his head in. I could barely see the outline of it through the frosted glass doors of my shower.

"You scared me," I said, laughing with relief.

"Sorry. I just wanted to let you know I was here."

"Okay, I'll be out in a sec."

"Want some company in there?"

I paused for a second. "In here. In the shower?" I'd never had sex in the shower. I'd tried to once with a college boyfriend, but his roommates were all in the other room, and it was about the least sexy near-sexual encounter I'd ever had. I'd lasted about two minutes before he'd accidentally knocked a shampoo bottle on my head, and I told him I was out. It wasn't a scenario I'd ever contemplated repeating. But . . . Leo.

Something told me he'd have a bit more skill.

"Brooke?" he said again, and I realized I'd been lost in thought.

"Sorry. Just thinking." I slid the door open just enough to peek out at him. "I'm kind of shy. It's very bright in here."

He smiled. "I could close one eye so I can only see half of you. Come on. Where's your sense of adventure?" He squinted in demonstration, and I couldn't resist. By most people's standards, shower sex wasn't considered an adventure, but it was for me.

"Close both eyes," I teased.

"Okay, but understand that means I'll be *seeing* with my hands," he answered as he pulled his shirt up and over his head, giving me a wonderfully enticing view of flexing abs. I watched as he quickly divested himself of the rest of his clothes and I realized that my insistence on dim lighting had done him a disservice. Even in universally unflattering bathroom light, he was divine.

"You really have a beautiful body," I said out loud, surprising myself. Blame it on the alcohol.

"So do you. Can I see it?" His eagerness made me laugh, and I slid open the sliding door.

"Come on in," I said. "The water's fine."

I wrapped my arms around his shoulders as he stepped in and under the showerhead. Water ran over his skin in rivulets, and I followed them with my mouth until the two of us were creating more steam than the hot water was. He kissed my mouth and shoulders and the little spot right behind my ear that drove me simply wild. He hadn't shaved today, and the scruff was scratchy, adding to the myriad of delicious sensations coursing through me. The rasp of his whiskers, the soft heat of his mouth, the water, his hands. It was wet and wild and wonderful and I decided, then and there, that even if Leo Walker eventually broke my heart, it was worth it.

Chapter 25

Leo and I watched a movie while lying in my bed with food containers from Carmen's Café strewn all around us. Macaroni and cheese, an Italian-style panini, barbecued chicken tenders, french fries that I'd reheated in the oven, and oversize chocolate chip cookies. A smorgasbord of comfort food that we fed to each other while laughing. Leo had brought two bottles of wine, and although I probably didn't need any more alcohol, I drank anyway, leaving me tipsy and loose but not so intoxicated that I wasn't fully aware. I loved the glow that I was wrapped in, being here with him, enjoying such simple pleasures. Cheese- and carb-laden food, a farcical, brain-candy movie where the boy would most certainly get the girl, and slow, steamy, wet sex that started in my shower and ended on the floor of my hallway because we simply couldn't wait to get all the way to the mattress.

This night was just what I needed to relieve the tension of earlier. Dmitri had been miles away from my mind until Leo asked, "So what kind of community service did you do today?"

It was an innocent question but was like a club to my senses, pushing memories of my afternoon to the forefront of my mind. What to do about Dmitri? My concerns must have been obvious because Leo reached over and tucked a strand of hair behind my ear. "Are you okay?"

"I am." I paused, mind tumbling. I needed advice, and it occurred to me that Leo was the best one to ask. He had no loyalty to anyone on the island. He could give me an objective opinion about how to proceed. Plus, if I was being honest, I was dying to tell him. I've never been any good at keeping secrets, and although I was sure I could keep this news from all the other locals, Leo and I were intimate now. Emily said she told Ryan everything. Wouldn't it be okay to share this with Leo? If I could share my time and my bed, and honestly, my heart, with Leo, I should certainly be able to trust him with a story like this.

"I found out something today that you're not going to believe, but if I tell you, you have to promise to never breathe a word of it. Not to anyone."

Leo chuckled. "Brooke, who would I tell? Other than mild pleasantries, you're basically the only person I talk to around here."

"I found out who the jewel thief is."

He shot forward from the pillows and looked at me in shock. "You did? How?"

"You know Shari from the post office?"

"No."

"Well, my friend Shari works at the post office, and after we talked to that private investigator, she started thinking about the name Jimmy Novak. It had sounded familiar to her, but she just couldn't place it."

Leo sat forward even farther, his body like a coil ready to spring. He was a good audience.

"Then she remembered that in the back room of the post office, there's a box of old letters that no one's ever picked up, and with no return addresses, so they couldn't be returned. She went and looked through them, and guess what she found?"

"What?"

"A stack of letters addressed to none other than Jimmy Novak. They were postmarked from the mid-1980s."

"No fucking way," he said slowly. His disbelief was palpable as he pushed a few empty food containers to the side and twisted toward me, as if to not miss a single word.

"So . . . who is he?"

I'd lasted less than twelve hours before letting the cat burglar out of the bag, but I'd gone this far. I couldn't really go back, and Leo's rapt attention made me want to draw the story out even further.

"Do you swear you'll keep this between us? Swear on your bartenders' oath of confidentiality or whatever?"

He hesitated only slightly before placing a hand solemnly over his heart. "As a bartender, you have my word."

"Dmitri Krushnic."

He exhaled loudly with a slump of his shoulders. "The beekeeper?"

"None other. I went to see him today and he confessed everything. Apparently, he robbed some heiress in the 1980s, and his partner got caught and ratted him out. Dmitri took off on the run and ended up here. He's been here ever since."

Leo ran a hand through his already-tousled hair and stared off into space as if trying to process this. I could relate to his shock.

"And what did he do with the jewelry?"

"He sold some of it. He's got a fence down in Florida who he goes to see once in a while, but he told me he still has some of it. You're never going to believe where the jewelry is hidden."

Leo took a long, slow breath. "Where's it hidden?"

"In the bases of his bee houses." I found myself laughing, now relieved of my burden and enjoying Leo's utter captivation. "Isn't that fabulous? Who the hell would ever think to look there?"

"I know I would never have thought to look there." He shook his head slowly. "I have to be honest. I kind of thought it was Sudsy Robertson, given all the stories you told me about him."

"Oh, that's the thing, though. Dmitri has been making stuff up for years, ever since he got here. He says he did it to direct suspicion away from himself. Diabolically clever, don't you think?"

"Criminal minds are usually pretty clever," he said, then looked at me intently. "What do you think about all of this? He's been your friend since you were little, right?"

My own sudden sigh was unavoidable. "I don't know what to think. I'd honestly kind of like your opinion on that. I know I should tell my father, because he has no idea, but Dmitri said the statute of limitations for all his crimes has expired, so it's not like my dad could arrest him, and he's been living here for thirty years. We all love him. I don't want to ruin his life over something he did when he was twenty-something years old."

Leo paused for a minute, then started stacking empty food containers. "I'm not sure that's true. If he fenced stolen property within the last six years, he could be picked up for that."

"He could? Are you sure?"

"Pretty sure. His best bet would be to turn himself in to the authorities and return whatever items he still has. Did he show them to you?"

I shook my head. "No, and I have no idea how much is left, or honestly, how much he even stole in the first place. Do you think I should tell my dad?"

Leo thought about this for a minute before saying, "I do think you should tell him. It sucks for your friend, but he stole things from people, and a crime is a crime. If the statute is up, then nothing will happen to him."

"Of course something will happen to him. Everyone on the island—everyone who's been his friend for the last thirty years—is going to feel betrayed. He might have to move after that, and he's fifty-five years old. If he gives the jewelry back, there goes his retirement."

Leo's expression told me he disagreed. "He hasn't earned that retirement, Brooke. Just because he's been sitting on that jewelry for half his life, that doesn't make it his. It belongs to someone else. And every time he fences something, he risks getting caught. Better he moves to another city and starts over as best he can rather than ending up in prison."

This conversation had taken a turn toward the serious, and I didn't like it. I wanted our fun, funny night back, but I couldn't deny the truth of Leo's words.

"What if he just, I don't know, anonymously returned the stuff?"

"Would he be willing to do that?"

"I don't know. He said if Mick, his accomplice, showed up and asked for it, he'd probably give it to him. Oh, that's the part I didn't tell you. Dmitri thinks that Bill Smith the private investigator may actually be his old partner, Mick."

"They haven't seen each other?"

"No, but he did say he feels kind of obligated to give what's left to his partner, since Mick did prison time, even though Mick is also the one who told the police about him."

Leo was silent for a few minutes as he got out of bed and started cleaning up the food boxes and leftovers. I couldn't quite read his mood. I thought he'd think the whole thing was a lark—the Beekeeping Hat Bandit—but he was somber. Did he think it was wrong of me to even consider protecting Dmitri?

I stood to help, gathering the refuse and carrying it down to the kitchen. I was wearing my dalmatian pajamas because Leo had seen them hanging in my bathroom and thought they were adorable. See, Emily didn't know everything. Leo was in his white T-shirt and boxers as he followed me downstairs with a now-empty bottle of wine.

I emptied the trash and threw the bag outside by the back door. Leo got us each a glass of water.

"What are you thinking?" I finally asked. "I hope you don't think I'm terrible for wanting to protect a friend. For what it's worth, I'm pretty conflicted about it."

He stepped close and draped his arms around my shoulders. "Of course I don't think you're terrible. I understand the predicament you're in, probably better than you'd believe."

"What do you mean?"

"I mean, knowing what the right thing to do is can be compromised by how we feel about someone. It's just human nature. Dmitri does seem like a good guy, even if he is a thief. Do you believe everything he told you?"

"I do. In spite of this one huge lie, and of course all the made-up stories, I could tell today that he was being completely sincere." I had believed that, but what if he'd played me? What if he was at his house right now, loading up piles of stolen treasure and getting ready to make a break for it? No. It just wasn't possible. I'd seen the tears in his eyes when I'd told him about Alice and Amelia. I'd heard the regret in his voice. And I'd spent the whole of my life with him. I might not have known who he was then, but I knew who he was now.

"I know it might sound naive, Leo, but Dmitri has been there for me a few times before, and despite this business, he's one of the best people I know. I just don't think I can destroy what he's built by telling my dad. And I don't want to make my dad have to make this judgment call, either. Does that make sense?"

Leo nodded and pressed his forehead to mine. "It does make sense. Let's talk about something else now."

I wrapped my arms around his hips. "Okay. Like what?"

He kissed my temple, then the corner of my mouth. "Let's talk about how beautiful you are."

I chuckled, feeling the tension ease. "That's going to be a short conversation."

"No, it's going to be a long one. It's going to take all night. Let's go back to your room so I can list all the things about you that are beautiful."

I let him pull me upstairs and into bed. I reveled in the whispered sweet nothings and the kisses and caresses. I gave as good as I got until we were breathless and dizzy and spent. And when we lay together afterward, tangled and tired and content, I looked into Leo's eyes and saw myself in them. His gaze back at me was tender and raw. And as I drifted off to sleep, he stroked my cheek, and murmured in my ear, "I'm very glad I met you, Brooke."

Chapter 26

Leo had left sometime during the night without saying goodbye, but he left a note on my pillow saying, *Hope you slept in. I didn't want to wake you.* There was a tiny heart drawn in the corner, but as far as I was concerned that little heart hinted at big things. He'd said he was glad he'd met me. He'd been particularly sweet and romantic and attentive before we'd fallen asleep, and my body was still tingling from it. I stretched like a kitty in the sun, feeling sensual and sublime. Leo Walker made me happy.

Apparently, he also made me a little decadent and lazy. It was nearly nine thirty in the morning, and I was usually up and out the door by eight. Sure, it was Saturday, but I couldn't spend the whole day lounging under the covers. Plus, I was scheduled to meet my sisters for lunch.

I got up and headed toward the bathroom, blushing at the memory of our slippery, soapy antics in the shower. My peach-colored towels sat in a heap on the white tile floor, and as I scooped them up to throw them in the wash something fell to the floor with a clatter. Leo's phone. It must have fallen from his pocket when he'd dropped his pants. No surprise, really. He had been in quite a hurry to get those jeans off. No worries, though. I'd have plenty of time to get ready and drop the phone off at Leo's place before I headed to the restaurant.

I thought about texting him to let him know I had his phone . . .

Yeah. That's not going to work.

I couldn't resist checking to see if he had a lock screen, and he did, so no surfing his photos. I probably wouldn't have done it anyway. Especially given our conversation last night about Dmitri. Clearly Leo's sense of morality was pretty strict, with the lines between right and wrong well defined. But that was a good thing. My lines were pretty specific, too. I didn't lie, cheat, or steal. If I had friends who did? Well, that was something I was still trying to work out.

I walked up the slight incline on Cahill Road a little while later, glad the sun was shining and the wind was calm. Leo had told me he was staying in the yellow cottage with blue shutters, so I knew where I was headed. I got to the front porch and heard voices inside. I paused with my hand raised, ready to knock, but something made me hesitate. It was a man and a woman talking. Not so loudly that I could make out the words but loud enough that I could sense the conversation was a heated one.

I stepped back from the door and cast a glance up and down the street. Was there a *different* yellow cottage with blue shutters? Had somebody painted? Not that I could see. A nauseating sort of premonition swirled in my gut. If Leo was in there with a woman . . . I didn't know what that might mean, but I knew it couldn't be good.

Squaring my shoulders like a superhero flinging my cape to the side, I stepped back to the door and knocked decisively.

The voices stopped, and a second later Leo opened the door. He blanched when he saw me.

"Brooke? Hi. What's up?"

"You left your phone at my place," I said, leaving it in my back pocket rather than offering it to him. "Who are you talking to?"

"Me? Nobody. It's just the TV. Thanks so much for bringing me my phone." He held out his hand.

I moved my foot forward. "Aren't you going to invite me in?"

He looked over his shoulder. "Um . . ."

"You're going to let me in." I pushed my way past him and walked inside the tiny cottage. There was a sitting room full of brown and tan upholstered furniture, a short hallway leading to a bedroom and a bathroom, and a rustic but serviceable kitchenette. And standing in that kitchenette next to a vintage refrigerator was the woman from the bar. Biker-Chick Barbie. She was leaning against the pine-topped counter, as casual as somebody just waiting in line for a bus. She was drinking from a paper coffee cup, and her expression didn't change one iota when she saw me. I doubt I could say the same for myself.

I turned to Leo. "Just the television, huh?"

Frown lines creased his forehead. "This probably looks bad, Brooke, but it's not what you think. I can guarantee it."

I crossed my arms and tapped my foot. "Okay, then. How about you tell me what it is?" There had to be at least zero good reasons for that woman to be standing in his kitchen. At least zero reasons that would stop this sinking sensation in my chest.

"What's she doing here, Leo?" the woman asked, as if I wasn't right there to hear her. I glared in her direction, trying not to notice today's outfit of tight jeans, knee-high black leather boots, and a black wide-necked top that was shifted to only cover one shoulder. The strap of a black bra peeked out over her other shoulder. It was a little early in the day for such a Saturday night kind of outfit. Skanky ho.

"What am I doing here?" I asked, staring directly at her. "I came by to give Leo his phone because he dropped it in my bathroom last night when he stripped off all his clothes to get in the shower with me." *Hah! Take that, skanky ho!*

She rolled her eyes. Loudly. "Jesus, Leo. Can't you keep it in your pants? And I'm not talking about your phone, by the way." She took a slug of coffee, and I swiveled back to him.

"Okay," he said, rubbing his hands together and looking all sorts of uncomfortable. "What we have here is a unique situation. And Brooke, there are things I should have told you about sooner but . . . I couldn't."

"Couldn't? Or just didn't? Either way, I suggest you tell me now."

"I can't."

God damn it. How did this keep happening to me? The first guy I'd fallen for in six years, the first guy since Jason, and there was another woman involved? Again? My stomach roiled, and the coffee I'd had for breakfast threatened to come back up. Whether I had the worst luck or the worst judgment, it appeared I'd been lied to. Again.

"You may as well tell her, Leo," the woman said. "She's going to find out soon enough anyway."

I didn't like the casual way she seemed to be in charge here. "Who *are* you?" I snapped.

"I'm Leo's partner," she said, finishing the coffee and tossing the empty cup into the trash can at the end of the counter. She sauntered over to the couch and sat down, knees apart with her elbows resting on them, hands dangling casually.

I shifted my steely-eyed stare from her to him. "Your *partner?*"

"Business partner," he clarified, as if that made any difference at all. "Remember when I said I worked with a friend I knew from Iraq? This is her. Gina, Brooke. Brooke, Gina." His attempt at polite introductions fell pointlessly flat, like introducing a cobra to a mongoose and expecting it to go well.

"I thought that company went out of business," I said. *And I'd assumed your soldier buddy was a man. Sexist me, I guess.*

"Not exactly out of business. We're just . . . transitioning into other things. Will you sit down, please?" He gestured to a chair, but I didn't want to sit down. I wanted to stomp my feet and start slapping people, but since that was socially unacceptable, even under these particular circumstances, I decided against engaging in blunt-force trauma. Instead, I reluctantly perched on the edge of one of the chairs across from GI Jane. I pulled Leo's phone from my back pocket and all but chucked it at him. He caught it deftly and sat down next to Gina. Not close to her. A full sofa cushion length away. Maybe it was just wishful thinking on my part, but there did not appear to be any kind of sexual connection between them. She clearly wasn't jealous of me, at any rate.

"I do have something I need to tell you, and you're going to be pissed, but before you get mad, let me tell you everything." He seemed earnest enough, but that was not a good preface. Clearly no one had ever explained to Leo the concept of a good news sandwich, where you start out with something good, sneak the bad stuff into the center, then end with something good again. He was going straight to the rotten.

"When I said I worked in private security, I meant it, but the part about me being here because I'd lost that job was false. I'm still working. Gina and I are sort of like bodyguards. We do personal protection, but we also do other kinds of security stuff when the situation calls for it."

"When the situation calls for it"? What in the name of sweet baby Jesus was he getting at? Gina fell back against the cushion, crossing her arms, crossing her legs, and letting out a fast, frustrated sigh. Clearly the disintegration of my relationship with Leo was boring her.

I really didn't like her.

Leo continued, and the slow, calm tone he was using made me want to grab his cell phone back and pulverize it with a hammer. I am not a ragey person, but I was ten kinds of humiliated right now, and ten kinds of mad. If anyone had good cause to demolish a device, or something equally as destructive, it was me.

"What kind of security stuff are you doing right now that meant you had to lie to me?"

He glanced at Gina, then back to me. "We work for the Wellington family," he said.

Wellington. Wellington. Why did that name sound famil . . . fuuuuuuuuck me. "As in the Marian Singer Wellington family? Marian Singer Wellington *the heiress?*"

He gave a single nod as he stared intently at my face, gauging my reaction.

"I don't understand," I said. At least not completely. "What does she have to do with anything?"

"When Mick O'Malley got released from prison, Gina and I were hired by Mrs. Wellington's granddaughter to find her stolen jewelry. Word on the street has always been that Mick's accomplice was sitting on it somewhere, just waiting for him to come and collect."

All the cells inside me seemed to expand and contract in an instant, and it didn't feel good. This was unbefuckinglievable. Leo was here because of the *jewel thief*?

"So, do you mean to tell me that you're here looking for Jimmy Novak?"

He nodded again, and I all but jumped from my chair and started to pace as I tried to recall everything I'd said to Leo last night. I'd been tipsy from the drinks, but had I told him all of it? The cells expanded and contracted again as certainty gripped me. I *had* told him everything. Everything, right down to the spot where Dmitri had hidden his stash. I'd betrayed my friend, and now he was going to lose everything. Maybe even go to jail for continuing to sell the stolen goods. Leo had used me, and worst of all, I'd let him.

"I would have told you sooner, Brooke. Honestly," he said, standing up and crossing over to me, "but it never occurred to me you'd have such a close personal relationship with the guy we were looking for."

I spun on him so fast I nearly did a full three-sixty. "Oh, really? It didn't occur to you that I have a close personal relationship with virtually every person on this island, you jackass? How did you think this was going to play out?"

The sheepish look on his face told me he hadn't given the notion much thought, and I couldn't decide if that was hurtful because he'd taken my feelings for granted, or hurtful because he hadn't bothered to think it through. Either way . . . hurtful.

"Did you even want to have dinner with me that first night, or were you just looking for dirt on all my neighbors? I must have been a jackpot for you, huh? Telling you everything about the people who live here. Now it all makes sense." And then it hit me. "Oh my God. You're not even writing a book, are you?"

That hurt, too. A lot. Him being an aspiring author was a big part of my attraction to him. Granted, he had plenty to offer, even without the book thing, but still, I'd really *liked* that about him. And it was fake. *He* was fake. I'd fallen for yet another guy who wasn't who he pretended to be, and suddenly I heard my mouth asking, "Are you married?"

He took a step backward as if I'd slapped him. "What? No, of course not."

As far as silver linings went, that one was whisper-thin, but at least I hadn't accidentally committed adultery. Again. Still, this absolutely sucked. "How could you do this to me, Leo?" I couldn't stop the catch in my voice as anger gave way to a tsunami-size sense of betrayal. Tears puddled up in my eyes, but I blinked them back.

"Drama queen much?" Gina muttered, picking casually at a cuticle.

"Shut up, Gina," Leo said. He turned to look at her. "Maybe you could go get another cup of coffee or something? Give us a little privacy?"

She arched a dark brow as if he'd just suggested she try eating garden slugs, which, come to think of it, was something I'd like to see.

"Yeah, no. I don't think so, Romeo," she said, her voice full of snarky dismissal. "First of all, you are emotionally and professionally compromised. Second of all, we can't let this one out of our sight"—she pointed at me—"or she'll go running straight to honeybee man and warn him. And third of all, you've already been on this Podunk island for well over a month. The Wellingtons aren't paying you to hang around and fraternize with the suspects. We need to wrap this up. We need to haul ass over to Jimmy Novak's house and get whatever is left of Marian's jewelry before Mick gets to him. That's what we're here to do. That's what we're getting paid for. We have bills, Leo, and other clients. Chop, chop. Wrap it up." She slapped the back of one hand against the palm of her other.

Leo's jaw clenched, the tightly coiled spring aspect of his personality coming out. "I need fifteen minutes here, Gina. Come on. Give me a break. Give me a chance to explain this to Brooke without your wiseass commentary."

She rolled her eyes again. "Fine, lover boy. I'm going to go stand on the porch for ten minutes. While I'm gone, don't let her use the bathroom."

"Why can't she use the bathroom?"

"Jesus, Leo. Because she might climb out the window or try to text somebody. Have you forgotten all your training?"

Climb out the window? Damn it. I wish I'd thought of that. I could jump out and run all the way to Dmitri's house. If there was any way to contact him, he could move the jewelry, and I could just say I'd made a mistake. That the jewel thief wasn't Dmitri at all. *Whoops. Sorry!* But this Gina person was ruining my plans before I could even make them. Have I mentioned that I really don't like her? I didn't like Leo anymore, either. Not at all. In fact, my heart was currently in a state of breaking into sharp, tiny fragments, but I had to figure out this Dmitri thing before I could indulge in that bit of clusterfuckery.

Gina stepped outside and slammed the door, and Leo stared at it for a long moment before turning back to me. His shoulders drooped, and he had the decency to look remorseful—but not nearly remorseful enough. He had a sort of *bad dog, I just ate from the garbage can* expression, but I wasn't buying it. This situation called for groveling, serious groveling. Not that any kind of apology would change the outcome.

"I never meant for this to happen," he said, in the weakest sort of mea culpa.

"Really? Maybe you should have thought of that before you kissed me. It's bad enough you pimped me for details at dinner, Leo, but all that phony seduction stuff was so beyond necessary."

His sigh was nearly convincing. He might actually feel bad, but it didn't matter.

"That wasn't phony. I know you don't have any reason to believe me, but Brooke, I want you to know, everything I said to you about *us* was true. I asked you out because you're beautiful, and I wanted to kiss you because I *wanted* to kiss you. Because you captivated me, not because I was trying to trick information out of you."

On the mea culpa scale, that scored a solid five, but it still certainly wasn't enough. "I don't believe you, and anyway, even if I did, you had to know that ultimately this situation was going to bite *me* in the ass. Eventually you were going to have to admit that the book stuff was a bucketful of shit, and the job stuff was all fake. There's just no way around the fact that you've been lying to me."

"I had to lie. I was undercover, but it wasn't personal, Brooke. It's just the job."

Just the job? Not personal? "It feels pretty damn personal to me, Leo! And what was all that crap about going on a job interview?"

He sighed once more and gestured again to the chair. "Will you sit back down? Please?"

I did. Not because he'd asked me to but because my whole body was trembling as if the house was suddenly floating on water. Maybe the island was sinking. It sure as hell felt like it was.

Leo sat heavily on the couch. "I didn't have an interview. I went to Florida to follow up on a couple of leads. That private investigator you talked to in the post office, by the way? Dmitri is right. It's Mick O'Malley. Gina's been following him for several weeks. He's back in Michigan again now, but he can't stay up north for very long at any given time because he has to check in with his parole officer in Orlando. In fact, he's actually violating parole by leaving Florida, but we're not reporting him because we need him."

"How resourceful of you. So I guess the law is only the law when it's convenient to you?" *Nice zinger, Brooke.* Heartbreak made me sassy.

He appeared chagrined by my comment. *Good.* I needed him to feel half as shitty as I did right now.

"We're keeping a very close eye on him, and as soon as we've gotten what we need, he'll be arrested again. Mick doesn't have the best luck, or judgment, and he'll be going back to jail very soon. The real question is . . . what are *we* going to do?"

He gazed at me expectantly, and I'm sure my gaze back said *go fuck yourself, I don't care what you do.* At least I hoped that's what he picked up from it because that was certainly what I was going for.

"I'm not sure I know what you mean."

He paused and leaned forward. "Brooke, Gina wasn't wrong when she said we can't have you going to Dmitri, but if he's willing to turn over the jewels, like you said, this could all be over very quickly. I'm not interested in sending him to jail. Shit, I don't even care if you never tell your father about this. I'm not the police. I'm a private contractor. I just want to collect what's left of the Wellington family property and close this case."

Close this case. I guess that would be good, to have this over and done with. But what then? Then Leo would go back to wherever he came from? Was he really from Chicago? Did it matter? No, because regardless, he'd be gone from Trillium Bay, and that would be that. No more dinners or drinks or decadence between the sheets. Chop, chop. Wrap it up.

Gina came back inside just as I was saying, "I won't tell him."

She chuckled, but there was little humor in the sound. "Not good enough, babe. You're going to have to come with us," she said.

"Come with you?"

"Yes, to Dmitri's place. Right now."

She was so rude and bossy. "I can't right now. I have lunch plans."

She pressed her lips together, looking at me as if I'd just said the stupidest thing ever. "Super sorry that you're going to miss out on green tea lattes and quinoa salad with your BFFs, sweetheart, but we either have to take you with us, or we have to lock you up in a closet until this is over with."

I'm pretty mild mannered, and thanks to thirteen years as a teacher I can take a lot of sass, but I'd officially reached my limit. This bitch was going down.

"You know what, *sweetheart?*" I said, rising from the chair and stepping right up to her. "I've had just about enough of your bad attitude. I don't deserve it. I am a victim here, in case you haven't noticed, dragged into this shit-show by him." I pointed at Leo as if there were any doubt to whom I was referring. "You want to lock me in a closet? Go ahead. That's kidnapping, and I happen to be the mayor, and my father happens to be the chief of police, so if you want me to cooperate, maybe you could quit being such a bitch."

Yes! That felt magnificent. I should rage more often. I should rage at Leo. He was the one behind all this angst. And he was currently staring at me with wide, startled eyes. I'd obviously surprised him with my sudden outburst, so it seemed we had both underestimated me.

Gina gazed at me for a second, and I saw her lips twitch into a near-smile. It seemed I'd earned some respect, if not my freedom.

"Fair enough. My bad. Will you please take us to Dmitri's house? Because Mick is in Michlimac City and probably heading over to the island today, and every time he comes here, we run the risk of him figuring out what he needs to figure out. The minute he realizes Jimmy Novak is hiding under a beekeeping hat, things are going to get a lot more complicated."

My options at the moment seemed pretty nonexistent. I didn't want Dmitri to know I'd revealed his secret to Leo, especially less than twelve hours after he'd told me, but I guess that ship had sailed. And sunk. If I led these two to him, at least they'd keep him out of jail. And better the jewels go back to the Wellington family instead of to his old accomplice. Dmitri had said Mick used a gun at his last robbery, so who knew how dangerous he might be now.

Leo rose from the sofa. "I'll make this up to you, Brooke. I promise."

I turned stiffly to look his way and hoped my disdain was evident. "You can't possibly make this up to me. I'll help you out for Dmitri's sake, but not for yours. Now let's get going, because I have *lunch plans.*"

Chapter 27

My lunch plans were clearly not going to happen.

According to my *captors*, recovering stolen property might take a bit of time, what with Dmitri Krushnic, a.k.a. Jimmy Novak, an uncertain element in this process. So, under close supervision, I texted my sisters saying I had an upset stomach from too much wine last night. That wasn't even technically a lie, because all the alcohol from the prior evening was not currently sitting well. I just omitted the part about helping to apprehend a jewel thief before another jewel thief showed up to steal the stuff that had already been stolen. No way I could have texted that with any clarity. That sort of thing definitely demanded a phone call.

Leo, Gina, and I made an interesting threesome, trudging toward Dmitri's house. As we made our way down Cahill Road toward Southville, I thought about taking them on an extra-long trek through the woods, maybe making a break for it or at least ensuring that their walk was a little extra miserable because God knew they deserved it. Especially Leo. But Gina's warning about Mick getting to Dmitri first had me worried.

Then I thought about what it might mean if I convinced them to let me call my dad. He could have deputies watch the boat dock and arrest Mick as soon as he landed. He'd broken parole, after all, and we didn't need him to lead us to Jimmy Novak. We already had Jimmy Novak, but calling my dad would mean telling him everything, and in the back of my mind, I was trying to create the least amount of collateral damage. If Dmitri gave the leftover jewels to Leo and Gina, he'd be broke, but at least he wouldn't be in jail. Gina had promised to go along with Leo when it came to not doing anything about recently sold items. It seemed their only priority was returning the stolen items to the Wellington family so they could collect their payment for services rendered. Anything above and beyond that was not their concern. This job was just a paycheck, not some assignment with a higher moral purpose. I guess that made me glad for Dmitri's sake but also a little sad, because I'd thought Leo was more principled than that.

Apparently, he wasn't.

Damn it. We were so over.

"Is this entire island uphill?" Gina muttered.

"Oh, sorry, *sweetheart*," I answered. "I guess you should have worn more practical boots." I heard a tiny snort of amusement, and if I didn't know better, I might say she was starting to like me. The feeling was not mutual. I couldn't wait to get this over with and send these two douche-canoes back to wherever with their freshly confiscated jewelry.

It was nearly noon when we stood on the front step of Dmitri's modest cabin. The sun was still shining, the wind was still calm, but a storm raged inside me. How was I going to admit to him that this was my fault? I'd promised to keep his secret, but I guess loyalty was in short supply around here. Betrayal seemed to be the soup of the day. I'd betrayed Dmitri. Leo had betrayed me, and when it got right down to it, Dmitri had betrayed everybody. We were all karma's bitch today.

I tapped lightly on the door, and then tapped again. I finally heard some movement inside, and Dmitri opened the door. He looked surprised and then nervous, and no doubt he was, seeing me there with Leo on one side and Goth-Barbie Intimidatrix on the other side.

"Brooke?" he said slowly and carefully. "Um, sorry, honey, but now's not really a good time. I'm sort of in the middle of something."

"This won't take long," Gina said, pushing open the door so fast that it bumped against him. She plowed past, and Leo and I followed. I mouthed the words *I'm sorry*, and Dmitri's face fell. Even without knowing the full truth about Leo, Dmitri surely knew this wasn't a friendly social call.

"What can I do for you folks?" he asked, his eyes never quite landing on any of us and his distress evident. As my grandmother might say, he was as nervous as a whore in church.

"We'll keep this simple, Mr. *Krushnic*," Gina said, pronouncing his name with a hint of drama. "We'd like the Wellington jewels and any other contraband you've stolen over the years. Hand it over without any fuss and we'll keep the police out of it."

A breath escaped Dmitri, and he grasped the back of a kitchen chair for support. My heart twisted.

"I'm sure I have no idea what you're referring to . . . miss?"

"I'm Gina Gonzales. I believe you've met my partner, Leo Walker? We've been retained by the family of Marian Singer Wellington to retrieve the items you stole from her on the night of July seventeenth, 1987, and any other items still in your possession. We have at least two sources who can verify that you are indeed James Novak, but if you want us to publicly prove that, we can, and we will."

Dmitri's eyes finally flickered over me and landed on Leo. "Is that so, kid?"

Leo's face flushed as he gave a single nod. "I'm afraid so, sir. For what it's worth, I enjoyed our fishing trip."

Dmitri offered up a rueful chuckle. "Yeah, me too, but life is like that sometimes, I guess. You think you know a person . . ." He paused as if waiting for us to respond. We didn't, so he added, "But, you see, here's the fascinating part. I don't have anything left. It's all gone."

"Mr. Novak," Gina said, dropping the name pretense and frowning, "we know that's not true. Do you want us to contact Chief Callaghan about this matter? And then he'll have to contact Judge Murphy to get a search warrant? And then we'll have to tear up your whole house before we finally find what we're looking for in your *bee houses*."

Damn, she was harsh.

Dmitri's face filled with pain and disappointment as she mentioned the bee houses, and I felt awful because I was the one who knew about that. I was the one who'd told Leo last night about Dmitri's awesome hiding spot. Obviously, Leo had told Gina.

"Dmitri, I'm so sorry," I said. "I didn't have any idea who Leo was when I told him those things. He promised to keep it to himself, but he lied." I cast a scathing glance Leo's way, but since I'd been glaring at him for the past hour, he'd become somewhat desensitized.

"Don't beat yourself up over this, honey," Dmitri responded. "I know a thing or two about lying. It starts out simple and then it gets complicated. But Miss Gonzales, something tells me you might know my old friend Mick O'Malley? He was here just yesterday and demanded his loot. He had a gun, so naturally I felt I had no choice but to give him all the jewels I had left."

Her smile was patently insincere. "Thirty years of living a false life has given you a very convincing manner, Mr. Novak," Gina said. "But you're right. I do know Mr. O'Malley. I also know he couldn't have been here yesterday because he didn't arrive in Michigan until very late last night. Well after the ferry service stopped running. He's in Michlimac City now, or at least he was this morning. It's quite likely he's on his way here now, and if we see him, we'll have no choice but to turn him in to the police for parole violation. My guess is he'll have some things to tell us about you if that happens. So how about you just give us what we want and we'll leave?"

Dmitri's expression was strained. He spoke slowly, enunciating each word. "Please believe me when I say that Mick O'Malley has the jewels." He held a hand up to his chest and very subtly aimed his index finger toward a closed bedroom door. Then he lifted his thumb . . . like a gun, and pointed it up toward his temple.

I glanced between Leo and Gina, and the realization was unanimous. Mick O'Malley was in the other room. With a gun. That was not good news. My heart thumped wildly in my chest as Leo started to slowly make his way across the room while she continued talking.

"I think that's very convenient timing, Jimmy. I mean, here we are to collect, and you say that somebody beat us to it? Doesn't your old partner realize that if he gets caught this time, and he's sure as hell going to get caught, his ass will go straight back to prison for a very, very long time? If he had any sense at all, he'd stay far away from you and far away from any stolen merchandise."

As she talked, we all watched Leo ease his way toward the closed bedroom door. Gina motioned for us to move over by the windows, maybe so if Mick started shooting we'd be out of the path of the bullets? What the actual fuck? Was I about to be shot at? Was Leo about to be shot at? I was still mad at him. Very mad, but that didn't mean I wanted him to get shot. Punched? Sure. Kicked in the groin? Maybe. But definitely not shot.

Mesmerized, I observed as he slowly reached his hand down to carefully wrap his fingers around the doorknob.

"Are you going to stick to that story, Jimmy?" Gina said, motioning for Dmitri to say something in response.

"Uh . . . I can see why you don't believe me," he said as Gina also started moving toward the door. "I mean, I have been known to tell a tall tale or two, but you have to understand about Mick and me. I owed him those jewels. Sure, he gave my name to the cops, but I don't blame him for that. I'm sure the cops tricked him into telling them more. I never held any hard feelings against him."

Ten seconds stretched into an eternity, and I stopped listening to Dmitri's words. He was rambling, anyway. Just killing time. My brain flinched at the cliché. Killing anything right now seemed like a lousy idea. I heard the faint sound of a horse taxi traveling past the house and caught the scent of bacon and coffee. Dmitri's breakfast. Just a normal

Saturday morning for Trillium Bay, the town I was the mayor of, and yet my world had been reduced to these four walls, and whatever was about to happen next. I reached over and clasped Dmitri's hand.

Gina had reached the doorframe by now, and she pressed her back against the wall. Leo made eye contact with her and nodded once before suddenly twisting the knob and throwing the full weight of his body against the door. I heard a bam and slam and the sound of Mick's body making contact with the wood.

"Ow!" he howled like a kid getting hit with a baseball.

Dmitri and I jumped in tandem as Leo rushed into the room, followed by Gina, but a millisecond later, they both backed out of the room with their hands raised.

"You could have broken my nose, you bastard," Mick said, pointing a handgun right at Leo's chest. My heart skittered to a halt, then jump-started into an erratic pounding against my rib cage.

"I'm sorry I didn't," Leo answered. "A broken nose would be the least of your problems."

"Well, that's not a very nice thing to say," Mick answered. "And it looks like you're the one with the problem. Because I'm the one with the gun." He smiled his dingy-toothed grin, and I thought about fainting. I always hoped I'd be extra brave in the face of danger, but it turned out that even the hint of bodily harm was enough to make me want to cry and pee my pants.

"Don't do this, Mickey," Dmitri said. "No amount of money is worth going back to prison for, is it? You heard what they said to me. If we give them the jewels, you and I are both in the clear."

Mick scowled at him for a second before returning his gaze, and the barrel of the gun, to Leo. "I don't think that's what they said, Jimmy. And anyway, what would you know about prison? I'm the one who spent half my life in there. I'm not going back. Fortunately, those shiny stones you were foolish enough to save are just what I need to get my new life started."

"Don't be a fool, O'Malley," Leo said. "There's no way off this island. The police know you're here."

Leo was bluffing, but Mick stared at him hard, then looked to Gina. "You just told Jimmy you hadn't called them yet. So, which is it?"

"I called them," I said, not at all certain I should be saying anything but choosing to follow Leo's lead. "I texted my father before we got here so he'd know we were coming for Dmitri." A total lie. I had just told a total lie to the convict with the gun—which was now pointed at me. I was in no way a fan of that. I definitely should have kept my mouth shut.

"You, little girl. I've met you. You come over here by me."

"Leave her out of it, Mick. She doesn't have anything to do with this," Dmitri said.

I stayed frozen to the spot, not out of bravery or defiance. Quite the opposite, in fact. I was essentially paralyzed with fear. I was about to start hyperventilating. I needed a paper bag, but now hardly seemed like the time to ask for one.

"Nothing to do with this? Sure she does. She's my insurance policy."

He crooked a finger at me. I took a reluctant step forward, and Mick grabbed my arm and twisted me around, pointing the gun at my midsection, poking me with it a little. Time moved in surreal slow motion. I was not brave. Not by any stretch of the imagination, but falling apart right now would only make matters worse. And I had two soldiers with me. Surely, they'd figure out something? Something that included Mick being knocked unconscious and me walking away with no extra ventilation? My eyes met Leo's, and he was calm in a way that gave me strength. He was going to fix this.

"You are making an epic mistake," Leo said, his voice low and gravelly.

"No, you're making a mistake if you think I'm leaving here without my payoff." Mick's voice had gone from friendly to threatening, and he poked me again.

"Whether we called the police or not, you'll never make it off the island," Gina said.

"I will if I take this pretty little mayor with me. You might think I don't have an escape plan, but I do. I'm smarter than I look."

"You'd have to be," Gina muttered.

"Take me instead," Leo said. "Think about it, Mick. She is the police chief's daughter. You think he's going to let that rest? No, he's going to want revenge. You'll be looking over your shoulder for the rest of your life."

Mick's chuckle lacked humor. "I'm going to be looking over my shoulder for the rest of my life anyway, buddy."

"Sure, but speaking of looking over your shoulder . . . what's that?" Leo exclaimed and abruptly pointed behind us.

Mick twisted to see, and the next thing I knew Leo's body had slammed into us both. I went flying from the impact and landed with a *woof* on the floor, with Leo half on top of me and Mick half underneath. I coiled reflexively as I heard the sounds of punches being thrown and a gun skittering across a hardwood floor. At least, I think it was a gun skittering across the floor. That's not a sound I'd ever heard before, but I dared to open my eyes just in time to see Gina stomping a black-booted foot down on the top of—sure enough—the gun.

"Oh my God," Gina said, glaring over at a now-incapacitated Mick. "I can't believe you fell for that. You are *so* not smarter than you look."

Chapter 28

"Violating parole is going to get you into serious trouble, O'Malley," Leo said to a now-handcuffed Mick. Not surprisingly, Gina had supplied the cuffs from inside her jacket. "But possession of a firearm will get you thrown back into the slammer for good. We're willing to make a deal. You leave the island with us, promise to never come back, and forget everything you ever knew about Jimmy Novak or Dmitri Krushnic, and my partner and I will escort you safely back to Florida just in time to meet your parole officer, end of story."

"I'm supposed to believe that? Why would you let me go free? What's to stop me from getting another gun and coming back here for my share of the take?"

"There won't be anything left of the take," Dmitri answered. "I'm turning over everything I have left to these two so they can return it to the Wellington family. I'm about to become a law-abiding citizen."

The matter of Mick having pointed a gun at all of us, especially at me, seemed to be of secondary concern to everyone. "How about we arrest him here?" I said. "That seems like a *better* idea to me."

Dmitri's face fell. "I know it's a lot to ask, Brooke, but I'd still like to keep Harlan and the law out of this."

That seemed like a *bad* idea. This guy was more than a menace—he was a dangerous menace—but after all was said and done, I had the chance to keep Dmitri's past in the past. Not sure I owed him that, considering the fact that he'd lied to me and everyone I cared about for the past thirty-some years. But then again, I couldn't ignore the reality of what Dmitri, the Dmitri I knew, meant to me. "I guess," I said with a sigh.

Gina motioned me to the side a few minutes later. "Don't sweat it," she murmured in my ear. "We're going to deliver Mick straight to the cops as soon as we hit the mainland. The only *jewels* in Mick's future will be the ones shaken in his face during shower time for cell block eleven. We just want to keep him quiet and compliant for as long as possible."

That was a mild relief, although the "quiet and compliant" part hinted at what Leo had done to me, and a fresh wave of hurt and dismay washed over my skin. How could I have been fooled again? Did I have *gullible* tattooed on my forehead? Technically Leo had saved my life today, what with him flinging himself into harm's way to knock down the man with the pistol, but Leo was also the reason I'd been in that predicament to begin with. My emotions were in chaos. This was going to require some serious self-reflection about my life choices. And a lot of vodka.

"Is this everything?" Leo asked a few minutes later, surveying the kitchen table now laden with the most beautiful pieces of jewelry I'd ever seen in my life. There were diamond-encrusted necklaces, chunky emerald bracelets, teardrop ruby earrings. I hadn't seen so much sparkle in one place since I'd watched the Oscars on television last year.

"That's everything," Dmitri said, looking more sad than remorseful. "After Brooke was here the other day, I moved everything from the bee houses and cleaned it up. My plan was to move it all to a safety deposit box in Manitou, but I guess that won't be happening."

I couldn't resist picking up one of the more garish necklaces and holding it up to my throat in front of the mirror on Dmitri's wall. I caught Leo in the reflection standing behind me.

"That looks really pretty on you. Sorry I can't let you keep it."

I pulled the necklace away and turned around. "Yeah, well, given all the other stuff you should be sorry about, that's pretty low on the list."

He took a step closer and lowered his voice so only I could hear. "Brooke, I can't begin to tell you how sorry I am about all of this. I wish I could go back to the beginning and have it happen some other way, but . . ." His voice trailed off as if he was waiting for me to jump in and say it was okay. That I understood. Sure, I understood. I understood that he'd started a relationship with me under utterly false pretenses. So even if the *feelings* we'd shared had been real, the foundation of everything was false. The bad canceled out all the good, and the fragile trust I'd offered him was irrevocably broken.

"How can I make this up to you?" he asked.

"You can't."

"I'm going to try anyway. I have to get these items back to Mrs. Wellington, but when all this is over, I hope you'll forgive me, and maybe we can start again?"

Had he conked his head when he'd jumped on Mick? Did he have a concussion? Because he wasn't making any sense.

"When all of this is over, Leo? It is over, and so are we. We are so very over. Go ahead and take all this gorgeous crap back to where it belongs, get your paycheck, and then don't come back here. I don't want to see you again."

"You don't mean that." His refusal to take me seriously just added to my anger.

"Oh, I do mean that, and it's the most polite version of my feelings that you're going to get, so unless you want to hear me start swearing and calling you every vile name I can think of, you will back the fuck up and leave me alone."

Leo may have been keeping his voice down, but I had not, and the others turned to stare. Mick snickered, earning him a cuff on the head from Gina.

"Ow," he cried out melodramatically. "That's police brutality."

"I'm not the police, you moron," she said, draping a coat over Mick's handcuffed hands. "And remember, keep your mouth shut from the moment we leave this house until the moment we deliver you back to your parole officer, or we will turn you in for having a weapon and possession of stolen goods."

"I don't have any stolen goods."

Gina picked up a bracelet laden with garnets and diamonds and dropped it into the front pocket of Mick's shirt. "Possession," she said.

She and Leo left soon after with a backpack full of very expensive jewelry, and each with an arm looped around one of Mick's elbows. Leo cast one last glance my way.

"I'll call you, Brooke," he said.

"Don't bother. I won't answer." And I meant it.

Dmitri sighed beside me as the door shut behind them. "Don't be too hard on the kid. He was just doing his job."

I walked into the kitchen and pulled the cork from a bottle of red wine. "He lied to me, Dmitri. About some pretty important stuff."

"Yes, he did," he said, joining me in the kitchen and pulling two glasses from the cupboard. "But for what it's worth, I think he really cares about you. Don't underestimate the value of that. I left behind a woman I loved and have regretted it every single day since. Don't make that same mistake."

"Our situations are totally different, Dmitri. You avoided Alice because you wanted to protect her. Leo did the complete opposite. He didn't think at all about how any of this was going to affect me." I filled the glasses with wine and took a gulp. This was not an occasion for sipping.

"I suppose, but there's no way he could have anticipated any of this. And I want you to know how sorry I am for my part in it. I let you down, Brooke. You deserved better."

I did deserve better, but somehow that didn't make me *feel* any better. Leo was gone, and I knew what lay ahead. Weeks of heartache while my brain and my heart went to war with each other. I took another slug of wine and shoved those thoughts away. This wasn't the time to indulge in tears. I'd save that for later.

"I expect a lifetime supply of free honey," I said instead.

Dmitri lifted his glass to toast. "Done. Here's to a lifetime supply of free honey for you and a life free of crime for me."

We drank, and suddenly an expression of realization crossed his face. "Oh my goodness, Brooke. Do you know what this means?"

"What?"

"I don't have to wear that stupid beekeeping hat anymore. No one is looking for me." His bright smile exposed that gap between his teeth. "And do you know what else this means?"

"What?"

"It means I can take a little vacation down in Florida. I'd like to figure out a way to meet my daughter."

Chapter 29

"Well, if this isn't the cutest, most adorable, tiniest little onesie I've ever seen!" Gloria Persimmons-Kloosterman exclaimed, holding up a mint-green baby garment to show off to the gals at Drunk Puzzle Night. Her engagement/wedding/baby shower had been postponed until after the holidays, but my sister had loaded up a wicker basket with a dozen baby-centric items to present to the newlywed/mom-to-be. A little stuffed elephant, brightly colored rattles, and assorted soft and fuzzy outfits that made my eyes well up and my midsection feel oddly hollow. I wanted a baby. I wanted a husband and a baby and cozy nights by the fireplace and stroller walks to the park. I wanted the diamond ring and the promise of forever.

But Leo was gone. It was just a week ago that he and Gina had carted off a sullen Mick O'Malley. I hadn't said anything to anyone yet, having spent the last several days pretending to have the flu just for the privacy that afforded me. It wasn't hard to fake illness because I pretty much felt like I was dying anyway, and I'm not sure I could have gotten out of bed if I'd needed to. Instead I indulged myself with days spent in my ratty pajamas watching maudlin, sob-inducing movies and taking long fitful naps with all the curtains closed, and I discovered that a meal comprised of spiced rum poured over vanilla ice cream tastes pretty fucking good.

True to his word (ironically), Leo had tried to call several times, and each message he left was the same. He was sorry. He wanted to make it up to me and wondered how. And I believed he was sorry, but I also knew I'd never feel the same way about him ever again. How could I? I didn't even know him. I had jumped without looking and had landed on rocks. So I didn't return his calls.

And now I was at Drunk Puzzle Night, where someone was most certainly going to ask about him. I had a story all ready, though. I'd tell them he got a job in Washington, DC. I'd say I was bummed that we hadn't had more time together but that I'd always understood we were just a fling, and that nothing very significant had happened between us anyway. Sure, I'd miss him, but I was practically already over him. I mean, how hard could you fall for someone in so short a time, anyway? At least that's what I'd planned to say. It's what I'd rehearsed in my head a dozen times.

So when Marnie White finally turned to me as we all sat in the cozy living room of Eva's house and said, "So, what's the latest with Sexy Bartender Guy?" I did the only thing I could do. I burst into tears. A full-on ugly cry with the snot and the hiccups. I'd never cried in front of anyone before, but instead of me being horrified, it felt oddly cathartic. I couldn't tell them all the stuff about the jewel thief, of course. I just said he'd given up on writing the book and had taken a job assignment someplace else, and every woman in the room did the *tsk, tsk, tsk* and shaking of the head and the *shame on him*. They were unanimous in their support of me, and the solidarity was something I'd never experienced before. Gloria got me a huge goblet of wine, and Eva got me a fresh box of tissues. My sister sat next to me with her head on my shoulder and assured me that Leo was the one losing out. I'd arrived that night with a broken heart, but sitting there among my friends, I'd never felt so loved. It was a small but priceless consolation. And it would have to be enough.

Chapter 30

"You're not going to believe this," Sudsy Robertson announced to the city council as he burst through the door. He brushed a generous portion of late-December snow from his winter parka and onto the floor of the Palomino Pub.

It was the Wednesday between Christmas and New Year's, and my life had settled into a calm if somewhat predictable routine. I continued to mark time with *life before Leo* and *life after Leo*, but it had been a full month since he'd left town, the phone messages had stopped, and my heart, although not really mending, had at least stopped with the incessant aching. I'd chosen to fill the cavernous void left by his absence with meetings and research and studying our local laws. Gertie continued to be a great resource, but I was starting to surpass her. I couldn't catch up to her thirty years of experience, of course, but I was smart, and with absolutely nothing else in my life to distract me, I was dedicated.

"Won't believe what?" asked June Mahoney. She was wearing an ugly Christmas sweater, but I didn't have the nerve to ask her if she meant for it to be ugly or if she just had bad taste.

"Remember how our community center project got delayed a few weeks ago because we couldn't find the funding for the necessary repairs?"

I tamped down a sigh. The community center, my pet project, was floating dead in the water. Ryan had found some structural issues with the foundation, and until we could afford to fix that, we couldn't proceed with the rest, and the money just wasn't in the budget.

"Well," Sudsy continued, "we have a benefactor."

"A benefactor?" Vera asked.

"Yes, someone by the name of . . ." He pulled a letter from the pocket of his kelly-green pants—because even in the winter, Sudsy wore golf clothes. He unfolded it carefully. "It says here . . . Marian Singer Wellington."

"What?" I gasped, exchanging a glance with Dmitri.

"Yep, she's some rich old broad from Illinois. Not sure why she's taken an interest in our little town, but she likes you in particular, Brooke."

"Me?"

"Uh-huh." He adjusted his glasses to read from the paper in his hands. "She says she hopes we'll accept her charitable gift and that the monies should be used at the discretion of the mayor, Brooke Callaghan, with the intention of completing the renovation of our community center."

"Who is Marian Singer Wellington?" Olivia Bostwick asked. "I've never heard of her."

Dmitri and I exchanged another discreet glance. "She's an heiress," he said. "She stayed at the Imperial Hotel a few summers ago. I had a lovely chat with her one day when she was visiting the butterfly garden. She said the charm of the island made her feel twenty years younger."

That was a complete fabrication, of course, but now I was onto Dmitri's style. A little lie here, a little lie there, just to keep the general public confused about the truth. It was really quite effective.

"Oh, I remember her now," I said. "She and her granddaughter came for the Lilac Festival, and we had a long conversation about . . . lilacs." I wasn't nearly as good at lying on the fly as Dmitri was. I hoped it wasn't a skill I needed to develop.

"What kind of donation?" my father asked. He was making an appearance at today's meeting. Actually, he'd been to all of them since Leo's abrupt departure. And he'd started showing up at my office with lattes or the occasional doughnut from Tasty Pastries. I knew what he was doing. He felt bad that my relationship with Leo had gone pffffft. I'd never discussed it with him, and he'd never asked. All he knew was that suddenly the bartender was gone, and I was sad about it.

"What kind of donation, you ask?" Sudsy responded. "That's the part you really won't believe. This woman donated twenty-five thousand dollars."

"Twenty-five thousand dollars?" Every person in the room, except for Sudsy, said it at the same time. Clancy looked up from his spot at the bar. He was down a bartender, so it was just him again.

"Twenty-five thousand dollars," I said again. "That's . . . crazy."

What had possessed her to be so generous? What had Leo and Gina told her about our little island that had made her want to do that? I'd have to send her a thank-you note, but I didn't even know where to start. *Thanks for the donation. Sorry my friend swiped your jewelry all those years ago?*

Vera clapped her veiny hands together. "Twenty-five thousand dollars? Looks like I'll have my bat display after all."

I listened to the excited chatter as everyone in the room started talking at once about the fabulous new center we'd soon have, with its computer labs and classrooms and a shiny new visitors' center. This *was* very good news, and I should have been thrilled. I *was* thrilled. I guess. I just wished the funds hadn't come at such a cost. My heart was on the mend, but still, I wished I'd never heard of Marian Singer Wellington or her fancy jewelry. I wished I'd never met Leo Walker. He'd disrupted my life and reminded me of all that it was missing, and he'd stolen my courage to trust someone. He was a far worse thief than Dmitri had ever been.

Chapter 31

New Year's Eve on Wenniway Island was typically celebrated inside at various locations, but this year things were a little different. Gigi had some dead husbands to launch into the sky, and so some of the festivities were being held outside. Bonfires crackled along the beach, the smoke thick and white against the dark sky. Lawn chairs had been hauled out from various sheds, and people wrapped in wool and fleece blankets waited while sipping peppermint schnapps and hot chocolate. On the lake, not far from the shore, sat a boat with an assortment of fireworks. The first to go up would be my grandfather, John Callaghan.

I huddled up next to Chloe with Emily and Ryan on the other side of her. Lilly hadn't made it back to Trillium Bay for Christmas, and missing her was a sharp pain inside me. I welcomed it, though, because missing her was a nice distraction from missing Leo. She'd sent me a text last week saying she wasn't ready to give up on Tag yet. Love doesn't always make sense, her note had said. Maybe it never makes sense, but when it's good, it's soooo good. I wasn't sure how to respond to that because I had nothing to compare it to. Love hadn't been good to me. Not ever, but if it was good to her, then I was glad.

Everyone was talking and laughing as snow came down in big, fat clumps. My dad arrived to stand next to me. Gigi was in front of us wrapped in a big, downy blanket, a paper New Year's Eve hat perched on top of her knit winter cap. Gus was standing off to the side, respect-fully giving her a chance to say goodbye while surrounded by her family.

"Are you sure you want to do this, Mom?" my dad asked. "It's not too late to put these guys in the cemetery where they belong. Or we could just, you know, dump them all back into their jars." I could tell he was teasing. He still didn't love this idea, but he'd come around to it.

"I'm certain. Your father is going to love this, Harlan. Stop being a party pooper."

"Ooookay," he said, and took a hearty swig from a flask in his hand. Moments later the sound of bagpipes floated over the crowd, and up went my grandfather, followed by Bert and Conroy. The swishes and the pops were nearly instantaneous as the pyrotechnics exploded up above. And damn if my grandmother wasn't right. This was a beautiful shimmering display filling the night sky. I tried not to think about all those ashes floating overhead as everyone oohed and aahed. A bunch of other fireworks went up next, just to make a real show of it. There was applause muffled by mittens and more conversation and laughter. The sky shimmered gold and pink and green. Maybe being sent up into the sky wasn't such a bad way to go. It really did look pretty.

"I'm thinking about hiring a new assistant deputy," my dad said as the last firework faded from view and people started making their way to the pubs to welcome the new year in warmth. We were headed to the Palomino. "I have one candidate in mind," my dad continued. "Seems like a pretty good guy. Maybe you'll like him."

I shook my head vehemently at my father's attempt at matchmaking.

"No, thanks. I won't like him. Not if he's Captain America, Tony Stark, and Thor all rolled into one." Maybe someday I'd give that whole dating thing another try, but certainly not now. Not yet. And anyway, I was busy being mayor.

"Okay," he said, and let it drop.

We stepped inside the pub, and Gloria hugged me, her belly start-ing to plump with that Kloosterman baby. There were the Drunk Puzzle

Night girls and Emily's construction crew. Gertie and the O'Douls. Lots of friendly, happy faces. Seemed that everyone wanted to say hello to me tonight, and they wanted to congratulate me, too, because word of the donation had spread, no doubt embellished by Dmitri, and suddenly everyone had a hazy memory of maybe having met Mrs. Wellington here during that nonexistent visit she'd never taken to Trillium Bay. Funny how that worked.

I got a drink and mingled a bit, finding a nice warm spot near the back. It was standing room only, and the crowd was ready to celebrate.

"Did you make any New Year's resolutions?"

The voice was low in my ear, but I knew it in an instant. My heart burst like one of those fireworks. Filled with a dead guy. How appropriate. Something beautiful and shimmery and magnificent that fades away to ash, and then you realize it was made of something rather unpleasant. Leo was back.

Leo was back.

I could ignore him. Pretend I hadn't heard, but I wasn't a teenager. I didn't need to play games. I just needed to be honest with him and ask him to take his questions and the rest of himself elsewhere. I turned to do just that, but I made the mistake of making eye contact, forgetting, somehow, just how blue and hypnotic his eyes were.

"What are you doing here?" I'd meant to sound standoffish and impersonal, so that tone of hopefulness in my voice was completely misplaced. I didn't want him here. I didn't want him back. But here he was. Standing before me cloaked in all his Leo-esque charm. He'd gotten a haircut and was clean-shaven, to better showcase his dimples, no doubt. So unfair.

"I'm here because I missed you and you won't return my calls."

I'd missed him, too. So much, but I'd stuffed that down, like the way you bank a fire. I knew the heat was down there, but from the surface, it just looked cold and gray, and I wasn't prepared to admit anything to him. No stoking allowed.

"Um, I haven't answered your calls because I don't want to talk to you. We don't have anything to say to each other."

"I do. I need to tell you some things, Brooke. Will you at least listen?"

I didn't want to. Not because I was mean or unforgiving but because I *wasn't*. Truth be told, I had forgiven him. I'd forgiven Dmitri for a lifetime of deceit; I could certainly give Leo a pass for just doing his job. But telling him that would only complicate this misery. Because he didn't live here. Because if the jewel thief issue hadn't broken us apart, something else would have, but my hesitation in answering seemed to offer enough encouragement for him to continue.

"Christmas sucked," he said. "And do you know why?"

"You got coal in your stocking?"

"No, it sucked because for the first time in years I had somebody I wanted to spend it with, and I couldn't. Gina told me I should man up and get over it, but I realized something. I don't want to get over it, Brooke. I don't want to get over *you*. If missing you is all I have left of us, then I guess that's what I'll hang on to, but I'm hoping to turn things around."

"Hey, kid," Dmitri said, appearing at my elbow and handing me a much-appreciated gin and tonic. His interruption gave me a chance to absorb Leo's words.

"Mr. Krushnic," Leo answered. "It's good to see you. Especially without the hat."

"The hat served its purpose faithfully but has recently been retired. I find myself no longer needing it."

Leo raised his bottle of beer in a toast. "I'm glad to hear that, and speaking of retirement, you might be interested to know that I escorted an old friend of yours back to his previous place of residency. He'll be living there for quite some time, I'd imagine. Sort of a forced retirement from the glamorous life he'd aspired to."

He meant Mick, of course, and I couldn't deny the sense of relief I felt at hearing that he was back in prison. I don't think he ever would have shot me, but in the weeks since that incident I'd woken up more than once from the grip of a nightmare in a cold sweat. Ironic, really. The most dramatic moment of my life, and I couldn't even tell anyone. Just like I couldn't tell anyone the real reason Leo had left so suddenly. Now he was back, and here we all were, chatting like friends on the surface while underneath my emotions were churning and erupting like an active volcano.

"I also delivered that package you were holding on to, and the recipient was very happy to get it back," Leo said.

Dmitri smiled. "So I gathered. She sent a note of appreciation to the mayor."

Leo glanced at me. "She did?"

"Twenty-five thousand notes, to be exact," Dmitri added.

Leo's gaze turned to surprise. "Seriously? Well, she's a very generous person. In fact, she was so generous to me that I can afford to take a break from working. I've decided to try my hand at writing that novel after all. I heard that winters here are the perfect time and place."

He looked over at me, observing as the words sank in.

"I'll just be going now," Dmitri said. "Seems like you two crazy kids might have some other things to chat about."

My heart raced as I watched Dmitri melt into the crowd. Reluctantly I looked back at Leo. "I'm not falling for that a second time," I said. "And you can't just come back here and expect everything to fall into place. It doesn't work that way."

He looked around. "It's crowded in here. Will you go outside with me?"

"It's freezing outside."

"Please?"

Well . . . shit. He had said please, and it *was* a little stuffy in the pub. Maybe a bit of fresh air wouldn't be so bad. We made our way to the front door and stepped out into the frigid air. The moon was high in the cloudless sky, and the stars were bright and twinkling. A perfect setting to fall in love, if only it wasn't ten degrees out. And if only my heart wasn't locked up inside a steel box and wrapped in chains.

Leo turned to face me, and I let him clasp my hands in his. You know, because it was cold. His eyes were warm on my skin, his expression wary but hopeful. "I did a shitty thing, Brooke. Regardless of my reasons, I hurt you and I can't take that back. I just need to know how to make it up to you. Will you let me try?"

"Why? I mean, what happens after you finish that book? What if you give it a try and decide you don't like it here and realize you need to move back to Chicago or Washington, or just anyplace but Trillium Bay?"

He sighed, his breath misty in the cold air. "I don't want to make specific promises about that, Brooke, because I'm not certain. But what I do know for certain is that the way my life felt before I met you wasn't half as good as the way my life felt when I was with you. And now my life is just plain miserable, and I want to change that. I do like it here, and I like you. In fact, I have a sneaking suspicion that I might even be in love with you. I probably am. Gina says I am, by the way, and she finds it completely annoying."

Gina. Maybe she wasn't so bad after all. Still, I needed more information.

"Are you really here to write a novel?"

"I am. And in the spirit of full disclosure, I've also been offered a job here. Turns out the chief of police is looking for an assistant deputy."

Ohmygosh. He didn't. My father offered Leo a job just to get him back here for me? That was either the most pathetic attempt at landing me a husband or the sweetest thing ever. Who knew that under Harlan's gruff exterior beat the heart of a true romantic?

"I believe my father may have offered you that job under false pretenses."

"I don't care. All I know is that it gives me another excuse to hang out around here because, as of yet, you have not asked me to come back."

The chains around the locked box of my heart rattled in my chest and fell away. "I'm not going to ask you to come back. I don't need you, Leo. I'm pretty happy being the mayor. However, if you do decide to come back . . . I might be willing to go out with you again." Ah, what the hell. What was one more broken heart? I guessed I was willing to jump just one more time.

"You would? Does that mean you've forgiven me?" He gave my hands a squeeze.

"It means I'm willing to consider it. Because I do like you, and in the spirit of full disclosure, I have a sneaking suspicion I might actually fall in love with you, if you play your cards right. But you should know, Leo Walker, I'm not looking for temporary. I'm looking for forever."

"That's okay." He smiled and pulled me close. "I like the sound of that. I think I'd like your kind of forever."

The hurt I'd been cloaked in melted away. Leo was back. And he'd come back just for me. Because I wasn't just someone special. I was someone special *to him*. It was nearly midnight, but I couldn't wait for the countdown. Leo was in front of me, and he probably loved me. I probably loved him, too, so no sense waiting for the ten, nine, eight . . .

I wrapped my arms around his shoulders. "If we jump, there's just no telling where we'll land, you know."

"I know," he said, pulling me tight against his chest. "But no matter what, we'll land together."

And then he kissed me.

Cheers erupted from inside the Palomino Pub, and in the back of my mind, I wondered if midnight had struck, but it hadn't. They were cheering for us, faces pressed against the windows, watching. So much for keeping this a secret. But I didn't want to keep it a secret, anyway. This time I wanted everyone to know. Brooke Therese Callaghan was about to take a lover.

ACKNOWLEDGMENTS

First and foremost, I want to thank you, my lovely readers. Your support and enthusiasm are the best part of my job and the reason I do what I do. I hope my stories make you smile and bring joy to your day. Thank you, Shari Bartholomew, for letting me use your name. Hope you enjoyed the bit about the pasties!

Thank you, Montlake Romance, and my editors, Megan Mulder and Melody Guy, for your patience and expertise. It's an honor and a privilege to work with you. Thank you, Nalini Akolekar, for being my most resounding cheerleader and a cherished friend. My Ouija board says we have great times coming our way.

Thank you, Catherine Bybee, Tiffany Snow, Marina Adair, Shelley Alexander, and all the Rocky Mountain Babes who offered ideas, support, friendship, and much-needed laughter. Thanks to all the talented and generous authors at Fiction from the Heart. I learn from you each and every day, and I am blessed by my tribe.

Thank you, Jane, for reading and reading and reading again. You're the best.

Thanks, Mere, Sue, Christy, Jenny, Samhita, and Jenny. We need to go on vacation now.

And of course, thanks to Webster Girl and Tenacious D, without whom nothing else matters. You amaze me every day, and I love you. You know how far.

ABOUT THE AUTHOR

Amazon and *Wall Street Journal* bestselling author Tracy Brogan is a three-time Romance Writers of America RITA® finalist for her Bell Harbor series. She writes fun, funny stories about ordinary people finding extraordinary love, and she lives in Michigan with her two brilliant daughters and their two intellectually challenged dogs. She loves to hear from readers, so contact her at tracybrogan@att.net or check out her website at www.tracybrogan.com. You can also follow her on Facebook at www.facebook.com/tracybroganwriter.